I0526659

Sin City Alibi

by

Sophia Ryan

Sin City Alibi

Contact Information: info@thewildrosepress.com

Cover Art by *Diana Carlile*

The Wild Rose Press, Inc.
PO Box 708
Adams Basin, NY 14410-0708

Visit us at www.thewilderroses.com

Publishing History
First Scarlet Rose Edition, 2015
Print ISBN 978-1-5092-0424-3
Digital ISBN 978-1-5092-0425-0

Published in the United States of America

**Her boss is dead. She was the last one to see him alive.
Her only salvation is her Sin City Alibi…**

She spun around at the sound of the elevator door banging open. His solid body was keeping it from closing.

"Hey," he said. "Do you wanna go have some fun?"

Did he mean sex? Did all their teasing remarks about handcuffs and whips make him think she was ready, willing, able, and up for kink?

"Define fun," she said, one eyebrow rising.

He grinned as if he could read her thoughts. "Nothing that fun. Dinner, drinks, maybe dancing if you don't mind my two left feet. No strings, just company."

Dani's heart pounded—at his offer, at the decision before her. She could spend the night drowning her sorrows with some Hollywood hunk on pay-per-view or begin the healing process she sorely needed by spending a few fun hours in the company of a real-live hunk.

"Dinner and dancing? Hmm. It's not the whip and handcuffs you promised earlier…" She stepped closer, and he moved back to let her in. "But deal me in."

Laughing, he released the door. Like a freed bird it wasted no time, whipping its wings closed and flying them to their destiny.

"This is my first visit to Vegas so I don't know the protocol," she said. "Is this the point where we give each other our fake Vegas names?"

She hadn't meant to infuse her words with a sexual subtext, but the heart-stopping, panty-soaking, lip-biting, sexy-as-sin smile he gave her told her he'd read it clearly.

He held out his hand. "I'm Matt."

His low, sex-filled voice heated her face, but she didn't avert her gaze as she slid her hand into his. The simple touch lit a fuse that led straight to the tinder box between her legs.

"Hi, Matt. I'm Dani." Her body was already tingling with anticipation for the *fun* ahead.

Dedication

To Lollipop, for her belief in this story,
the characters, and me.

Chapter One

"Baby, that...was...amazing."

Baby, aka Dani Parker, snuggled deeper into her lover's embrace, her mouth lifting into a contented smile. "You said that last time, too." She cupped the hand at her breast when it brushed across her sensitive nipple. "And the time before that."

"You're everything I've ever wanted. Smart, beautiful, sexy, loving. You make me feel like..." Elliott chuckled. "Like Superman."

Her hand trailed down his heaving chest to his half-stiff cock and stroked him. "Mmm. My man of steel."

He slanted his grin over her mouth, the slick friction between them already rebuilding the heat burning low inside her belly. "I love you, Dani."

Smiling up at him, she was about to respond when he extricated himself from her arms. "Which makes what I have to say so difficult," he continued. "I'm..." His eyes left hers and he sat up, leaned back against the headboard. "My wife and I are reconciling."

The words were a torrent of icy water to her flames, and a tide of nausea swelled in her stomach as her world came to a complete and abrupt stop.

"You said the marriage was over," she managed to choke out as she eased into an upright position. "You showed me the signed divorce papers."

"They were signed, but we hadn't, um," he

swallowed hard, "filed them yet. She begged me to reconsider, said we shouldn't throw away our marriage."

His words wrapped around her heart like a vice, squeezing the life from it and making her head feel like it was going to explode. "You seduced me into a relationship you knew you wouldn't commit to? How could you?"

"I didn't twist your arm," he said, inspecting his fingernails instead of giving her the respect of looking her in the eye. "You wanted this, too. As the boss' lover, you enjoy perks other employees don't get."

She blinked at the absurdity of his statement. "Our relationship has—had—nothing to do with work. And I never asked for or received special treatment, from you or anyone."

He chuckled, a low sound that scraped her raw nerves like a dull, jagged blade. "Who do you think approved all those conferences you attended—including this one—opened doors to the plum assignments, got you on the short-list for the team-lead position you enjoy today and then for the open assistant director's job? You may not have asked for perks, but you certainly benefitted from them."

His words, like boulders sitting on her chest, squeezed the air from her lungs. Could what he was saying be true? Had she only risen to her current status because he paved her way? Orchestrated her gains?

Her five years at Meganlin rushed past. The 50-hour-plus workweeks. Rarely taking time off and even working from home some weekends to keep her edge, to ensure she was always on top of things. Taking advantage of every possible opportunity to strengthen her existing skills and learn new ones. Frequent and ongoing networking to build critical relationships that would benefit the company.

No. It was her own hard work and dedication that led to outstanding performance ratings every year and accompanying raises and promotions. Not Elliott. He'd only been at the company for two years, and despite being president, he didn't wield that kind of power. He reported to a board that would be on the lookout for occurrences of special treatment.

Indignation stiffened her spine. "Don't you dare try to take credit for my accomplishments. I *earned* every benefit that came to me. And I deserve the assistant director position because I'm more qualified than the other candidates, and you know it."

"Despite your obvious," he eyed her naked body, "assets, I never seriously considered you for the position. I gave it to Nathan Gerber."

Her body went numb under the force of his betrayal. In a blink of an eye, she'd lost the man, the promotion, and the future she thought was hers. How had she been so wrong? And so stupid! *Stupid, stupid, stupid*, she castigated herself as she made herself breathe and move.

She flung the sex-scented sheet off her sex-flushed body and started for the edge of the king-sized bed, but Elliott grabbed her and pulled her back into his arms before she could go further.

"C'mon, Dani." His arms gripped like chains around her, his breath a snake's hiss at her ear. "Let's don't ruin our last night together with a silly tantrum."

A silly tantrum? A silly tantrum! He called her reaction to his life-changing betrayal a silly tantrum?

Bastard! She'd never seen him act so cruel. Was he intentionally trying to make her despise him? If so, it was working.

He held her chin and tried to kiss her, but she turned her face. The pain and anger surging through her merged to give her the strength to jerk from his embrace and scramble out of bed.

Shame prickled her skin as she gathered her clothes scattered on the floor where she had tossed them an hour ago in her rush to lie in her lover's arms. Fighting to hold on to the shreds of confidence and dignity whirling away like confetti tossed in a hurricane, she dropped the pile onto the bed and with cold, numb fingers fumbled to dress. Lastly, she stepped into her heels, grabbed her still-packed suitcase, and rushed toward the door.

An overwhelming desperation to be gone—from him, his hotel room, the out-of-town conference they were attending together—shook her, filling her with nausea. But she swallowed back the churning bile and forced herself to stop. To turn back. To take a good, hard look at the mistake in that bed. To remember the lesson of this moment. To remember her promise.

She steeled her eyes at him, his damned hot six-pack and rock-hard pecs glistening after their fiery bout of sex, his sexy lying lips still wet from her cum and kisses, his cock still magnificent where it hung well-used between his powerful legs. As far as mistakes went, he was a pretty bad one. He'd promised her love and commitment and had delivered sex and betrayal. How had she been so wrong about him? Her heart tumbling to her knees, she turned away and grabbed the door handle.

"A little free advice before you go." Elliott's words had her turning back to hear the rest. "If you want to keep your job, you'll keep quiet about…us."

"If anyone should be worried about losing a job, it's you," she said. "There are any number of people who'd be interested in what I have to say about us…boss."

Her blade-sharp bluff sliced away Elliott's smug veil to reveal what looked to her like fear. His eyes narrowed and his face paled as if his brain was spinning thoughts of what the scandal could do to him. "Don't go there, Dani. You'll regret it."

She already did, she thought as she forced a wicked grin to her face and opened the door. "So will you." She let the door slam shut on his retort and probably on her career.

****

Elliott lay in bed, channel surfing. The breakup had been harder than he'd imagined, and in the aftermath, he found he'd needed time to just chill. To think about what he'd done. And why. Which is why he was still in the room, still naked, still in the bed where they'd fucked three times before she'd walked out a couple hours ago, a nasty parting threat on her lips…something about reporting him to someone. He didn't think she'd really do it—it wasn't her style—but the threat weighed heavy on his mind, prompting the need to chill and plan. He was in no mood to attend the remaining two days of the conference, but he would stay the night in the hotel on the company's dime instead of heading back to Albuquerque.

At the knock on the door, his first hope was that it was her, come to tell him she'd do anything to be with him, even carry on a secret affair. But that hope quickly faded. He knew her well enough to know she'd never do that. However, it wouldn't surprise him a bit that she'd come back to give him a royal tongue lashing—and not in a good way. That *was* like her...rarely backing down from an argument until the other side caved from sheer exhaustion. He started to smile at the thought but lost it. He hoped like hell it wasn't her because this time he couldn't give in. He'd have to hurt her even more than he already had.

He climbed out of bed, not even bothering to wrap the sheet around his waist, and peeked through the peephole. "Fuck," he muttered but opened the door and stared into the eyes of the last person he wanted to see. "What do you want?"

"You can start with ditching the attitude," came the snarky reply as the visitor pushed past him into the room.

"If you don't like my attitude, you can get the hell out." He closed the door and went back to bed, pulled the sheet up to his hips, then grabbed the remote and resumed surfing, keeping his eyes on the TV, ignoring his visitor.

"You're such a fucking bastard, you know that."

Elliott's head swung up at the insult, eyebrows furrowed, a nasty retort of his own ready to fire. That's when he saw the gun, lengthened with a silencer, aimed at his chest. His eyes flew wide, and he scrambled back against the headboard, as if that would protect him from what was coming. "What the fuck are you doing?"

"What the fuck do you think?"

The evil in the mocking voice froze his heart and deflated his lungs. His brain was flooded with fear, and his balls had crawled up into his body. "I know you're upset, but you don't want to do this."

The visitor laughed. "No, I do. I really do. Goodbye, Elliott." The gun fired with a muffled thwump.

Elliott gasped at the jagged pain ripping apart the inside of his chest as the hot metal slug bore through skin, flesh, and organs. Wild-eyed and panicked at the red gushing from the wound, he reached for his cell on the lamp table, but his hand wasn't working right, and his jerky movement knocked it off onto the floor. He clawed for the hotel phone cord, getting a finger on it and knocking off the handset, but before he could lift a finger to dial 0 for help, the stores of energy surfed out of his body on the wave of blood. His arm dropped useless on the bed.

He slumped over, his cheek pressed to the edge of the bed, his gaze fixed out the window where the lights of The City Different twinkled at him.

"Why?" His voice, so unlike his own, sounded like it came from far away, as if everything that made him who he was had already left his body.

The shooter walked into his line of vision and stood there, watching him die. "A lot of reasons, really. The main one being that I don't trust you to keep our secrets."

Elliott laughed then, though it cost him. Blood splattered on the sheet as he erupted into a coughing fit. He pulled on ragged, gurgling breaths.

"I have to hand it to you," said his killer. "When I pictured this moment, I never thought I'd be hearing laughter...yours, anyway."

"I gave...someone...proof. Against you...us."

Elliott knew he was using up his last precious breaths on words, but they were important as far as last words went. "You'll…go down." He managed a weak grin, both at his accomplishment and at the sound of the sharp intake of breath from his murderer.

"You don't have the balls or the brains to be that calculating."

"Surprise." Elliott coughed again, bringing up more red. Panic raced through his body at the knowledge that he was choking on his own blood. Hearing footsteps headed away from him, his gaze went to the window that reflected the door, where his murderer stood, ready to leave.

In a moment, he would be alone. And dead.

The fear of dying alone roused the last surge of energy in his body. "Don't go." Blood-soaked words gurgled out in a pleading tone. His body already felt like ice, like an empty shell, and his lungs weren't working right. In the window's reflection, he saw the door open.

"Dani," he cried out, the sound sighing out as a whisper as the door closed.

****

Dani barreled down I-25 toward Albuquerque, Elliott's words of betrayal echoing in her ears, making her head feel like it was going to explode. One hand swiped at the tears that refused to stop, the other white-knuckled it on the steering wheel. A gritty mix of humiliation, anguish, and rage sat like cement in her chest, limiting her ability to concentrate on the road ahead. After accidentally driving out of her lane and nearly hitting a passing car, she swerved off the road and slammed on her brakes. The car skidded to a gravel-pitching stop.

Her fists pounded the wheel until they throbbed. "Damn you, Elliott." Regret and sorrow poured from the gaping wound in her heart. She had allowed herself to love a man who didn't love her, a man who lied, a man who couldn't commit to her.

The sight of blue lights flashing in the rearview mirror pulled her out of her virtual attack on Elliott's dismal character. *Fantastic. Just the cherry I need to top this dessert of a night.* She quickly wiped her streaked cheeks, and when the knock came and the badge appeared, she rolled the window down half way.

"License, registration, proof of insurance, please."

"It's in my glove box," she indicated her actions to the officer, then retrieved and handed over the materials.

The officer walked to his car, returning a few moments later.

"Ms. Parker, I clocked you doing eighty-six in a seventy-five-mile-per-hour zone a half-mile back, and you abruptly veered off the road." He flashed his light on her tear-stained face as he handed over a citation along with her driving documents. "If you're too upset to drive your vehicle safely, I can call someone to assist you."

"No, I'm fine." She took the ticket and documents and placed them in the glove box. "Just a little disagreement with my boy...with my boss." She tried to give him a smile to lend credit to her claim, but her mouth wouldn't cooperate.

He nodded. "Slow it down, Ms. Parker. Have a good evening."

"Yes, officer."

Only after he'd pulled away did she fully succumb to the pain galloping through her and release the deep, wracking sobs tearing her apart. When her insides were wrung dry and raw, she made two calls and a plane reservation, and after a quick stop at her condo, drove to the airport.

Chapter Two

"How does it feel to be the most beautiful woman in the bar?"

Dani sighed and rolled her eyes. In the past hour, she had deflected every line from, "That dress looks good on you. So would I" to "Can I borrow your phone to call the cops. You've stolen my heart."

This latest was the most flattering, but it still made her want to toss the contents of the highball cupped between her hands into the man's face. All she wanted was to drink in peace, let the heat of the liquor numb her to the mistake that pushed her to this Vegas weekend. She brought the glass to her mouth and tipped.

Damn. Empty. Again.

She raised her eyes in time to glimpse her suitor in the bar-back mirror, signaling the bartender for a refill.

"Make this your last one," he whispered at her ear as the bartender brought the bottle of whiskey over and warmed the ice in her glass. "When we get to my room, you're going to want to be able to feel everything I do to you."

Dani sized up the man. Mid-twenties, with just enough scruff to roughen his baby face. Blond finger-combed hairstyle that probably cost as much as her car payment. Clothing a billboard for some designer label. Full lips and a rock-hard pocket rocket that promised he'd be an entertaining way to pass the night for someone.

But not for her. She was already past her three-drink and one bad-judgment-call limits for one day. Adding a one-night stand, no matter how tempting, to her towering pile of mistakes could topple it, crushing her in the process.

Pulling her wallet from her purse, she fished out some bills and slipped them under the untouched refill. She stood and met his hungry eyes. "I'm going to my room, and you're going to stay here and try those lines and that smile on a woman who can appreciate them."

She had turned toward the exit, even gotten a few steps away, when Baby Face grabbed her from behind and spun her around. One muscled arm slid around her waist and hauled her against his chest, and one hand grabbed her ass to hold her there.

"I'll make you so appreciative you can't breathe." To prove it, he flexed his hips into her, stabbing her with the hard-on in his jeans.

This close, wisps of his spicy cologne curled up her nose, making her want to stop breathing. Raising her hands, palms against his pricey shirt, she pinned him with her stare. "What's your name?"

"Shane."

"Well, Shane. Get your hands off me before I break your fingers."

He laughed. "Now, that's not very friendly." The confidence projected in his straight, white grin never faltered.

She released another annoyed sigh. She didn't want to resort to physical force that would leave his body in agony and his ego in shreds. But if he continued to hold her against her will, she wouldn't hesitate to pull out the new move she'd been practicing in her self-defense class all week. She'd stop before actually breaking his fingers. She grinned. Maybe.

****

Matt Collins stood just inside the bar, allowing his eyes time to adjust to the dim light before choosing a place to sit. At least four dozen people sat at the scattered tables, mostly couples but almost as many groups of women or groups of men. A third of that sat on stools rimming the bar. Half a dozen couples danced to the pulsing techno music.

Joining those at the stools, he ordered a whiskey, neat. One sip and the smooth liquid fire began to work its warm magic, unknotting ropes of tension put there from the expected but monotonous goings-on of his former college roommate's bachelor party.

He'd expected the hookers and strippers, nonstop drinking, pleasure-enhancing drugs, looping porn on the big-screen TV, gambling, and asinine behaviors of caged men given a heartbeat of freedom, but this party blew out all the stops. The whole damn crew was two joints and a rebel yell away from spending the remaining hours of their wonderland in jail.

He rubbed his tired, red eyes. When had he gotten so old, in thought if not body? Sad thing was, he could answer that question. Could identify to the year, the day, the hour, the early demise of his youth. He poured back a huge swallow of his drink, the biting taste almost strong enough to mask the resentment and grief that clawed his chest when he thought about that day. About her.

Not wanting to get lost in thoughts of his dark past,

he turned and faced the room, letting his gaze travel the crowd and pinpoint every seductive gaze zeroed in on him. The redhead in green. The blonde in red. His gaze stopped on the pixie with short purple-streaked hair flicking her tongue stud against her front teeth. His cock jumped at the thought of that ball on his slit, running down his shaft. Damn.

He hadn't come here to the hotel bar to find someone to ease back his memories, to numb his pain. Tonight, all he wanted was to drink, then go to bed...alone. But with the bountiful selection before him, all looking eager, able, and ready, heaviness settled in his groin, stroking the base of his cock, the familiar, welcome feeling tempting him to choose one. Any of them would do as well as the other.

His eyes connected with the pierced pixie for a long few seconds before he fished a ten from his pocket and left it on the bar. As he turned to join her at her table, a leggy brunette headed his way caught his attention and knocked his ass back to the stool.

The turquoise dress she wore was made to make a man's cock stiffen. Like two firm hands, the thin, clinging fabric cupped her breasts, lifting them into luscious moons that crested at the deep-cut neckline of the dress. The outline of her puckered nipples was embossed into the silky material, and he wanted to flick his tongue over them, suck them into his mouth, see how hard they could really get.

From there, his eyes took in her slim waist, traveled the slow route over her smooth stomach, down the long length of her toned, tanned legs, legs that would wrap all the way around the man lucky enough to win her attention.

Inching back up her body, his gaze locked on her dark eyes filled with passion and anger. Then on her mouth. He wanted to run his tongue over those full berry lips. He wanted them hungry against his. Hell, as long as he was being honest, he wanted them wrapped tight around his cock.

A buff frat-boy behind her grabbed her and pulled her around to face him, making her long hair swing behind her like a dark chocolate curtain, and his hands grabbed her perky round ass.

Matt enjoyed a handful of curvy tight ass as much as the next guy, but something about that guy's handling of her made his teeth grit.

Gripping his glass tight in his hand, he tipped it to his mouth again, willing himself to control the adrenaline racing through him and just keep his ass on his barstool. The disagreement going on between the beauty and her beast was none of his business. They wouldn't thank him for his interference in what might be nothing more than foreplay between them. He'd learned that lesson the hard way, a few years ago receiving a broken nose and a knife cut to the chin that left visible reminders.

But when the beauty began to fight hard against the man, demanding he release her, Matt decided to make it his business. He downed the rest of his drink and pushed away from the bar.

****

"Leave. Me. Alone." Dani yelled the command, but the pulsing techno music drowned out the intensity of it. Her body was trapped between the solid wall of Shane's chest and the solid bars of his arms, but she managed to slip her hand between their bodies and twist the sensitive skin between his nipple and underarm.

"Shit!" He yelped and pulled back, releasing his hold on her for an instant. She took advantage of the opportunity to dart away. He reached out for her, but another man's arm slipped possessively around her waist and hooked her away.

Dani turned furious and surprised eyes toward the intruder but then stopped, not just her body but her heart, her lungs, her mind. Wild sensations swirled hot and low in her stomach at his touch.

"Sorry I'm late, honey," he said, in a voice as smooth and deep as the top-shelf whiskey she'd tossed back tonight, with a slight twang that made her insides vibrate like the plucked string of a steel guitar.

To say the man was easy to look at would be an understatement. Tiny crinkle lines, from the sun, from laughter, fanned the outer corners of his long-lashed eyes, putting his age at late twenties, early thirties. A thin white scar that stroked a half-inch of a scruff-free chin and a nose straight and strong except for a crooked little jog near the bridge suggested he was no stranger to fist fights. That sumptuous mouth was there for one primary reason—kissing. Brown hair, licked here and there by the sun, teased the collar of the buttonup shirt spanning his wide shoulders. Dark-wash Wranglers fit him like they'd been tailor-made to enhance his athletic build, and on his large feet were—oh my—cowboy boots. A genuine cowboy in Vegas. Now she'd seen everything.

Her gaze returned to his. They sparkled with what looked like humor or desire, and she really wanted to find out which. The air crackled around them, between them, as they locked gazes.

The moment dissipated when Shane stepped forward. "Get lost, man. She's with me." He grabbed Dani's arm again, tried to reclaim her, but her hero tucked her into his side, smiling as if he found Shane's tenacity amusing.

"You're ditching me for another guy on our wedding night?" The smile and wink he gave her released something hot and achy inside her.

Understanding dawning, Dani smiled and slid her arms around his neck. "You were late. And I was tired of waiting."

"You're married?" Shane's eyes darted from Dani to the man and back in disbelief.

"And eager to consummate it," the man said, tightening the arm around Dani and turning them toward the exit.

Shane grabbed her left hand in a final attempt to hold on to her. "I don't see a ring."

Her hero's patience disappeared faster than his smile. A grim line where his smile had been, chips of jade for eyes, he shifted her behind him and advanced toward Shane, his hard-as-stone stance and gaze warning him it was his last chance to back the fuck off voluntarily.

Shane let her hand slide free, but he didn't back off.

The two were nearly bumping chests when Dani stepped between them. "Shane, I'm sure you're a nice guy, but as you can see, I'm with someone."

Her stranger circled her waist with both arms. "Someone who has already kept you waiting too long to get you into bed." He drew her away from Shane and flush into the front of his very hard body. "And is willing to accept whatever punishment you care to dole out."

His words slid up her spine like a warm, lapping tongue. Heat flushed her face, and her hands clasped the hands on her stomach like she'd done it a million times.

"Hope you mean that," she said over her shoulder, loud enough for Shane to hear, "because I packed the whip."

Hero lowered his head and touched those sinfully hot lips to her neck, right below her ear, shooting hot and cold shivers across her skin, making her nipples stand up hard and tight against her dress. "And *I* packed the handcuffs," he said it too softly for Shane to hear, which meant it was just for her.

An unbidden purr, low and sensual, tumbled from her parted lips, and her hand lifted to his head to hold his mouth closer to her scorching flesh. She wasn't into the BDSM lifestyle, but their talk of it made her hum with anticipation. "I can't wait."

"Then let's get to it, darlin'." He turned her in his arms and again steered them toward the exit. She could feel Shane's eyes on them, as if he still didn't quite believe their story. Nevertheless, when they'd made it out of the bar and the door shut behind them, he hadn't followed.

Away from the bar, Dani extracted herself from her rescuer, slow inch by slow inch. Her muscles, along with her bones, seemed to have melted from the heat of having this man so near. Once standing on her own, she drew in a deep breath and knew the clean scent swirling crazy ideas in her mind came from the man standing inches from her.

"I appreciate your help." She was surprised to find she could talk with all the lust lodged in her throat. "But after that performance I was beginning to wonder who was going to rescue me from you."

Passion sparked in his smiling eyes as they brushed over her body. "I had to be bold, otherwise he'd think he had a chance. Now he knows you're mine."

Something about the way he said *mine* made her wish it were true. Realizing the foolishness—and the danger—of the thought, she lifted her chin slightly, stepped back, and threw in a raised eyebrow to cool the words that followed. "You and I are not going to sleep together."

Those delicious lips parted and curved into a sexy grin. "I don't remember asking you."

The heat in her face thickened her tongue, and she stumbled over the "I know" that tumbled from her mouth. "I just wanted to make sure we were on the same—" She tripped on her remaining words when he scooped her up in his arms. "What the hell are you doing?" squeaked from her throat.

"Lover boy's back for round two," he whispered. "You really must have made an impression for him to risk an ass-kicking."

Dani's heart spun as her faux-husband carried her across the hotel lobby and toward the elevators. There was something seductive and naughty about being held and touched so intimately by this handsome, sexy stranger. And, God help her, she liked it.

"He's still following," she whispered against his neck and wondered how far he'd be willing to go to keep up this farce. She got her answer when he carried her into an open elevator and punched the button for the top floor.

Shane halted outside the doors, looking as if he were going to step inside with them and make them prove their tale. She did what she had to do.

Grabbing her hero's face, she pulled him in for a kiss as the doors slid closed.

Somewhere between the bottom and top floors, that fake kiss took on a feel of reality. Lips softened, explored. Hungry mouths opened, slanted to find the best fit. Tongues tasted, twirled. Desire rose through her faster than the elevator through the shaft.

Only when the doors dinged open at the top floor did her hero slowly break off the kiss. She searched her desire-fogged brain to recall when it was he had set her on her feet and aligned their bodies so perfectly together.

"That was close," she said, affecting a breezy tone and easing some room between their steaming bodies. "For a minute, I thought we'd have to prove we're lovers. I'm hoping that kiss was proof enough, and he won't follow me around all weekend."

"It would have convinced me." Arms crossed, legs crossed at the ankles, he leaned against the elevator wall, watching her. "What floor do you need?"

For a few hazy, crazy seconds when she was struggling to remember that piece of information, she thought about simply saying "yours," but then common sense and her memory prevailed. "Seven. Your performance wasn't half bad either."

"Half bad?" He chuckled as he stabbed the number on the panel. "It was significantly better than *half bad.*"

She chuckled, too, and stepped close to him. Reaching out, she wiped her berry lipstick from his mouth with her thumb. His performance had been so good she'd never be able to wipe away his lip prints singeing her mouth. Which was fine because she didn't want to.

Standing there, too close to him, her thumb on his mouth, she realized she had to either kiss him again or move the hell away. She stepped back but didn't let her gaze break from his.

"If you hadn't stepped in, I would've had to hurt him." She shrugged at his raised eyebrow. "His pride, at least."

"We all know how fragile the male ego is," he said.

They continued to stare at each other even as silence surrounded them like hands trying to push them back into each other's arms.

The ding of the elevator door opening to her floor shook her from the spell locked around them. *Exit the elevator and never look back*, her brain insisted, but her body refused to take that first step. It was as if something inside her knew this moment was important and wasn't letting her walk away from it. But she couldn't just hang around in the elevator with him. It wasn't like he'd asked her to continue what they'd started.

"Well, goodnight." Dani took a step forward. Glanced back with a smile. "And thanks again." Took another step. Let the door close on her heavy heart.

She spun around at the sound of the elevator door banging open. He had stepped forward, his solid body keeping it from closing.

"Hey," he said. "Do you wanna go have some fun?"

Did he mean sex? Did all their teasing remarks

about handcuffs and whips make him think she was ready, willing, able, and up for kink?

"Define fun," she said, one eyebrow rising.

He grinned as if he could read her thoughts. "Nothing that fun. Dinner, drinks, maybe dancing if you don't mind my two left feet. No strings, just company."

Dani's heart pounded—at his offer, at the decision before her. She could spend the night drowning her sorrows with some Hollywood hunk on pay-per-view or begin the healing process she sorely needed by spending a few fun hours in the company of a real-live hunk.

The door buzzed loudly, protesting its forced captivity and screaming at her to decide. The *yes* dancing hot on her tongue rushed adrenaline through her body, filling her with bravado.

"Dinner and dancing? Hmm. It's not the whip and handcuffs you promised earlier..." She stepped closer, and he moved back to let her in. "But deal me in."

Laughing, he released the door. Like a freed bird it wasted no time, whipping its wings closed and flying them to their destiny.

"This is my first visit to Vegas so I don't know the protocol," she said. "Is this the point where we give each other our fake Vegas names?"

She hadn't meant to infuse her words with a sexual subtext, but the heart-stopping, panty-soaking, lip-biting, sexy-as-sin smile he gave her told her he'd read it clearly.

He held out his hand. "I'm Matt."

His low, sex-filled voice heated her face, but she didn't avert her gaze as she slid her hand into his. The simple touch lit a fuse that led straight to the tinder box between her legs.

"Hi, Matt. I'm Dani." Her body was already tingling with anticipation for the *fun* ahead.

Chapter Three

"So what's the story with lover boy?" Matt whispered against Dani's ear.

His arms circling her waist, hers looping his neck, their bodies shuffled in rhythm to the soft strains of the slow blues swirling like smoke around the handful of couples on the dance floor at the cave-like private club. When they'd arrived an hour ago, they'd found a table, ordered a drink, but after one sip, he'd taken her hand and pulled her into his arms on the dance floor, where they'd stayed, his muscular thigh insinuating itself between her legs every step, his strong, warm hands sizzling her skin wherever they touched, marking her through the thin fabric of her dress.

She met his eyes with a wry grin. "I told him I was there to have a drink, alone, and he took that as meaning I wanted his hands all over me." Her voice sounded soft and smoky to her ears, like she was in a dream. A dream come true.

His gaze dipped to her breasts pressed tight against his solid warm chest before it returned to her face. "Can't say I blame him." The thorough look he'd given her felt like a caress, and her nipples beaded in response.

"Are you justifying his actions?" She slid her hand to the back of his neck and teased her fingers in the hair riding his collar. The devil on her shoulder whispered in her ear to grab hold of that thick hair, pull his face down to hers, and take his lips. The angel said wait, insisting they needed to talk first.

"I'm saying any man with a heartbeat would want his hands on you."

Suddenly, she was all too aware of his hands. They had left her waist and were at her hips, holding on tight, his fingers gripping her flesh, controlling every movement of her hips against his. A seizure of tingles danced there, where her pelvis met his, and was growing. Desire tickled her throat, and she wasn't sure words would actually come out when she tried to speak. "Do *you*?"

"Where are my hands?" His hands smoothed down over her ass as he spoke.

Shivering at the feel of his hands on her, she gave him her best I'm so into you grin. "Right where I want them to be."

"Then I take it he just wasn't your type?"

"No, he wasn't."

"Am I?"

She slid a glance to his hand gripping her ass and raised an eyebrow as her gaze returned to his. "Where are your hands?"

"Right where I want them to be," he growled and eased her even deeper into him, into the hard ridge in his pants pressing against her mound.

The feel of him made her pussy ache with the need to be touched—with his hands, his tongue, his cock. The fast-burning desire building inside her would have to be extinguished before the night was over. She had packed her vibrator, but the way things were going, she might have a better option. She'd never had a one-night stand. It wasn't her style. But barring some disaster, she was about to have her first.

"Why Vegas?" he whispered a moment later.

The simple question evaporated the breath in her lungs, leaving her throat dry and stealing the contentment she'd found in his arms. She could feel him looking at her, waiting for an answer, but she kept her gaze focused on the top of his shoulder so her eyes wouldn't give away any of the inner turmoil she'd brought with her.

She shrugged, hoping it would lift her weak voice. "Why *not* Vegas?"

"You don't strike me as the type of woman who'd choose Sin City as a solo vacation spot."

She forced a smile to her face. "Yet here I am, on vacation, alone. Just out of curiosity, what vacation destination does a woman like me choose?"

"I'm thinking Italy, Spain, maybe France…but not Paris. Too cliché," he added.

"It wounds my ego that I'm so easily pegged by a stranger, but you're right. I'd have chosen to walk the footprints of Michelangelo and Leonardo in the streets of Florence or even play in the sand and surf of the French Riviera. Vegas was a spontaneous escape."

"From?"

Aw, shit. Wrong choice of words. Unwelcome memories and images of her last moments with Elliott flooded her mind, and she stiffened against Matt's body.

As if feeling the change in her, he eased back a bit to look at her. "Did I hit a nerve?" His hands held her firmly, as if to give her support, comfort, and time to exorcise whatever demons had stolen the magic.

"Let's just say I needed time away from the grind of reality to clear my head," she finally said.

"I understand."

Something in his voice told her he did understand. She dropped her hand to his chest. The steady thump of his heartbeat against her palm calmed her. "Are you escaping reality, too?"

"Just the opposite." One corner of his mouth lifted into a wry smile. "I'm here for a bachelor party that's gone so wild I'm trying to escape *into* reality. If that makes sense."

She traced an invisible pattern on his shirt over his muscular pecs. "Not the party animal type?"

"Apparently not anymore," he said. "This weekend was supposed to be about cramming in as much fun as I could, only it hasn't been that fun. Until now."

She couldn't stop the little smile taking over her mouth. "And why do you need to cram in fun?"

"I'm starting a project next week that will siphon all my time and energy for months. Until it's done, the word *fun* won't be in my vocabulary."

Matt's tone was defiant but resigned, and the gaze that met hers was intense, almost angry. Clearly, the project was a thorn jabbing a tender spot.

What was it about this man that had her wanting to chase away the unhappiness suddenly clouding his eyes and consuming his thoughts? She caressed his cheek and trailed her thumb across his mouth, wanting to bring him back to now—to joy, to fun, to her—and really wanting his kiss again. "Why don't you and I push aside all thoughts of yesterday and tomorrow and just focus on tonight?"

He caught her hand and kissed her palm. "And

fun?"

"Yes. Lots and lots of fun." The kind that goes all night.

He eased her closer, and she could feel his wholehearted acceptance of her suggestion. His mouth lowered to hers, hovering so close they shared breaths. His hooded eyes held hers. "I don't want to wait any longer."

"For?"

"To kiss you again."

The low rumble of his voice slid between her legs and tugged her clit, and it felt so good she could barely speak. "Then don't," she said and leaned in.

His mouth touched hers, flipping on to high every nerve inside her body. He increased the pressure, sliding his mouth across hers, not just touching, but tasting, layering sensation upon sensation that only increased her hunger for more.

He ran the tip of his tongue along the inside edge of her top lip, encouraging her to open her mouth fully to his exploration. She did, and his tongue tangled with hers, setting loose a moan inside her.

His hand moved to the back of her head and held her to him while his mouth enveloped hers in a kiss that brought in lips, tongues, teeth, and breath. Her fingers slipped into his hair and brought him closer to catch the moan sliding from his mouth into hers.

His fingers tangled in her hair, too, to hold her mouth tight to his. His other hand gripped her ass and drew her even closer, locking her against his body. Feeling his dick hard and ready seared the oxygen from her lungs and bathed her body in tingles.

He eased back, letting their lips cling softly before

disconnecting. Sometime during their kiss, the air around them must have become thicker and heavier because her heart was jackhammering in time with his, and his breathing was as unsteady as hers.

"How's that for fun?" he whispered on a low, shaky exhaled breath.

"A decent first step," she said, surprised she had enough breath to speak. As she stared deep into his eyes, he into hers, she knew the truth. Tonight would be about giving pleasure and taking pleasure, not waiting for it. About living in the moment, not looking back or ahead. About the two of them having fun, not regrets. "But I bet we can do better." She arched into him and pulled his head down for another taste.

After leaving the club, they could have shared a chocolate confection at an all-night paniere. But they didn't. They could have climbed to the top of the rotating observation tower—the tallest in the country— to witness the city spinning below them. But they didn't. They only glanced at the famous fountain and its dramatic background of music, water, and light. Like agents on a mission, they raced back to their hotel. Wrapped around each other, they stood near the bank of elevators, waiting to ride the elevator to their destiny.

"You tired?" He dropped a kiss on the crown of her head.

It was two in the morning. She'd had a busy, stressful, emotion-wringing, confidence-destroying day that should have her falling-on-her-face exhausted. But she wasn't. Not when Matt's very essence raced through her veins like a drug, keeping her high and happy, eager for whatever was next even while anxious to let go of what was.

She lifted her face to him and shook her head. "No. I'm so full of energy right now I could go all night."

His eyelids grew heavy, almost as if his shining green eyes could see the energy charging through her and what that could mean for them. "That makes two of us."

The words trilled across her glowing heart like the skilled fingers of the blues musician on his piano keys. She wanted what Matt promised in that thorough gaze of his that touched deep inside her, searching the depths of her eyes, caressing the slope of her cheeks, the rise of her nose, the curve of her lips in a spinning whirlwind of feeling. But a nagging voice inside her head taunted her. *What are you doing, jumping into bed with a stranger? Did you learn nothing from the disaster with Elliott, the one that sent you running here, the scraps of your pride dangling behind you like soiled toilet paper stuck to your shoe?*

Matt's lips brushing the delicate skin at her neck silenced the naysaying voice and chased away thoughts of Elliott, of mistakes and mistrust. She slanted her chin to give him better access to her neck, and his lips moved to her ear.

"I want to make love to you all night," he whispered, then nibbled and tugged on her lobe.

His words triggered a chain reaction of pleasure that rippled through her, tweaking her already puckered nipples, pulsing the already wet, swollen flesh between her legs.

Tonight, there was only one thing she was certain of. Right or wrong, she wanted this man, needed this man, deserved this man. She would love him tonight and leave him tomorrow, and that was as it should be. Giving her body to this stranger was safer than giving any man her heart.

As if the universe was in accord with her plan, the elevator doors sighed opened. She eased from his arms, took his hand, and entered the car, him right behind her. He punched a button on the panel, then his arms captured her fully, yanking her against him as the doors closed. She wrapped her arms around his neck and kissed him, revealing her passion, her intention, in every move, every taste, every caress, every moan she couldn't swallow.

He walked her backward until her spine was against the wall. She curled her leg around his thigh, and he pressed his body deeper into hers. His mouth opened on hers, his tongue swirled with hers, and little moans rose in her throat with every kiss. He grabbed her thighs and lifted her, as if she weighed nothing. She wrapped her legs around his hips, causing her dress to rise way up. Her pussy straddled his cock, and a blazing heat spread through her. He rocked into her, massaging her clit, every gyration sending her to the brink of an orgasm.

"I need you inside me. Now," she said, her hoarse whisper showing her desperation to be fucked.

"Hold on, baby. We're almost there," he whispered before his mouth was back on hers.

She sensed rather than saw them leave the elevator and rush down the hallway, Matt carrying her, but then they were there, inside his room, their lips and bodies still locked in a consuming embrace. He had left a lamp on low in his room, and it cast a soft light over their actions.

As soon as her feet touched the floor, he unzipped

her dress and it fell to the floor. Arms around her waist, his mouth and tongue explored her exposed neck and shoulders. Electricity raced through her, heating the spot between her legs and making her nipples tingle for his touch.

Her panties stood between her and his hand, but that didn't stop him. He nudged them aside and plunged a finger inside her wet-with-need pussy. She groaned against his shoulder, and his mouth moved back to hers to swallow the low sounds rumbling from her throat.

She clutched at his shirt and tried to pull it off. "Take off your clothes."

Releasing her, he grabbed the back of his shirt and whipped it over his head without unbuttoning it. As it fell, she rushed forward, back into his arms. She trailed her hands down the wide, muscular expanse of hard chest. She took time to kiss and lick it, before her hands moved on to caress the subtly defined six-pack of his stomach. He was hard, virile, all male, and all hers—for a few hours anyway.

Her quick but trembling hands worked open his belt and jeans and shoved them down his legs. Her hands came together to palm the tent straining his boxer briefs and stroke it the way he'd stroked her. A groan left his throat, and he drew her to him again. He kissed her, his large hand cupping her breast.

His mouth was on hers, his hands touching her, but something was distracting him, his concentration not on her, and his legs were jerking in little sporadic kicks. She broke the kiss and met his eyes. His eyebrows were furrowed in frustration. She grinned. "Everything okay?"

"Uh…" He chuckled. "Shit."

"It feels like you're having a seizure down there,"

she said, her gaze dropping to his legs where his jeans were balled up at his ankles.

"I can't get my jeans past my fucking boots," he said, shaking his head in humor and frustration.

Laughing, she put her hands on his shoulders and gently pushed him down onto the side of the bed. "Let me help you with that."

"I swear I usually handle these types of situations with a lot more finesse and seduction," he said as she gripped the heel of one boot.

"Uh-huh. What happened this time?" She pulled hard until the boot came off.

"You happened."

Her gaze met his, and she grinned. "You're blaming me for your epic striptease fail?" She grabbed the other boot and tugged it off, dropping it beside its mate, then tugged the legs of his jeans until they slid off him and puddled on the floor next to his boots.

"Since I met you," he said, and leaned over to strip off his socks, "the blood supply to my brain has taken a hard detour south."

"South?"

He stood. The massive tent in his boxer briefs drew her gaze, and she stood mesmerized as he slowly pulled down his underwear. His cock bounced free of the waistband and pointed directly at her, as if saying you're mine.

She licked her suddenly parched lips and heat rushed through her body as she pictured him filling her pussy with that…masterpiece. "I did that, huh?"

He eliminated the boxers with none of the trouble from before and sat on the edge of the bed again, legs spread, cock standing at perfect attention up by his belly, his thumb and finger stroking the bulbous tip. "Yep. All you."

She slid her hands into the sides of her panties and slowly lowered them past her ass, her hips, her thighs, her legs. They pooled around her feet, and she easily stepped out of them. Fully naked, fully aroused, she stood before him, her nipples so hard they hurt, the ache low in her belly growing stronger as her eyes caressed every inch of the fully naked, fully aroused man in front of her. "I do good work."

"So do I." He held out his hand. "Come here."

Her heart jumped into her throat at his low, sexy drawl. She took his hand, and he drew her to him. Standing between his legs, his cock twitching just inches from her pussy, she couldn't wait any longer to touch him.

As if he could read her mind, he led her hand down between them. Their hands still linked, their eyes still locked, together they stroked his shaft. He was hot and pulsing, and she could smell his pre-cum before her circling thumb felt drops of it at the slit. Her inner muscles clenched at the sight and feel and smell of this man.

Leaving her hand to continue the stroking, both his hands settled at her hips. He leaned in and kissed her belly button, up her stomach, toward her breasts. "I want to make it up to you for my epic striptease fail." His voice brushed her skin, creating delicious waves of pleasure. His hands smoothed up her body, palmed her breasts, and brought them to his mouth. He sucked her nipples, first one then the other.

She groaned and arched into him, one hand grasping his thick hair, the other his thick dick. "Make me come three times before sunrise, and we'll call it even."

He stood. Wrapped an arm fully around her waist. Cupped her face. His eyes danced over hers, as if trying to find a way in. "We won't be stopping at three."

Her heart fluttered at his promise and then harder when he lifted her in his arms, carried her to the side of the bed, and lowered her onto it. He settled next to her, facing her, skin to skin, heart to heart, breath to breath. His eyes dark green and shining, he caressed her face, smoothed his thumb over the edge of her lips. He kissed her, nipped at her mouth, all the while trailing his hand over her shoulders, arms, ribs, and stomach. He lowered his head and sucked and laved her nipples. Dizzy with the tornadoes of pleasure swirling inside her, Dani was glad she was lying down, his expert touch anchoring her to the bed.

Inch by inch, his hands continued their slow exploration, across her stomach, and she shivered beneath his slow, thorough loving. When his hand reached the tiny patch of dark curls at her mound, her legs parted eagerly to him, willing his fingers to explore her. He pressed a finger inside her, stroked her, his thumb riding her clit. It was good, but she needed more. Never had she needed to be filled so badly.

To speed things up, she reached between them and wrapped her fingers around his fullness. Drops of pre-cum leaked at the tip, and she wanted to lick it, get her first taste of this man who was going to rock her world, but she'd have to sit up, and that would interrupt the out-of-her-mind pleasure his hands and mouth were giving her.

So she circled the wetness with her thumb, spreading it and using it to lube her strokes. With each stroke, she tugged him toward her, willing him to find her opening and fill her with his heat. Finally, finally, he settled between her thighs, holding his weight on his arms, the blunt head of his thick cock at her entrance, ready to take her, ready to satisfy her, ready to make her scream.

Then he froze and pulled back. "Hang on," he whispered, his voice rough, husky, as he eased off her.

"Matt, no." She groaned her disappointment and clutched at his shoulders, but neither stopped him from leaving the bed.

He opened the suitcase sitting nearby and dug into the contents, tossing out clothes and other things until he found what he was looking for. He pulled out a long strip of foil squares. She couldn't believe she hadn't thought about protection. But he had. Another reason to not regret her choice tonight.

Ripping open a package, he rolled the condom into place and returned, again covering her body with his, supporting his weight on his forearms. He kissed her mouth, and she guided him where she wanted him.

She held her breath as he slid in slowly, taking his time, letting her feel every millimeter. The friction and fullness of his huge cock stretching her slick tunnel drove her mad with want, and she arched against him, trying to bring him all the way in. She clutched his ass to pull him closer, but still he wouldn't rush. She wanted to scream at the need scratching at her insides.

When he was in, as deeply inside a woman as a man could go, he stilled, as if demanding they savor this moment. "By the way," he said, his breath ragged, showing the great control it took for him to take this pause. "Matt really is my name."

She wrapped her legs around his hips and locked her

feet. "And Dani's really mine."

He pulled out, letting her feel the full length of his rigid shaft before pushing forward again. And again. Slowly in, slowly out. She needed to come. Desperately. And at this pace, she'd go completely crazy before it happened.

"It feels great, Matt." Her words came out breathy and needy. "But if you don't mind, let's save slow and easy for our second time. Right now, I need hard and fast."

Lust burned in his eyes, and he gave her a sinfully hot grin that said she was about to get everything she'd asked for and more.

His mouth slammed down on hers and devoured it as he took her hard, again and again, faster and faster, in a fevered pitch that had the headboard banging against the wall in time with their slapping flesh. Her high whimpers joined his low grunts. And each pounding thrust drove her higher and higher, toward the state of oblivion where nothing mattered but the feel of Matt's body inside her body, of his mouth on her mouth, of the soul-healing orgasm about to go supernova.

Her heart thundered in her ears, but she heard his harsh whisper. "Come for me, Dani."

She wanted to scream his name, assure him that she was there, but she hadn't the breath for it. Already her tightened muscles were releasing, exploding, the strength and effectiveness of their rough fucking tossing her high.

A cry of pleasure ripped from her throat as her orgasm hit, sending her hips arching into his, every nerve buzzing like a hot wire. A loud, primal groan left his throat, and his wild thrusts transformed into long stabs as her gripping pussy stroked every last drop of his cum from his cock.

He stilled, gasping for breath like her, his chest heaving like hers, and dipped his head to rest on her sweaty forehead. Their sex sweat, on their chests and stomachs and pelvises, sealed them together. The scent of his cum and sweat mixed with hers and swirled in her nostrils, her body already recognizing it as their scent, making her want him again. God, had she ever been fucked like that before, she marveled as she slowly came down from her high, still trembling in the aftershocks of her orgasm. No, she decided and released a shaky sigh of bliss.

At her sigh, he met her gaze, and a leisurely, sexy grin appeared. "Was that fun enough for you?"

Grinning back, she gave a weak nod. It had been more than fun. It had been just what she'd needed. Joy bubbled out of her in a chuckle that soon turned to a laugh. He laughed, too, and brushed back the strands of hair sticking to her face. She wished she'd asked for more than three orgasms. She wished she'd asked for a whole weekend of orgasms…with him.

The grin still on his face, he met her eyes, kissed the tip of her nose, her cheek, her mouth. "Stay with me all weekend."

She bit her lip to keep from releasing the too eager yippee ki-yay dancing on her tongue. "I'll stay."

Then he kissed her, gently, lovingly, and she tumbled into afterbliss, clutched in his arms, connected to his body, floating in a cloud of satisfaction she'd never known before, never wanted to give up.

****

Dani awoke just after dawn Sunday, the weight of

a muscular leg curled possessively around hers, a large hand cupping her breast, and morning wood jutting against her ass. In the tiny span of time it took her to recall who the appendages belonged to, desire settled heavy between her legs, the pink flesh already swelling and tingling at the mere thought of what had transpired between her and Matt and what would transpire in the few hours they had left.

Ah, Matt. Matt. His name vibrated inside her like the beating wings of a hummingbird, awakening her senses, her cravings. They'd spent all Saturday in his room, naked, learning each other's desires and making them come true. Smiling, she stretched, her body more relaxed and satisfied than it had been in all of her twenty-six years, thanks to the dozing man who lay entwined with her on the destroyed, sex-painted bed.

She turned to face him. The morning sun had stolen into the room via the filmy curtains, and as she watched the play of dappled light across his body, a hunger rose in her to kiss the spots that warmed his mouth, his chin, his chest, his stomach. But she resisted, just so she could watch him unaware and stretch out the moment a little longer.

"We could call room service."

At Matt's low, rumbling voice, her eyes flew to his, and she smiled at her temporary lover. "What?"

"You look hungry. I said we could call room service."

Heat climbed her chest and settled into her cheeks as his hand trailed down her side and settled possessively atop her bare hip like it was where it had always belonged. Knowing she would soon feel him pulsing inside her was enough to slick her pussy with wetness to prepare his way. She thought about taking him in her mouth again. She thought about straddling his face again so his mouth could devour her pussy. That was all good and would stave her cravings, but what she wanted most was him inside her. Connecting them.

"Room service doesn't have what I'm hungry for." She grabbed a condom from the nightstand, ripped it open, and rolled it on him, watching him watch her. "But you do."

In one easy motion, she straddled him and slid down on his fullness, sighing. Sitting deep, she kept her eyes on his, her hands on his chest, and rolled her hips in a tantalizing rhythm. Fuck, they were so good at this. Already she was feeling the first tight tingles of an orgasm building.

He sat up, kissed her, and rolled them over so he was on top. Lifting her leg over his shoulder, he drove deeper into her, filling her, his thumb riding her clit. His eyes locked on the spot where they joined, as if he were focusing on committing to memory how their bodies looked as they came together. Her gaze went there, too, and she groaned at the sight of his thick wet cock thrusting in and out of her pussy. His gaze lifted to hers, eyes hooded and dark, and he pumped harder, as if his prime mission was to make her come.

The intensity of everything she was feeling was almost too much, but it was his deep, delicious, possessing kiss that pushed her over. She growled into his mouth as her body contracted in orgasm, hips bucking up against his thrusts, hands clenching his back to keep him as close as possible, pussy squeezing his cock to pull him along with her into bliss. Even before she was finished, she could feel his cock swelling inside her, a sign she now knew meant he was close.

He broke the kiss to drag in a sharp breath. His jaw tightened, his eyes squeezed shut, and he came, too, thrusting harder for a few more strokes before his movements slowed and stopped. His eyes slowly opened and found hers. And he grinned, looking like a little boy who had just hit his first home run.

Lowering her leg from his shoulder, he collapsed against her. He chuckled against her neck, which triggered hers and drew his gaze. Eyes and bodies locked, they laughed at the pleasure and happiness flowing between them.

She'd never been with a guy who laughed after coming, and she didn't know whether it was something he always did, or whether it was something he did only with her, but hearing his laughter touched her heart, because she knew it meant that he'd enjoyed her as much as she'd enjoyed him.

She would miss it—would miss him—when she left this fairy tale to reenter the real world.

****

Dani sat curled up with Matt in his bed, naked, finishing their room-service breakfast. Conversation had been light and easy, avoiding the topic of their impending goodbye. But when he set their empty plates on the tray, their last meal together over, reality crept in.

He grabbed the bunch of grapes and settled back against the headboard, pillows propped behind him. He fed her a grape before popping a couple into his mouth.

"When's your flight?" he said.

"Two o'clock." She chewed the words alongside

the grape and both were like ash in her mouth. "I'll leave here at noon to get to the airport."

She had known going into this Vegas affair that it would have a short life. No strings. No looking back. No wishing for what might have been. She had her life, and he had his. Still, leaving him was harder than she'd thought it would be.

The getaway to Vegas was meant only as a salve for a broken heart. Never in a million years did she believe she would indulge in a red hot fling while here.

But she had.

Her first.

And it was more than she'd hoped it would be.

Matt had swept her off her feet, literally and figuratively, and had fulfilled her every sexual fantasy. In their short time together, she realized she liked him. His humor. His easy mood. His intelligence. His quick laugh. His almost gentlemanly demeanor. His everything. He was the kind of guy she had always wanted. And unfortunately, he had quickly set up residence in a corner of her heart, where she harbored dreams of him declaring the passion they shared was more real than the loveless practicalities of a fling. That it deserved a chance to live beyond Vegas.

In her rational mind, however, she knew it wasn't going to happen. Couldn't happen. Wouldn't happen. She had never been one to believe in fairy tales—not with the childhood she'd had—but he was the first man who made her wish she did believe in cotton-candy sentiments like love at first sight and happily ever after and true love always wins.

The touch of his hand on hers brought her back to the moment. He drew her to him, and she crawled into his lap and rested her head on his wide chest. In his arms, she allowed herself the luxury of believing in the fairy tale. For just a little longer.

****

Matt had been with more women in the three years since his life fell apart than he cared to remember. Saying goodbye to them had never been a problem. But this chance encounter with Dani had left a mark on him. If he could live out every man's fantasy and custom build a woman like he would a car or a bike, she would be the end product for him. She possessed everything he wanted in a woman—intelligence, beauty, passion, confidence, independence, compassion, spirit. Just his luck she would come along under these circumstances. A Vegas fling. King of the cliché hookups. The odds that anything more could come of it were against them. He knew that. But it didn't stop him from thinking about it.

In a few hours, they would leave each other and all that would remain of their time together would be memories. Memories like the softness of her skin that smelled like a field of flowers, or that she tasted like an exotic fruit he couldn't resist, or her smile that lit up his heart, or how they fit together so perfectly, or how they both laughed after making love. Was that something she did with all her lovers or just with him? The women he'd been with thought laughter after sex an insult. So he'd stifled it. But he couldn't with Dani. And, fortunately, he didn't have to.

How many times in the last thirty-six hours had he tried to convince himself to ask for her last name, her number, her email address, any means of contact that would allow them to continue this flash of lightning sparking between them and fusing them together so perfectly? But the moments when they talked instead of fucked, she avoided his every attempt to discuss any topic, disclose any information that could lead to discovery of who she was outside this fantasy world they'd created. He didn't blame her. Flings came with an unwritten and unspoken set of rules both parties silently agreed to that precluded all discussion of reality. Which was part of the fantasy and the appeal.

Maybe between now and noon he'd come up with the right words to convince her to take a chance on them, on discovering whether what they had conceived in their few hours together was worth nurturing into something more. Any little thing he could learn would help him apply his company's resources to get the information he needed.

Her nipping at his bottom lip broke through his thoughts. The nip turned into a suck, and then they were kissing with such urgency and desperation that it made his heart ache. The goodbye neither of them was ready to say, and the silent physical conversation, held more emotion than either of them should have for the other.

For now, while he had her in his arms and in his bed, he would pleasure her, take some for himself, and give her a reason to ask for more before she left him.

****

"Come by for a drink," Liz Lujan said when Dani called her to let her know she had made it home. "I'm dying to find out about your trip."

"Raincheck...I'm blasted," Dani said as she lifted her luggage from the trunk of her car. Liz's "but" had her quickly adding, "We'll talk later. I promise."

"Details?"

"Most of them."

"*Most* of them? I like the sound of that. I guess I can wait a few more hours," Liz said on a sigh. "But give me one thing to live on til then."

"Vegas was just what I needed," Dani said, trying to keep the *I had sex all weekend* out of her voice as she said it but failing...at least to her ears. "So thanks. I owe you."

Liz had been one of the phone calls she'd made after her breakup with Elliott. When Dani told her everything, her best friend had suggested a quick trip to Vegas to get her mind off her troubles. She'd even offered to go with her, but Dani had said she needed to be alone.

"Good! Hey, you going to be okay tomorrow? Seeing Elliott?"

Dani heard the worry in her voice, and it triggered some of her own. "Yeah. I'll be fine. Really."

In truth, the hours in Matt's arms had replenished her reserves of confidence Elliott had depleted, and although she would need every ounce to get through tomorrow, and the next day, and the next, she would do it. Because that was who she was.

Chapter Four

Dani arrived at the office an hour or more before most of her co-workers began trickling in. Her department director, Karen Rutledge, was already in her office, head bent over a pile of paperwork. Dani rapped on her open door. "Good morning."

Karen flipped the top sheet over on its face and removed her reading glasses. She waved Dani inside. Karen had been call number two, letting her know she was leaving the conference early to deal with a personal matter that had come up. "Did everything work out all right? With your personal issue?"

"Yes, thanks for asking. Thought you were off to Florida this week?"

"Something came up to delay it. Please shut the door and have a seat."

There was something urgent about her boss' words and tone, and she couldn't help but feel a bit anxious. She took a seat in one of the twin upholstered chairs stationed in front of the massive mahogany desk. "Is everything okay? It's not Walt, is it?" Karen's husband, Walt, had suffered a heart attack a few months back and was still not one hundred percent yet.

Karen's demeanor softened slightly. "No, Walt's fine." She rose from her heather-gray leather executive chair like a queen rising from her throne. With that royal grace, she walked around to perch on the corner of her desk, facing Dani. "Acting on an anonymous tip several months ago that there were some irregularities in our books, the board conducted a cursory investigation. That investigation uncovered evidence that suggested Elliott Gibson might be involved."

Dani reeled, surprise flooding her senses. Financial irregularities almost assuredly meant embezzlement. Although she wasn't one to relish the misfortune of others, she allowed herself an internal smile at Elliott's expense. The smile vanished when she remembered the gifts he had given her during their short-lived affair, including the silver and turquoise locket gifted during dinner of their last night together. The locket that was still in her purse. Had he bought it with stolen company money?

"To get to the bottom of it," Karen continued, "the board engaged the services of a renowned financial investigation firm out of Dallas to conduct a thorough review of the books. That investigation begins day after tomorrow."

"Will the investigation team be seeking input from staff, or primarily management?" Dani asked.

"Primarily management, but as team lead you may be questioned. But that's not the reason I asked you to join me. Before Elliott left for the conference, he put in paperwork to award the assistant director position to Nathan Gerber. However, the board has now suspended all decisions Elliott made over the past six months, including those related to staffing."

Karen paused in her oration as if to give Dani time to soak in the information. It would have been a painful shock had Elliott not already told her he had given the job to Nathan. Karen seemed to notice her lack of expected response, but she didn't comment on it.

"You know I supported you for the position," she continued. "I still believe you are the better choice, and I intend to recommend that the board select you to fill it when the time is right. You've been a superior employee with this company since you joined us five years ago."

"I appreciate your continued confidence in me," Dani said. This was the first time she'd been happy that Elliott hadn't kept his promise to give her the promotion. But her desire to dance on Karen's desk at the possibility of again getting the position was tempered by the fact that she had been involved with Elliott. And by the fact that, if the affair came out in the audit, it would cast doubts on Dani's reputation, and she could kiss any job with teeth at this company *adios*.

"However," Karen said, "even a hint of involvement on your part in wrongdoings in this company could jeopardize your career."

"I can assure you, I know nothing about Elliott's financial dealings." Dani's stomach clenched with guilt at her response. Though it was true she knew nothing about his financial wrongdoings, she did know about his other wrongdoings—his extramarital affair with her. Maybe now was the time to confess. Before Karen went to bat for her. Before the investigation team pulled it out and branded it as something else, something more damning than a simple affair that had nothing to do with their work relationship.

Karen studied her, as if she were trying to read the truth scribed in light on Dani's soul, making her wonder whether she already knew about the affair. "You'll inform me immediately if you recall anything that could assist the investigation team with its work."

Dani nodded. "Of course."

Karen walked back to her chair, sat, and put her glasses back on, the signal that the conversation was over.

Dani rose to leave, then sat back down. "There is one thing I think you should know."

True to character, Karen maintained her poker face and her silence throughout Dani's confession of her short-lived affair with Elliott that ended at the conference, prompting her desire to leave early.

"I wondered whether you'd come forth about the affair."

The quiet words shocked Dani to her crimson toenails. "You knew?"

"I suspected. Six months ago."

"We were only together two months. How did you—"

"Elliott was a big talker who didn't know when to shut up, especially about his private achievements. About six months ago, he said he was divorcing his wife for 'the one' and went on to extol the lucky woman's finer attributes. He never mentioned your name, but from his description I was sure he meant you."

"He pursued me for nearly a year. I admit I was drawn to him, but I don't date unavailable men, and I told him so. When he told me last month he'd signed divorce papers—even showed them to me—I thought he was free to start a relationship. Otherwise, I never would have."

"Why did it end?"

She looked down to get control over her emotions,

to clear her voice. "He and his wife are reconciling." After a moment, she brought her head up, her eyes level with Karen's. "Could the affair affect my position with the company?" Her voice was stronger than she imagined it would be.

"If it comes out, we'll remind any accusers of the inequity of power present in the working relationship. I'm in no way excusing your part in it, but he—as your superior and as the married man—carried the larger portion of any blame to be handed out."

Karen's comment eased the burden weighing Dani's conscience, allowing her to respond with a nod. "I understand completely if you want to pull your support of me for the position."

"That won't be necessary. But to be honest, Dani, retaining your job might be the least of your worries," she said, her voice as serene and staid as her gray suit.

"What do you mean?"

"Elliott was found murdered in his hotel room the day after you left the conference."

"What? No!" The room tilted, slamming her against the chair back. Her yogurt and fruit breakfast spun in her stomach, and her heart pounded white-hot in her brain. Her lungs were being squeezed so hard she couldn't breathe. Her body felt empty, like everything inside her had been flushed out. "Oh, God." Tears burned her eyes. She covered her face with her hands and let them fall.

"The police have launched an investigation into his death. And you, my dear, may soon be at the top of their suspect list…woman scorned, and all."

****

"I told Karen about my affair with Elliott."

Ignoring Liz's wide-eyed and open-mouthed stare, Dani broke open a shell and popped peanuts into her mouth, chasing the saltiness with a draw of frosty beer. The overhang of the bleachers blocked the heat of the sun as the two friends took in a baseball game the following night.

"Why would you do that?" Liz asked.

"She's putting her reputation on the line for me. If—when—the affair comes out, it could call into question her ethics as well."

"In protecting Karen, you're needlessly putting yourself at risk. All I can say is, dibs on your office."

Dani tossed a peanut at Liz. "Bitch!"

Laughing, Liz dug the nut from her ample cleavage and popped it into her mouth. "You worried?"

Dani's gut had churned the worry into a solid lump of agony since she'd first learned about Elliott's death. "The investigation team might assume that because of the affair I'm connected to or at least knowledgeable about Elliott's shady dealings. The police might assume I killed him because he dumped me. At best, I could lose my job. At worst, spend time in prison. So, yeah, I'm worried."

"You trusted the wrong man, but I can't see how they'd be able to use that to pin his financial wrong-doings or his murder on you."

"Having an affair with a married man, no matter what he said or promised, suggests that I condone and participate in questionable behavior. And he died in the hotel room where we had sex, so my fingerprints and DNA are all over the room and him."

"Everyone knows you're an honest, ethical person. This one mistake won't sink you."

"I hope you're right."

"Aren't I usually? Now. Change of topic. You never told me about Vegas."

She hadn't told Liz. She'd wanted to keep the memories inside so they'd stay alive longer. "Vegas." The screaming fans, the hawking vendors, the players on the field, Elliott's death all faded away to allow the image of Matt to float before her eyes. As the memories flooded her body, she couldn't halt the smile spreading across her face. "It was…good."

Liz squirmed in her chair, barely able to contain her eagerness. "No way! You met someone. Tell me, tell me, tell me."

"I met someone."

"Who?"

"Matt."

"Did he come with another name?"

"We agreed to first names only. And before you ask, we also didn't discuss addresses, phone numbers, professions, politics, or religion."

"What's left to talk about?" Her eyes opened wide as Dani's grin grew. "Oh, my God! You *didn't* talk. You had sex all weekend!"

Heat flushed Dani's face at the inquiring faces that turned toward her at Liz's outburst. "A little louder," she whispered. "I don't think the shortstop heard you."

"Your first one-night stand," Liz said, her voice lower than before. "Aww, my little girl is growing up." She wiped a fake tear from her cheek.

Dani grinned at her friend's theatrics. "I hadn't planned to. You know that's not my thing. But when the moment came, it seemed the most natural thing to do." She turned her eyes back to the game, trying to gather her swirling thoughts. "And it lasted all weekend, not just one night."

"A fling. Even better." Liz leaned in, her smile gleaming. "Tell me, and don't leave anything out."

Dani relayed the events that led up to her fling, from the rescue in the bar, dinner, and dancing in the private club, and the ride up the elevator to his suite. She glossed over the thirty-six hours spent in his bed. And she concluded the story with their sad goodbye in the hotel parking lot as they waited for her cab to take her to the airport. She'd refused his offer to take her because she'd known extending it would only make parting more difficult.

"It sounds like you two made a real love connection."

A connection? Yes. Love? No. She shook her head. "It was salve for my wounded ego and broken heart. An escape from the reality of a busy life for him. A little fun and excitement for us both. Neither of us had any illusions about it being anything more."

"Something that hot could have easily grown into more given half a chance."

"In the harsh light of reality, our brilliant diamond probably would have turned out to be nothing more than cheap glass. And that's not how I want to remember it. Or him."

In truth, it had been harder to let Matt go than she'd thought it would be. Her decision to have fun, hot sex with no ties and no future sounded perfect at the time, just what her crushed and bleeding heart needed. But the more she thought about him and their weekend, the more she wished they'd exchanged numbers so they could have, like Liz said, explored whether what they started could have lead to more.

Ah, Matt. An image appeared of making love to him that final time, arms and legs around each other in a desperate, tangled embrace. Of his luscious mouth kissing, his hands caressing every inch of her body. Of them becoming one in a single flowing motion. Of hearing her name ease from his lips like the answer to her prayers.

A rush of pleasure swept over her on that stiff stadium chairback seat, shaking her and hardening her nipples beneath her T-shirt. She pressed her thighs closed against the intense heat mounting between her legs. Her body craved Matt. His touch. His kiss. His taste. But Matt wasn't here. Wasn't ever going to be.

"...satisfied at night." Liz's voice yanked her out of her internal carnality.

"Sorry, what?"

"I said memories—no matter how perfect—won't keep you warm and satisfied at night."

"They won't break my heart, either."

"You're talking about Elliott aren't you?" Liz pulled deeply from her straw, sucking down the tangy strawberry margarita.

Dani took a drink of beer to gather her feelings, analyze them, before sharing them. "He was a dishonorable bastard, I guess, but I cared about him, and I believed him when he said he loved me and wanted a future with me. My bullshit meter must have been malfunctioning." She took another drink to wash down some of the sorrow.

"Speaking of dishonorable bastards," Liz said. "I could hardly contain my glee when I heard Nathan's promotion was reversed. The guy's such a snake."

"The snake could still get it. Especially if I'm in jail or fired or both."

Liz squinted into the distance, as if she were listening hard to whispers three rows down. Then her face relaxed. "Nope. He's not getting the promotion. I think fate has something else in mind for him. I see him being...pulled in another direction."

Liz's "impressions" were legendary. Feelings or images came to her, like whispers on the breeze, she said. And more often than not, they came true. Dani noticed Liz didn't say that she wasn't going to jail.

"Karen put my name in the ring for the assistant director job again."

"You should've had it to begin with. After all, you *are* the most qualified."

"Let's hope the board thinks so."

"They will. But enough about that. Tell me more about Matt. You zipped past the two-days-in-bed scenes way too fast. I haven't had sex in three weeks, so be specific."

Chapter Five

Dani arrived at her office the following morning, wondering why most of her co-workers were already at work, when usually she was the only one of a handful who was in at seven-fifteen. When she spied Karen talking with a tall, dark-haired stranger in an impeccably cut brown suit down the hall near Nathan's office, his back to her, she remembered. The investigation would start today. And the man? Lead auditor extraordinaire? What was his name? She didn't recall Karen ever saying.

She went into her office and turned on her computer. As the two made their way down the hall toward her office, Karen introducing him to the others on the floor, Dani heard something in the man's voice that stirred feelings of familiarity that made her heart flutter. Before she could pinpoint why, Karen stepped through her doorway, the man a step behind her.

Dani stood to greet him, a ready smile in place. But as she took in the face before her, the green eyes staring at her, her smile cracked, and not even the power suit she donned this morning could hold in the strength evaporating from her body. Her heart slammed into her ribcage, stealing her breath and dropping her back into her chair. Memories fast-forwarded past as she stared wide-eyed at him, and she was sure the whooshing sound in her ears was her brain exploding.

No wonder the man's voice had sounded familiar. It had whispered in her ear, across her skin, in her mouth, three days ago when she'd had wild and frequent sex with him in his Vegas hotel room.

Matt froze for an instant, too, as if his brain couldn't make sense of what his eyes were seeing. Then his polite smile transformed into something warm and real. That mouth had traveled every inch of her body. Numerous times. His eyes glowed with pleasure. Those eyes that had seen her naked more than they'd seen her clothed. The tousled hair she had run her fingers through was now tamed into a professional style, but there was the same tiny scar on his chin he'd gotten in college while defending a woman. That same tiny scar she'd traced with her fingers, her tongue, her lips. A quick glance down told her he wore the same boots she'll pulled off him that first night, right before she'd stripped him of his jeans. She swallowed and remembered to close her mouth.

"Dani, this is Matthew Collins, leader of the audit investigation team. Matt, this is Danielle Parker, a team lead in our new-client services department."

Barely realizing that Karen was making introductions and not hearing much after Matthew Collins, Dani bunched what was left of her muscles under her, slowly rose from her chair, and crossed the few feet to take his outstretched hand. She tried to speak but couldn't.

Their hands touched, and she was back in Vegas, enveloped in a full-body flush of desire. Did she really just shiver?

"Nice to meet you, Ms. Parker."

The fire in his gaze, his words, his touch made her

head spin. Needing to disengage from the magic flowing between them, she tried to step back, but he held on, subtly caressing the palm of her hand with the tips of his fingers. His body radiated heat that swirled around her, looking for an entrance. She had to say something.

She swallowed again and forced out the first thing that came to mind. Well, the second thing. "Welcome to Meganlin, Mr. Collins."

"Please, call me Matt. And do you prefer Danielle, or Dani?"

Hearing her name on his lips again sent a surge of desire sweeping through her. Her tongue felt glued to the roof of her mouth, but she managed to answer without choking. "Dani."

"Dani." He nodded as he said her name. "One of your co-workers mentioned you'd just returned from Vegas. Did you have fun?"

The only co-worker who knew she'd been in Vegas was Liz, and there'd be no earthly reason for her to mention it, so his mention of it was deliberate, to see her reaction. Her face flushed, and she bit her lip to staunch a smile but kept her eyes locked on his. "I did."

"You must not have hit the jackpot."

Oh, I hit it big. And often. A small smile nudged onto her lips at the memories of their loving. "Why do you say that?"

"You're hard at work instead of lazing on a beach somewhere in the French Riviera."

She was clamping down on her lip so hard she expected to taste blood soon. She wasn't sure which comment was causing her sudden need to be fucked on her desk—that he remembered her comment about vacation spots or his clever double entendre about hitting the jackpot. She tried not to drop her gaze to his crotch, but hearing the words *hard at work,* what was a horny woman to do? There was a definite bulge to the front of his tailored trousers, showing he was the one *hard* at work. Not her. No, she was *wet* at work. Very wet. Wishing-she'd-brought-a-change-of-panties wet.

"Maybe I did hit it," she said, her voice low. "Maybe I just love my job so much I'd choose to continue working regardless."

"Maybe that's it," he said while his eyes ripped off her clothes and fucked her.

Soon she felt other eyes boring into her, and her gaze shifted to a point just behind Matt, where Karen stood. Her mouth was a tight line on a stern face as she listened to the low, humid exchange, her eyes keenly taking in Dani's hand still held tightly in Matt's and their protracted stare.

Dani pulled her hand away and stepped back, resisting the desire to check her hand for scorch marks.

"Matt, we should get to the rest of the employees," Karen broke in.

"Of course." His voice sounded harsh, as if something were blocking his throat. Something like passion, desire, lust, whatever one wanted to call it. At least, that's what was in hers.

His crystal green gaze captured hers, and that sexy smile played at the corners of his mouth. "I look forward to working with you, Dani."

"Me, too, Matt."

He turned to Karen. "Lead the way."

With a final look at Dani, Karen preceded him out the door.

Dani's control crumbled, and she stumbled to her chair. With her elbows on the desk, she covered her face with her hands and took deep breaths to quiet the moans in her body. Despite her earlier bravado in facing Matt, she was as weak and defenseless as a newborn.

Matt? Here? No, no, no! I had wild, hot sex with the man investigating wrong-doings in this company, the very man who has my job, my future, in his hands. They got that slogan about Vegas wrong! What happens in Vegas doesn't stay there...sometimes it follows you home!

Liz rushed into her office and closed the door. "Oh, my God! Did you *see* him?" She rolled her eyes and sighed. "I'm warning you right now. I'm making a play for him so don't even get in line. He is going to look so damn good laid out on my king-sized bed, with me draped over him. Mmm-mmm-mmm!" She must have seen the *I'm going to vomit* look on Dani's face because she moved closer, concern on her face. "What's wrong?"

"That investigator..."

"Yeah?"

"Is Matt."

"Yeah, Matt Collins."

"No. Matt. My Vegas fling Matt."

Liz's eyes and mouth flew open. "You're joking."

"Would I joke about something like that?"

Liz laughed. "Oh, this is just too good to be true. What did he say? Was he surprised to see you? Did he mention Vegas?"

"Oh, yeah." Dani dropped her head to the desk and moaned while Liz guffawed over her. "It's not funny! I all but melted into a glob of lusty pudding at his feet. He probably thinks I'm incompetent."

"No, he thinks—and hopes—you're hot to continue your fling."

"I doubt that. We ended things in Vegas, and I imagine he'll want to keep it that way to avoid any impropriety. My only option now is damage control—and hope that the shit hitting the fan doesn't bury me."

Liz crossed her arms and made a face. "Look, against all odds, he's here. If that isn't a sign you should be together, I don't know what is."

"I need him to see that the Dani who works at Meganlin is nothing like the wild fling he bedded in Vegas, so that when he finds out about the affair with Elliott, he won't automatically connect me with anything he finds out about him. My job is important to me, and—"

"This isn't about your job. It's about taking a chance on the man you obviously connected with. He's the one, Dani. You can't let him get away."

"What do you mean, he's the one? He's not the one. He can't be the one. How do you know he's the one?"

Liz scoffed and rolled her eyes. "Are you really asking me that?"

Dani sighed, a little afraid to press Liz for details. "He's probably as freaked out about my being here as I am about his being here."

"No. That one's thinking he hit the jackpot. Again."

****

Matt removed his jacket and dropped into the sumptuous overstuffed leather chair, leaned back, loosened his tie, and gathered his spinning thoughts. He couldn't believe fate had worked this one in his favor. What were the odds of finding the one woman who had rearranged his orderly existence in a single weekend, flipped his life upside down with her insatiable passion, and haunted his every waking and sleeping hour since?

He'd almost had a heart attack when he walked into that office and saw Dani, looking even hotter than he remembered. He'd wanted to grab her up, sweep everything off her desk, drop his pants, rip that suit off her so fast her head would spin, and pitch her onto the desk, her four-inch high designer heels plunging into his ass cheeks as he plunged into her wet pussy. Not the most appropriate thought to indulge in while in the office, judging by the instant hard-on that filled his pants.

Matt cursed as the reality of their situation settled in. It would be damn near impossible to work with her without thinking about the taste of her skin and mouth, the feel of her hands and mouth working their magic on his cock, the feel of being tight inside her pussy, the sounds she made when she came around his rod.

He moved his hand to his swollen cock and shifted it. Why should he deny himself the pleasure of being with her? They were consenting, unattached adults. Rekindling their fling would in no way compromise his mission unless... Were she suspected of any of the wrongdoings, well, that would be a reason to keep his distance. But Meganlin's reports contained only glowing praise for Danielle Parker. She was a highly valued member of this company, a rising star, who was destined for a top position.

Top position. Bottom position. Side position.

Standing position. Fuck. They'd tried them all. She had excelled at them all.

His cock grew as his mind flipped through and dismissed the possible obstacles. No, there was no problem, no reason why he and Dani shouldn't resume where they'd left off in Vegas, if it was what they both wanted. He wanted it. And by the way she looked at him today in her office, she wanted it. She wanted him. As much as he wanted her.

With that thought in mind, he felt happier than he'd ever been since arriving in Albuquerque to investigate signs of wrongdoings at Meganlin.

He turned his chair to face the window. Would Dani come to him tonight? He believed she would. Their Vegas fling had been too intense and was too unfinished for her to pretend it hadn't happened. She would be in his bed again. Of that, he was certain. He'd see to it. And although she'd be surprised when she later learned he was also the owner of Meganlin, the first business his grandfather had started fifty years ago—a business that upon his father's recent death had passed to him—she would understand his reasons for not immediately divulging that truth.

Turning back to face his desk, he ignored his throbbing cock and instead rolled up his sleeves, scooped forward a stack of files, and dug into work so he could be free to dig into her when she arrived, hot and horny for him.

****

Walking the dim hallway toward the corner suite of offices that had belonged to Elliott, Dani knew Matt would be there even though the floor showed no signs of life. As she rounded the corner, she saw him. The

Sophia Ryan

blinds were up on the wall of windows separating his large suite from the other offices, and he was seated at the desk, pouring over the scattered stacks of files and papers covering the polished wood surface.

Shirt-sleeves rolled to his elbows, the knot of his tie loosened at his neck, he grunted something unintelligible from her vantage point and ran his hands through his thick hair, making it stand on end.

How many times had she raked her fingers through that hair when ecstasy bloomed deep inside her at the things his hands or mouth or body was doing to her? How many kisses had she given those full lips that were now set in a firm line? How many times had they whispered sweet, erotic, dirty, tantalizing expressions of lust and love into her ears, her skin, her mouth? More than she could count or forget.

Dani hadn't seen this serious side of Matt in Vegas, but she knew she'd enjoy getting to know him as much as she had enjoyed getting to know his other side.

As if sensing he was being watched, Matt raised his head. His gaze fused with hers, making her body tingle. He rose from his chair as she walked through the door. A sexy, inviting grin on his face, he eyed her intently as she silently placed a to-go cup of coffee on his desk and dropped her purse in one of the two chairs facing his desk. They exchanged no words. None were needed. The heat and intensity in their eyes, the electricity zapping between them, said it all.

She went into his arms, he in hers, in a familiar, easy motion, and hugged each other. It was like she'd made it home after a long time away.

"I've missed you." His voice was so soft and loving it touched her heart. He kissed her and held her tight.

The bulge in his pants grew hard against her, and she wanted to take it in her hands, her mouth, her pussy, which had craved him all day as she relived everything they'd done to each other in Vegas. But she wasn't here for that.

"I've missed you, too," she said and gently eased back when his hand found its way to her breast and she was a heartbeat away from relinquishing control of her body to her passion. Her gut clenched at the disappointment flashing across his face. What she had to say would probably blindside him. She knew it, hated it, but it was necessary. For both of them.

She shifted from his arms and nodded toward the desk that looked like a tornado had touched down on its surface. "From the look of things, I'd say the rumors of Elliott's disasters weren't exaggerated." Before he could open his mouth to speak, she added, "I don't expect you to answer that."

He would have pulled her into his arms again, but she turned, picked up the cup of coffee and handed it to him. "Maybe this will help you get through it tonight."

The confusion in his eyes told her he knew something was amiss with their reunion. When he'd fantasized about their first time alone together, had he imagined they'd be half naked and on their way to nirvana by now? She had, even while knowing it couldn't happen.

He took the cup but did not drink from it. "Thanks."

She nodded. "Mind if we sit?"

He motioned her toward the two leather chairs and couch surrounding a small table in the corner of his office. She sat in a chair, not trusting herself to sit on the couch because she knew he'd join her and then she'd give in and do what she really wanted to do with him. He set his cup on the table and settled into the chair across from her, crossing his ankle on his knee.

"Did you come here just to bring me coffee?" he said, his voice low and full of heat.

"No." Though she fought to keep the sex from her voice, the smile twitching at the corners of his lips told her it had sneaked in and that he thought he knew exactly what she had come for.

He uncrossed his legs, leaving his tented lap an open and familiar invitation. His eyes closed halfway, but she could read fully what they told her. *Come closer. Touch me. Suck me. Ride me.* He held out his hand to her. Desire radiated from him, from his posture to the way his eyes were drinking her up. Her heart swelling in her chest released tingles of pleasure that tangoed through her. Her automatic response was to take his hand and accept his invitation, so it took everything inside her to keep her ass in the chair. She couldn't keep her gaze from his mouth, his eyes, his lap, though.

When she didn't take his hand, he withdrew it and let it drop to the arm of the chair. His head tilted. "Why did you come here?"

Choosing her words carefully, she leaned forward, narrowing the gap between them, her hands clasping each other for support and strength. "I wanted to talk with you before any more time passed, to tell you…to ask you…"

"Dani. Tell me what you want."

How many times had he uttered the same sultry

words to her in Vegas? How many times had she told him, in graphic detail? *Fuck me harder. From behind. On your lap. Up against the wall. Touch my ass. Eat my pussy. Kiss me. Bite me. Suck me. Harder. Slower. Faster. Again. Now.* What she wanted right this minute was to pull open his pants, lift her skirt, yank aside her panties, and ride to hell on his sinfully delicious cock.

Garnering all her control, she faced him full on, licked her dry lips. "I want you to forget what happened between us in Vegas."

His eyebrows furrowed, his eyes darkened and narrowed, and his mouth tightened, clearly suggesting he was not pleased by her request. "Why?"

"The man I had a Vegas fling with is a memory that keeps me warm at night. The man sitting before me is investigating the company I work for."

He moved to the edge of his seat and leaned forward. Only inches separated them, and she got a whiff of his sexy scent that sent her restraint on a long vacation. "Who I am is the man who loved you breathless."

Breathless. Oh, yes. Even now, just thinking about him loving her, her breath balled up in her throat and shivers danced along her skin.

He took her hands. "And you're the woman who satisfied my every desire. Not in a million years will I forget what happened between us."

He had released something in her in their short time together that wouldn't allow her to forget him either. Ever. There, in the semidarkness, legs and hands touching, mouths aching to kiss, she wanted—needed—his touch, the weight of his body on hers, the feel of his mouth on her lips and skin, the taste of him in her mouth, the sound of his rough, joyful sex chuckle in her ears. She needed it like she needed air, water, food.

She shook her head to rid her mind of the inappropriate thougths weakening her resolve. "Matt. It was just a fling," she lied. "A slightly extended one-night stand."

A look of dejection and anger flashed across his face before he reined it in. "It was more than that." He stroked and caressed her fingers and palms as he spoke, causing fire to flare up and run the course of her body. "And I see no reason we can't continue what we started."

It took all her strength not to lunge at him and straddle the stiff orgasm-giving god between his legs. It took all her strength to remember why they couldn't continue what they'd started. Pulling her hands from his helped her resolve only slightly.

"That can't happen." She heard the rough edge to her voice. He did, too, by the way his eyes narrowed.

"Because…"

"You're here to investigate serious wrongdoings in the company I work for. You and I have been intimate." Fucked-each-other's-brains-out intimate. "If you don't see the ethical dilemma here, you're not as good as your reputation suggests."

His narrowed gaze was colder than she'd ever seen it. No, this Matt wasn't her Matt. "You're worried about your job."

She drew in a long, steadying breath and released it. "You have a job to do here, and so do I. I need to know that you can see me as a professional in this company despite what happened between us in Vegas."

"I have no trouble seeing you as the accomplished

employee your files and your management say you are. And as long as you weren't involved in your president's alleged crimes, you don't have to worry about your job."

She nodded her thanks.

"And I see no ethical dilemma about continuing what we started in Vegas. That's personal."

"Considering why you're here, I think it's best that we maintain a purely professional and platonic relationship, don't you?" *Even though we were lovers just days ago*. She didn't say it, and neither did he, but it was there in the room with them, screaming to be heard.

"What I think is best is to sweep everything off that desk and fuck you fast and hard until you scream my name like you did our first time together."

His words sent delicious shivers through her that made her nipples peak against her silky blouse and made her panties damp. Damper.

He moved closer, his lips so close she could almost feel them brushing hers as he spoke. "Then I want to take you home and slowly make love to you in my bed. All night. Like we did our second time. And third. And fourth. And—"

"Matt," she said on a gulp of air. Her eyes closed, and she fought to still her thundering heartbeat, calm the desire raging through her. But the lust she had seen raging in his eyes weakened her resolve to stay firm. Oh, how she wanted him right now. Wanted to kiss him. Touch him. Ease the tension in his body. And hers. Feel his heart beat inside her body.

"Dani."

She met his eyes. The words, "I want that, too,"

lodged in her throat, where they throbbed, fighting to get free, insisting that she undo the empty relationship pact she had asked for. Could they maintain separate personal and professional relationships, or would the one forever be seeping into the other, creating a bitterness that would eventually destroy both? Not if they knew the rules. Set up boundaries. Tried hard.

She opened her mouth to tell him so. But an unwelcome thought of Elliott surfaced. The pain and humiliation she'd mostly vanquished rushed into her throat. The night of their break up. His betrayal of her love and loyalty. Her sickening fear stemming from his illegal activities and his death. Like it or not, here, right before her, was another man in power who could do that to her, could take her job, maybe even trump up evidence to send her to prison.

She shook her head.

Every second of the protracted silence that followed her silent life-crushing *no* felt like a knife to her soul. Finally, he stood. Slowly. Kept his gaze locked with hers. "Thanks for the coffee."

His acerbic tone belied his courteous words. He walked back to his paper-piled desk, leaving the cup on the table, leaving her to grapple with the stark realization that unless she said something now to change course, she would lose him.

Her chest burned, evaporating the breath from her lungs and transforming her heart into a cold mound of ashes, rendering her unable to say the words that would save the relationship.

Nothing left to do or say, she stood, too, and faced him. "Goodnight, Matt." He ignored her so she turned to leave. She had reached the door when he spoke.

"Dani."

She halted, hand on the doorframe to steady herself, but didn't turn back to face him. She couldn't face him with regret and desire burning her eyes. He'd see it and convince her, with his mouth and his hands, that their platonic agreement was wrong.

The soft sounds of his steps coming closer tickled up her spine. He stopped right behind her, his front brushing her backside. His heat, his scent, rushed out and wrapped around her, and she felt her will slipping.

Oh, God, Matt. Please don't touch me again. I won't be able to—

His hands settled lightly at her hips, and a breath caught in her throat. She swallowed it down and took another, trying to ready herself for what he'd do next with those hands.

His lips ran over her neck and rocked a shudder through her. His mouth hovered at her ear and chills skated up her thighs. She trembled at his nearness, at her overwhelming desire, at the desire emanating from him.

"If I slip across our new platonic and professional boundary," he whispered as his hands slid slowly up her side, halting at the swell of her breasts, then inching back down where they eased around her waist, "I'll count on you to push me back until I learn how to treat you as someone other than my lover." At *lover* his hands traveled low on her abdomen, his fingers dipping lower to her sex to trace her throbbing clit.

A rough moan rolled from her mouth before she could swallow it back. Too breathless to speak, she could only nod. He let her go, and she wanted to cry out, to grab him to her, drop her panties and his pants, and beg him to forget what she'd said. Instead, she stiffened her spine and walked out the door, their agreement and her regret bubbling like acid in her stomach.

A purely platonic, professional relationship. That was what she had come here to ask for, and that was what he'd given her. And she'd never felt so empty or heartbroken.

****

Matt watched Dani leave his office. Only when he heard the elevator swish closed and head to the ground floor did he unplug his feelings.

"Fuuuuuuuuck!" He shouted the obscenity, long and loud, pounding the desk with clenched fists. This was *not* how he had imagined this going at all.

Here she was, within his reach again, as hot and dazzling as the first time she set fire to his life, and she was putting herself off limits. He'd been kicking himself for letting her go. And no matter what she said, no matter what he'd just promised, he wouldn't let her go again.

He breathed in the familiar intoxicating smell of her lingering in the air—a heady elixir of scents from her warm, soft skin, the floral shampoo she used on her silky hair, the exotic perfume she touched to her pulse points and between her breasts, the erotic scent of her desire for him—and he was back in Vegas with her, their bodies wrapped up tight.

From the moment he discovered that the sexy, fiery woman who had rocked his world worked for his company, a single burning thought controlled him, that they would resume what they had started. Part of the reason he was still at the office was that his focus today had been more about getting her back into bed than disarming the bombs Elliott Gibson had planted and getting this business whole and clean again so he could sell it.

The business he could fix with his eyes closed. The relationship specifics with Dani would take more effort to work out, but he was confident the passion they shared in Vegas would light their way to even greater pleasures here in Albuquerque. With her declaration tonight that what she wanted from him was a professional relationship that would protect her job, those preliminary plans fizzled.

He had overcome much more complex, even dangerous obstacles to get what he wanted. A love affair—even a slightly more complex one like theirs—offered far less challenge.

The women who had come before Dani had done back flips to share his bed and his company. Of course, the difference between those women and Dani was that, with her, he actually entertained the idea of something more permanent.

Their time in Vegas had planted in him a need to have her light in his life every day, her fire in his bed every night. He had realized that the afternoon she left him. He'd seen that same desire in her today. And he thought she had come here tonight to tell him, to show him. Instead, she had asked him to forget Vegas, to accept their new relationship—a hands-off relationship.

It would take more finesse on his part than he initially thought, but he would draw her back into his bed, into his heart. And when this job was done and he left the company in capable hands, he would have found a way to make her a part of his life.

Sophia Ryan

A smile grew on his face as a plan grew in his brain. He rifled the files on his desk until he found the one with her name. The file was amazingly thick for someone so young and with just five years in at the company. As he thumbed through the pages he was already familiar with—resume, job description, performance reviews, awards, salary increases, promotions, conferences attended, customer praise—a better picture of the woman he wanted materialized in his mind.

Dani was ambitious, taking on additional responsibilities at every opportunity, and highly competent, always exceeding the requirements of those responsibilities. She attended as many conferences and workshops as budget allowed, paying for some out of her own pocket, each time bringing new information or more efficient methods of doing things into the company and using them to improve her job performance and, as a result, her department and the company itself.

Her managers noted her professionalism in all situations and were eager to develop her already strong leadership abilities. However, despite her abilities and her director's overwhelming confidence in and support of her, the president, Elliott Gibson, passed her over for the assistant director promotion and gave it to Nathan Gerber, who, from what he could tell on paper, didn't hold a candle to Dani.

He would find out why. In the mean time, he would see that the board approve Karen's recommendation of Dani for the assistant director position. And he would ask Karen, as acting president, to appoint a trustworthy employee of high enough status to assist him with the investigation. He was sure she'd appoint Dani for that role as well.

He was hanging high hopes on that decision. That Dani would see that he absolutely did see her as the valuable employee she was. That it would give them more opportunity to work together. And that it would remind her how good they were together and could be again.

Chapter Six

Days later, Dani left Karen's office, the news of her promotion and new assignment blaring in her ears, and stormed down the hall to Matt's.

"Lisa, I need to see Matt."

Lisa Bowden brought up his calendar for his appointments. "He has a meeting in fifteen minutes with Luis from—"

"Thanks." Before the assistant could come up with an argument why she couldn't have five minutes, Dani rapped on Matt's door, opened it, walked in, and closed it behind her.

He was at his desk, phone to his ear. When he saw Dani at his door, he told the caller he'd phone them back. He moved around to the front of his desk where she stood, hands clenched in fists at her side, her body rigid.

"I have to know the truth." Her voice matched her body language.

"About?" He perched on the corner of his desk, arms crossed, eyes on her, as if eager to hear what had the passion spinning high and fast in her demeanor.

"You know perfectly well what about," she demanded, the fire burning in her pushing her to use a tone and words she normally wouldn't.

"Want to give me a clue?"

"Karen just told me I'm the new assistant director."

"Congratulations. Don't you want the position?"

"Yes, I want it."

"Then what's the problem?"

She put her hands on her hips and leaned toward him. "It's not the promotion. It's what comes with it."

"You mean assisting me with the investigation."

"That's exactly what I mean."

"Karen suggested it and the board approved it. Who am I to disagree?"

"Are you sure?"

His eyes sparkled with what looked like humor. Was he laughing at her? "What are you accusing me of, Ms. Parker?"

"That you set it up...us working together...in the hopes that..." She looked behind her to make sure they were still alone. "That we would continue our...relationship."

"Did you consider that it was your reputation as an honest, dependable employee that made you the perfect choice to take on the assistant director position and to help with the audit, and that my desire to get you back into my bed played no part?"

She had. For about a second. But it was overshadowed by the memory of his previous declaration that he wanted to continue their fling. In his defense, in the week he'd been here, he hadn't said a word about their relationship after that first day. He'd all but stayed away from her, talking to her only in meetings with others around. So maybe she had jumped the gun, just a little, rushing into his office and hurling accusations. Embarrassment heated her face and lowered her chin a fraction.

Matt stood and stepped toward her, put his finger

under her chin, and lifted it until she met him eye to eye. "I've made it no secret that I want you back in my bed, so I understand why you'd question my motives. But don't do it again." His voice was firm but kind—kinder than she deserved. "You insult your talent and my judgment."

His hand stayed at her face to touch her cheek, and she forgot to breathe. "Your judgment? I thought you had nothing to do with it?"

His fingers slid into her hair, his thumb dangerously close to her bottom lip. The touch softened the stiffness to her spine, and all she wanted to do was fall against his chest and feel his arms around her, his heart beat against hers, his lips taking hers.

"The board approved your new position, based on Karen's recommendation."

"And the assignment to work with you?"

"I need a trusted Meganlin employee working with me on this investigation."

"Did you ask Karen to appoint me?"

Then his thumb was there, on her mouth, tracing the edge of her lower lip, brushing over its plumpness, and she was seconds from drawing it into her mouth, nipping it, sucking it. His other hand palmed the small of her back and shifted her closer. A little whimper, a sharp quick intake of breath that screamed of need, escaped, and she flushed with heat, from her face to her tingling breasts, that it had come from her parted lips.

"I asked for the best," he murmured. "She immediately thought of you."

His ringing phone made her jump, and it pulled her from the fog she'd sunk into at the simple touch of his hands. She stumbled back a step or two, away from his touch. Ignoring the call, he stuffed his hands into his pockets...so he wouldn't be tempted to touch her again?

"If you know of any reason you shouldn't be part of my team, tell me now. Otherwise, get your sexy little ass to work." He softened his last remark with a smile.

"I have three things to say before I go. First, I apologize for storming in here hurling accusations with no facts to back them. Second, I appreciate the opportunity to help the company. Third, *sexy little ass* is way outside the boundary of appropriateness."

He threw his head back and laughed, and the sweet sound of it followed her as she headed back to her office.

****

The pace of her days-old job was demanding, requiring that she come in early, eat lunch at her desk or on the run, and work late. It was exhilarating, and she was learning so much. What was exhausting and frustrating was the constant fight to stay on the right side of the relationship boundary with her new boss.

She turned her gaze to his office, the one adjoining hers. Matt's office. Her first task in her new role had been to move next to him. She had protested, he had insisted, and she had moved in. She could hear him in there now, on the phone. His voice trilled over her skin, raising goosebumps like his hands used to. If only she could get the images of him out of her head, get his touch and his scent off her skin, get the feel of his kisses off her mouth, her body. Then she could handle anything the job threw in front of her.

Her phone rang, startling her out of her thoughts. She grabbed it. "Dani Parker."

"You ready for lunch?"

She looked at the phone ID screen, then at the time. It was Liz. And it was Eleven forty-five. She had been daydreaming about Matt for nearly fifteen minutes. She glanced at the pile of Elliott's files on her desk. She had dozens to go before she could call it a day.

"Dani? Are you there?"

"Yes, I'm..." She cleared the fogginess from her throat. "I'm here, Liz, but—"

"No. No. No. You are not going to cancel on me again. You need to eat, you need to get away from the office, and your best friend needs to see you. I'm headed to your office right now, and you better be ready or I'm going to drag you out in front of everyone. I'll do it, too. You know I will."

Liz hung up without waiting for a reply, and Dani set the phone down. If she took time for lunch, it would mean working even later tonight. At the same time, she really wanted, needed, deserved a few minutes away from the office. But Matt had such faith in her, so did Karen, and she didn't want to let either of them down.

Hell, it was just lunch. She was allowed. The work would still be there when she got back.

She grabbed her handbag and walked to the door. Waiting on the other side was a smiling Liz.

"I would have done it," she said.

Dani grinned, already feeling better about her decision. "I know you would have. Any ideas where you want to go?"

"You choose, since you're paying, Ms. Hotshot Assistant Director."

Dani chose one of their favorite places known for its locally brewed beer and some of the best green chile cheeseburgers in town. They sat on the patio to enjoy the weather and the eclectic sidewalk traffic consisting of young professionals like them, students and professors from the nearby university, residents of the area, and the occasional four-legged furry friend.

She leaned her head back on her chair and closed her eyes, luxuriating in the warm caress of the sun. "Thanks for getting me out of the office. I really needed this. It feels like forever since I've felt the sun on my face."

"Soak it in, baby. You're looking a bit vampish."

Dani snorted but otherwise didn't argue the point.

"I'm serious. You're pale, look like you haven't slept, and you've lost weight."

"So basically, I look like shit?"

"What's going on with you?"

Dani opened her eyes to face her friend and felt just a hair better at seeing the love and concern in her eyes. "I think it was a mistake to accept the job."

"Why? I thought you loved it?"

"I do, but—"

Liz wagged a green bean fry at her. "What's really going on?"

She was about to toss out a flippant remark but was too tired to even pretend a lightness about her feelings toward Matt. "I can't think straight, being so close to Matt. I spend all day in the same office with him, my mind replaying the memories of us in Vegas. I relive every word, every touch, every kiss, every moment." She closed her eyes. "And all I can think is how much I want it again."

"So do something about it."

"I'm the one who marched into his office insisting

on this platonic, professional agreement. I can't go back in there and tell him I was wrong and, oh, by the way, I want sex right now or I won't be able to do my job properly."

"You don't need to say anything. Go into his office, wrap yourself around him, give him the hottest, wettest kiss on the mouth, stick your hand down his pants and remind him he's your man. I guarantee he's not going to say no or insist you stick to your no-fucking agreement."

"Coming on to him now would only make him question my commitment." She glanced at her watch. "So will a two-hour lunch. Let's get back." She grabbed her bag and plopped down cash for the bill and tip.

****

Matt stood in Dani's office, desire turning to disappointment that she wasn't there. He'd been on that damn conference call all morning and rushed to her office as soon as it broke so he could see her. He needed to see her face, smell her skin, hear her voice, touch her hair. Hell—what he needed was her body ground against his for an hour or two of rough, consuming sex.

This absurd agreement of theirs was driving him insane. To be near her every day but not able to touch her, kiss her, make love to her was torture. It didn't help that his brain kept flashing him slide after slide of their weekend in Vegas. That he could focus on work at all was a miracle. What had he been thinking, insisting she move into the adjoining office?

It wasn't just sex he was after. If it had been just sex, he could have scratched that itch easily. It was *her* he wanted. Sex with *her*. No one else would satisfy his need. But he had agreed to honor her request to maintain a purely professional relationship. And if he pushed her too hard for something more, she might leave.

If there was one good thing about their agreement, it was that he was getting to know another side of Danielle Parker. In Vegas, he admired her wit, her enthusiasm, her passion. Since working with her, he noticed her intelligence, her leadership, her integrity, her tenacity—and the list just kept growing.

In Vegas, he realized he wanted her, with a hunger that burned deep. Here in Albuquerque, he realized he liked her. A lot. And that only made him desire her more. Yeah. He wanted her. Like he'd never wanted a woman before.

Did she know what she was doing to him? He knew what she was doing to him. Hell, anyone with eyes knew what she was doing to him by the constant hard-on the size of a nuclear sub in his pants when she was around him. And he was damn tired of it. Damned tired of drooling around the office like some hormone-driven high school boy stalking his latest crush.

If he wanted her, he'd have her. He'd been her lover once, and he could make it happen again. He *would* make it happen.

The sound of laughter floated toward him from down the hall. Dani's laugh. The sound trilled over his heart, soothed his inner tirade, like cool water trickling over warm stone.

She rounded the corner to her office, stopping when she saw him standing at her desk.

Her cheeks flushed pink, but her eyes still showed traces of exhaustion that had appeared shortly after she started working with him. A long, hard, soul-satisfying orgasm or three would take care of that, and he'd do it for her, if she'd let him. Her long, thick hair caressed her back, and she plucked away a strand that had caught on her glossed lips. He could have done it for her with his lips if she'd let him. The coral sleeveless dress she wore made her skin glow, and the silky material expertly followed the curves of her breasts, waist, and hips like his hands would do again…if she'd let him.

"Back from lunch?" The obvious was all he could manage.

"Yes, we are." Liz answered, but he kept his eyes on Dani. "It's such a gorgeous day I dragged Dani out to enjoy an hour of sun."

"Good. She doesn't get enough." Sex or sun.

He knew he was staring, ogling really, hell, fucking Dani with his eyes, but he couldn't seem to stop, couldn't tear them from her beautiful face. By the way she stared back at him, her gaze trying not to meet his but failing, he could tell the hunger probably showed in his eyes, had triggered her own, and she was trying to ignore both.

He took a breath to break the bond. "But now that you're back, I want to discuss your progress on that client list. Get settled, then come on in."

Without waiting for a response, he walked away, to his own office, before the urge to pull her into his arms and kiss her, despite his promise, despite their witness, overtook his good sense.

****

The hunger in Matt's eyes stripped the strength from Dani's body, and she rushed to the bathroom to freshen up before meeting with him.

Liz joined her as far as the elevator. "Remember," she whispered. "Tongue in his mouth, hand in his pants...or vice versa." She jumped into the elevator, laughing.

Dani brushed her teeth and freshened up. When she got to his office, he was on the phone. He pointed to the leather grouping they had sat in the night she brought him coffee and they'd etched their agreement in fragile glass.

She slid into the same chair and opened her master file, pretending to study her notes but actually listening to the sound of his voice. She took deep breaths in an attempt to still the hammering of her heart that being near him caused.

He soon joined her in the adjacent chair, that crooked little grin on his face that sent her head swirling. If she was going to melt into a puddle of steaming lust every time they were together, she might as well resign today.

He leaned forward, elbows on his knees, hands clasped between his legs. "So, how's it going?"

"I've been running through Elliott's files and I think I found—"

"No, Dani. I mean you."

His presence, his intimate question, filled her head with hot fudge and turned her organs to goo. "Excuse me?"

"How are you doing with your new position? Any concerns? Regrets?"

Uh-huh. Like she would tell him her regrets. "It's been challenging and fulfilling."

As if he had seen into her heart and glimpsed the truth, he pinned her with his eyes. "And?"

"And?" She raised her eyebrow and shook her head quizzically.

He chuckled. "The politically correct answer out of the way, tell me how you really feel." That white-hot smile had her considering Liz's earlier suggestion about tongues and hands.

She answered his smile with a shadow of her own. "A bit overwhelming at times. Not that I'm complaining. I'd appreciate any suggestions you care to offer on how to get it all done in a mere twelve hours a day."

"You don't. You do the best you can, remembering to reserve enough energy at the end of the day to have some fun, enjoy some good food, and get some sleep, so you can start all over again the next day."

She nodded and was surprised to see his eyebrow lift in humor.

"Not what you wanted to hear?" he asked.

"Actually, it's better than the answer I thought I'd hear."

"Which is?"

"That the board was on crack when they approved me for this job."

He laughed and she joined him. It felt good to be laughing with him. She missed the closeness they had shared in Vegas—humor and laughter had been a surprising byproduct of their sexual intimacy. Easy. It had been easy with him, and even though there wasn't a moment she didn't remember who had the power in their relationship, it had her longing for the life they'd lived in those few hours in Vegas.

"Like I said, I asked for the best person for the job. And I got her."

She stared into his eyes, seeing his sincerity in his words, his voice, his face. Something else was reflected in those all-seeing eyes of his, some emotion she refused to give name to but felt calling to her, tugging the strings inside her.

He reached out and scooped up her hand, and her chest tightened at the contact.

"Don't doubt yourself," he said.

She didn't doubt her ability to do her work, just her ability to stay away from Matt. She fixed her gaze on their linked hands. He caressed her fingers with his, sliding one long finger up one side of her finger, down the other to the vee where another finger began, then repeated the motion with that digit.

She should stop him. Remind him that this behavior was outside the boundaries of their agreement. But dammit, she didn't want to stop him or remind him. She wanted him to continue, to go wherever he was going and not stop.

"I don't doubt you," he said, his voice low.

He turned her hand over and brushed her palm with his thumb. Then, as if reading her thoughts, her hidden desires, he lowered his mouth and kissed it. Heat blossomed from the kiss he left and radiated up her arm and into the pool of heat between her legs. He nibbled her fingertips, pasting kisses from the tips of her short, manicured nails up to her scented wrist.

Her mouth parted in a sigh, and she shuddered with the overwhelming need for him to hurry, to take all of her now. At the sound of his responding low groan, her nipples peaked hard and hot in her lacy bra, and the real ache of want swirled deep inside her. She was already wet for him. So wet. So needy. So empty and ready for him to fill her completely.

His lips reached the sensitive spot on her inside elbow, and he licked it with the tip of his tongue. She moaned and closed her eyes in ecstasy, feeling the pleasure of that lapping tongue as far away as her pussy.

"Look at me, Dani." His whispered voice, rough with longing, prompted her heavy lids open, and she obeyed him. His dilated pupils darkened his eyes and told her he shared her passion. "I want to see how much you want me."

Chapter Seven

Matt's hand moved to Dani's face, the pad of his thumb brushing her cheek before moving lower to trace the full edge of her mouth. She licked her lips, touching the tip of her tongue to his thumb. His quick intake of breath made her bold, and she nipped the digit with her teeth.

He curled his hand around her neck, under the curtain of her hair, at the same time her hand reached out and caressed his face. He moved in. So did she, her soul crying out in joy at the breath-stealing kiss she knew was coming, the kiss she'd craved since their last kiss so very long ago.

"Matt." His whispered name fell from her lips like a plea, like a consent, like a promise.

"God, Dani, you're so fucking delicious," he said. "All I want to do is—"

"Matt, Glenn Marquez is—"

Dani jerked back immediately at Lisa's voice, but she knew the woman had seen enough in that split second to understand exactly what kind of business was going on between them, seated too close together, their heads too close for business-related activities, their hands on each other in a way-too-friendly touch.

"Sorry, I'll come back," she muttered and spun around to leave.

"Lisa," Matt said, his voice rough voice, stopping

her. "What about Marquez?"

"Uh, he's here. Says he has the data you wanted."

"Tell him I'll be down to his office in ten minutes."

"Yes, sir." Without another glance, Lisa rushed from his office and closed the door.

Dani didn't know whether to curse or thank Glenn for his timing, but she couldn't meet Matt's eyes with the need heating her face.

"Dani, I'm…I need to go," he said, his voice filled with regret.

Not trusting her voice, she nodded, gathered her files, and scrambled to her office through the adjourning door.

What was the matter with her? Had she lost every drop of self-control in Vegas? It scared her how easily she had been about to give in to her desires and destroy all she had worked for. It could *not* happen again. Especially at work.

****

Matt watched Dani rush off to her office, away from him, and he let her go before he lost what little self-control he had left and took her on the chair, her legs spread wide over the arms, or up against the wall, her legs high around his waist, or on the fucking floor, her bucking beneath him. Whatever position, all he wanted was to climb between her legs and release the pent-up passion putting her body and his on edge and making them tense and skittish around each other as if they could sense the coming explosion and were doing everything to shy away from it. Ah, the sweet instant when she had allowed the wall between them to drop, had let her desires do the talking. It gave him hope.

When his hard-on had calmed, he left his office

and headed to Glenn's office, trying to get Dani off his mind but failing. God, he missed her. If only he had handled things differently in Vegas. If only he'd gone with his gut and made clear to her his interest in continuing the combustion that had sparked between them like a flash of lightning. She would be in his bed now. He was sure of it. But all that didn't matter. If he didn't find a way past all her walls and into her heart, all that would remain of their fling would be memories.

Giving her up wasn't an option.

The IT manager was seated at his desk, into whatever was on his computer monitor, when Matt rapped on the open door and walked in. "Glenn, what do you have for me?"

"Hey, Matt." He spun his chair to face him. "I've uploaded the data from Elliott's computer onto this thumb drive and the erased data onto this one." He handed the two drives to Matt, who slipped them into his pocket. "Some of the data was corrupted and beyond saving, but there's still quite a bit to review. Emails, documents, spreadsheets, invoices... Hope it gives you what you're looking for."

"Great work. Thanks for getting it done so quickly."

"You bet." He turned back to his monitor as Matt headed for the door.

The rush in his step was as much about getting to see Dani again as it was getting to review Elliott's files. Maybe the breakthrough they were looking for was at hand. The sooner they solved the case, the sooner she'd have to toss her high ideas of right and wrong and come back to him.

****

Her knees weak from her close call with Matt, Dani dropped into her chair and released the frustrated growl she had been curbing, letting her head fall onto her arms.

"Job getting to you?"

She looked up to see Nathan Gerber leaning against the doorjamb, watching her intently and smiling at her display of frustration as if it pleased him.

In no mood to deal with him, she didn't even try to couch her annoyance. "What do you want?" She turned to her computer and opened her email.

He ambled into the room. "I wanted to congratulate you on your promotion and take you to lunch tomorrow to celebrate."

He kept his fake smile firmly on his face. He'd had work done—veneers from the look of him—but it hadn't helped his sincerity.

"That's not necessary."

"Maybe not, but it's only right, since we were both up for the job." He moved closer and perched on the corner of her desk, his crotch facing her. "To show you there are no hard feelings on my part." He put his hand on her hair.

Recoiling, she slapped his hand away and did her best to grind him into the floor with her stare. "Don't touch me, Nathan."

"Ouch! Withdraw the claws." He held his hands up in mock surrender. "Elliott always said how nice you were. Either he was lying, or you're only nice to the boss, whoever he may be."

She went cold, her blood freezing in her veins at his insinuation. What did he know? What had Elliott told him? They'd kept their affair hidden in the workplace. Her stomach churned as she stared at him, seeing a secret lurking behind his shit-brown eyes like a shadow. "I'm busy, and you're wasting my time with your riddles. If you have something business-related to say to me, say it and leave. If not, then just leave."

His gaze rose to the ceiling as if he were thinking hard. "Something business related...hmm." He scratched his head. "Okay." His eyes bore into hers. "You should wear that jewelry Elliott gave you. Add a little bling to your wardrobe."

Shit! How did he know about the necklace? She had never worn it or told anyone about it. Elliott must have told him. But why would he have? How much did he know about her affair? What was his game? To gloat that he could out her at any time? And for what purpose? To cast doubts about her character and suitability for the job, thereby getting revenge for her having won it over him? Would he then go as far as to suggest she had murdered Elliott in retaliation for his giving the job to Nathan?

She didn't know what he was doing, but she wasn't going to give him anything. Couldn't. Shock had sealed her mouth, preventing even one word or one sound from exiting her throat, but self-preservation kept it closed. The heavy silence weighed on them, and her brain was about to explode from wanting to scream and demand that he reveal his real agenda.

Arrogance lifted his mouth into a grin then lifted him from the desk. "Congratulations on your promotion. Good luck keeping it."

As he sauntered out, Dani rose, shut the door behind him, and pressed her back against its solidness. She breathed slowly to get her pounding heartbeat and temper under control then she pushed away from the door and trod across the carpet to her desk. She pulled her bag from her drawer, dug into the bottom of it, and found the box she was looking for.

Opening the lid, she glared at the silver and turquoise locket sitting undisturbed on its velvet bed, still pinned in place. The last gift Elliott had given her. It was odd that Nathan had called it bling. The necklace in question was pretty but could hardly be classified as bling. And it was the only jewelry Elliott had given her. Was Nathan just testing the waters, dangling comments to see which one she'd bite at? Unfortunately, even her silence had probably been enough of a reaction to his comment about Elliott giving her jewelry that he knew it was a definite bite.

Ah, Elliott. Seeing the locket brought back the memories of the pain of that day when she realized every sweet word coming from his luscious lips had been a lie. That every kiss given in love had been a lie. The necklace was a reminder of the mistakes she'd made. A reminder that she had risked everything to be with a man who was in a position to ruin her, a man who didn't love her, a man who only wanted to use her.

Sadness wrenched her in its unforgiving grip, and she put a steadying hand to her chest, not so much from the pain of losing Elliott, but from the sudden and sharp realization that she and Matt could not resume their Vegas affair.

Matt, like Elliott, could destroy everything she had worked for.

Matt, like Elliott, didn't love her.

Matt, like Elliott, only wanted sex from her.

Giving Matt up, for good, was her only option.

She snapped the lid closed and stuffed the box back into her bag.

****

Matt passed Nathan in the hall on his way back to his office. The man shot him a smug look and was in the elevator before Matt thought to shove him up against the wall and question what had put that smirk on his face. There was only one office he could have come from.

"Lisa, was Gerber in Dani's office?"

She looked up from her computer. "Yes, he just left."

"Why was he here?"

She scrunched up her face and rolled her eyes. "He said he wanted to congratulate her on her promotion."

He stuffed his hands in his pockets and fisted them. "I didn't realize they were friends."

Lisa's eyes darted toward Dani's office then back to him. "The word is they had one date, and she refused to go out with him again. I don't know what happened, but ever since, it's like they're enemies. Also, he was furious when his appointment to assistant director was overturned and she got it instead."

She leaned in and lowered her voice. "I wasn't there, but I heard he smashed up the Blue Note—it's kind of a Meganlin hangout—the day her promotion was announced. A friend of mine, who was there, said he was trash-talking her the whole time he was zinging back shots. Saying stuff like he couldn't wait until she got what was coming to her."

He pushed down the sick feeling swirling inside him, not only at listening to gossip about Dani in order to gain some insight into her and Nathan but also that

Nathan seemed to have a grudge against Dani. "If he feels that way, why would he congratulate her?"

Lisa shrugged. "Who knows what goes on in that sleazy mind of his?" She shivered. "I don't mean to speak ill of anyone, but he creeps me out."

He gritted his teeth, tightening his jaw. "Do me a favor. If he comes around again, send him to me. He has no business-need to be in her office."

Not waiting for a response, he strode into Dani's office.

She sat at her desk, nose in the computer monitor, her face a bit pale, her luscious lips zipped in a tight line.

"Ready to take a look at Elliott's files?" he asked.

She jumped at hearing his voice, and her eyes shot to his then back to her computer where she was furiously clacking away at the keys. "Yes."

He rolled one of the side chairs to her desk and sat beside her. He handed her the thumb drive of Elliott's files, keeping the one with Elliott's erased files in his pocket to give to his tech team to go over. She plugged in the device and scrolled through the list of documents.

"Let's start with spreadsheets," he said.

She opened the first file in that folder. It listed business names and addresses, contact persons, anticipated R&D projects, competitors' names and bids, pricing.

"I recognize a few of these names from the hardcopy files I found," she said. "However, there are quite a few new ones."

"Which ones?" Matt asked.

She called out one after the other. "I'll have to check to be absolutely certain, but I don't believe we've ever done business with these companies, at least not since I've been here. This is…." She turned to face him. "I'm pretty sure this is a list of our competitors' top customers."

He met her eyes. "Tell me, Dani. Why would a company give up its confidential customer list to its competitor?"

"It wouldn't."

"Right. So, how do you suppose this sensitive and valuable information landed on Elliott's computer?"

"He bought it or…." She released a deep breath.

Matt nodded. "Considering the size of this list, I'd say it's from more than one competitor. Try another file."

She clicked into another file. "These are invoices for supplies to those clients."

"Most paid in cash." He scooted closer to the monitor, eyes narrowing as he scanned every line in the list. "These invoices weren't in the books accounting supplied for the audit."

"Our clients don't pay in cash," she said. "So it's true? Elliott was stealing?"

"Too soon to know for sure."

She blinked at the black and white proof before them then turned her face from his. But not before he saw the sadness in her eyes. Sadness and something else.

"I don't understand. He was the president of the company. He didn't see clients, other than at special functions. Why would he have this information on his computer? Maybe it wasn't his. Maybe someone planted—"

"I know it's hard to believe someone you knew

being capable of this kind of deception. Unfortunately, it happens more often than you realize."

"I wonder if this information is what got him killed?"

"That's for the police to determine. Our job is to talk to everyone on this list to verify whether they were actually doing business with us."

"I know people at most of these companies. I can get an answer from them with a quick call. However, for the others, I recommend face-to-face meetings. Shows we're serious about maintaining the company's reputation and otherwise good business practices."

As Matt left Dani to her work, he wondered why he hadn't told her about the erased data.

Chapter Eight

Between her work demands, Matt's thinly veiled and constantly humming passion enveloping her, and Nathan's insinuations and sly glances, the weekend couldn't have come too soon for Dani.

When almost everyone else in the office had left at four-thirty to start the weekend early, she was still hard at it at seven o'clock, going over Elliott's files, making notes about who to contact for appointments and who could give her the information she needed with a simple call, which she would get started on come Monday.

The guilt she felt earlier at declining Liz's invitation to happy hour had been replaced with relief and satisfaction at getting so much accomplished. She closed the program, glanced through her fifty or so email messages and, seeing none that couldn't wait until Monday, shut down the computer.

The blinking red light on her phone caught her attention. She dialed in to listen to her messages and put the phone on speaker phone while straightening her office and putting her work away in preparation to leave.

"Hey, girlfriend!" A tipsy Liz shouted into the phone to be heard over the din at the bar, but her slurred voice came in loud and clear to Dani, and to Matt, who had appeared in her doorway just after the message began to play.

"We're at the Blue Note for another hour or so. So finish up whatever you're working on and get your ass down here. Unless you're working on Matt. In which case, leave your ass where it is. Nasty sex with Hardbody will do you more good than alcohol with your bitches." Liz cackled while Dani's skin burned with humiliation, especially when Matt grinned.

She rushed to the phone and jabbed at the keypad to disconnect from speaker phone. One hand on her hip, the other over her mouth, she shook her head and stared at the device that had just opened up a conversation she had been trying her damndest to avoid. He now knew she had talked about him to her best friend. He now knew she wanted sex with him.

It was Matt who broke the awkward pause following Liz's message. "We should talk about that."

She held up her hand. "No. We shouldn't."

He moved closer to her. "It's long overdue."

"You don't want to talk. You want me to give in and sleep with you again."

"I *do* want to talk. I want to talk about why we're wasting time avoiding something we both want."

Her nerves and patience and resolve were frayed ends. "I'm not interested in having a sex-only relationship with you."

"Great. I'm not interested in that, either." His calm voice only increased her anger.

"Oh, please." She rolled her eyes, not for a minute believing his statement. "Do me a favor and just drop this conversation."

"I'll drop it…on one condition."

That damn sexy voice. He thinks all he has to do is use that damn sexy voice and I'll lose my mind and fall

all over him.

She threw her hands up. "One condition? And what would that be? Fuck you right here, right now, in my office?" Her voice rose with every word, all her pent-up passion for him and frustration for the job coming out.

With one swipe, the few papers and pens on the desk flew off and onto the floor. "How about on the desk?"

She shoved her phone and computer to the far corner and sat on the firm wooden surface. She spread her legs, her fingers crawling into the material of her skirt, making it rise, higher and higher.

Heat flared in his eyes as they focused on her bare thighs, and she could almost feel his mouth sucking and licking at her trembling flesh. "Too small? As I remember, you like lots of room to move around."

She slid off the desk, letting her skirt fall back in place, covering her legs. "How about the floor?" She pushed over the chairs in front of her desk to open a space big enough for two lovers to ride each other to the passionate finale. Dropping to her knees, she clasped her arms behind her back. "Or maybe you want to tie my hands behind my back again so you can guide my mouth wherever you want it. I know you liked that."

His eyes were dark and fiery, his body tense. And his chest was rapidly rising and falling, suggesting he was affected by her performance. The bulge tenting his pants was a pretty clear sign, too.

"Oh, I know..." She stood and yanked the silky sweater over her head and threw it at him, then backed up until the window stopped her. "Up against the window so the homeless people at the mission below can have a show with their soup."

Her arms reaching over her head caused her breasts to rise full and high in the transparent cups of her bra. The friction of material and flesh puckered her nipples. Her outburst and disrobing set her hair to flying around her heated face, and strands hung across her eye, her cheek, her parted lips. "Is this what you had in mind, Matt?" She put her most seductive spin on her voice.

The room grew cool to her exposed and flushed skin as she awaited his response. And waited some more. The cold silence doused her angry flames, leaving in their place the realization that she had gone too far. She felt foolish and embarrassed and vulnerable standing there, half naked, fully aroused, in front of him. She crossed her arms over her breasts but couldn't avert her eyes from the desire burning in his. She licked her lips, then swept the wayward hair behind her ear to tame the just-been-fucked hairstyle.

He approached her slowly, his gaze locked on hers, a little grin on his lips that pissed her off as much as it turned her on, his hands turning the sweater she threw at him right-side out. When he stood in front of her at last, he held it out to her.

"Actually." The word broke as it left his mouth, so he cleared his throat and tried again. "What I had in mind was dinner. But I admit...I do like your suggestions better." His voice was thick and hot, like caramel sauce.

She snatched the sweater from his hand and turned her back to him while she pulled it on. "Sorry," she said over her shoulder, her voice low and apologetic. "I'm tired, I'm hungry, I'm embarrassed, and I overreacted." She kept her eyes averted as she picked up the papers and pens from the floor and set them on her desk and he righted the chairs.

He moved to stand beside her. "If we hurry, we can still make our eight o'clock reservation."

Shaking her head in disbelief, she slipped into her suit jacket and opened her leather satchel and added two files to it. "You haven't heard a word I've said."

He put his hand on hers to stop her actions. "I heard every word."

With a barely muffled sigh, she pulled her hand away. "If you had, you'd know that dinner together is not a good idea."

As much as she relished the opportunity to sit a few feet from him, enjoy delicious food with him, hear his voice, talk to him, stare at his beautiful eyes and mouth, she knew where it would lead. She would be in dangerous territory with him a mere arm's length from her, his eyes, his mouth, his voice, his scent urging her sensuous side to take control. She was a nudge away from falling into his arms, into his bed. She knew it and, worse, *he* knew it, and she couldn't count on him to apply the brakes. Hell, she couldn't even count on herself to have the good sense to stop.

"Dani, outside this office the labels, the roles fall away, and we're just two friends having dinner together."

"You and I skipped the *friends* stage." She snapped the satchel closed, lifted it from the desk, and gripped the handle.

"That doesn't mean we can't be. Two colleagues having dinner together is well within the boundaries of a professional relationship."

She rifled through her mind, trying to come up

Sophia Ryan

with something to refute his argument, and he used it to push a little more.

"We won't discuss—or do—anything you're not comfortable with." As if he saw the instant her will faltered, he smiled and added, "I promise."

"It's been a long week. I should just go home." The last-ditch effort to refuse him was lame, but it was the only thing she could come up with. This weekend, she'd write a list of responses for everything he might ask her. Then she'd be better prepared for situations like this.

"You have to eat," he said. "I have to eat. Eating alone isn't good for the digestion or the soul. And it's no fun. And as I remember, you like to have fun."

Heat swirled inside her at the reminder of their conversation in Vegas, but he was right. About eating, that was. The idea of going home to cook at this hour or picking up something to go didn't appeal to her, and she knew she'd end up just having a piece of fruit and cheese or not eating at all. But still she hesitated to say yes to something she so badly wanted but shouldn't have.

She hadn't realized he was so close to her until she felt his hands on her shoulders and he turned her to face him. Goosebumps covered her at his touch, and she shivered, but inside she was warm, one delicious feeling after another rolling through her, making her decision.

"Consider it an apology for working you late all the time," he said, his voice low, as if he were trying to ease her fears and suspicions."

"It's my job," she said. "No apology needed."

"Then think of it as a reward."

104

"I'm rewarded with a good salary and benefits for doing my job. Nothing extra is expected or necessary."

His soft chuckle crawled up her spine and cupped her neck like a warm hand. "Then take pity on me so I don't have to eat alone."

His persistence, his teasing, his smile, his charm made the flashing red lights and sirens going off in her head clang louder as she heard herself agree.

****

The restaurant Matt chose, which charged a small fortune for its high-end brand of dining experience, richly catered to the two dozen or so couples cuddled in the flickering and flattering candlelight.

The hostess escorted them to a secluded linen-topped table upstairs near the wall of windows that looked out on the dazzling nightscape. A blues band played softly in the far corner of the room, setting the mood with rich and sultry notes. And the mood was seduction, Dani mused as she sipped the delicious and way-too-expensive pinot noir Matt had selected. The nectar warmed her insides and bloomed hot thoughts in her mind about the man sitting across from her, about the sex-filled night she could have if she would but allow it to unfold.

He had made her fantasies come true in the past, and she knew he could do it again with one word from her. If she didn't slow down on the wine, she'd be saying that word to him before their friendly, platonic, professional dinner was half over, despite what was at risk if she did.

"So, Dani. Why you were at the office at seven-thirty on a Friday night instead of out with friends at happy hour?" He tipped the wine bottle and filled her glass for the second time. "Or on a date?" So much for her vow to slow down.

"I had planned to meet friends at five-thirty, but when the time came, I was so close to finishing that last file, I decided to stay. And I don't date."

The way Matt looked at her, his eyes burning into hers, his mouth turned up into a slight smile, made her feel as if he were laughing at her.

She sat up straighter in her chair and met his gaze unblinkingly. "I noticed you weren't out kicking it at happy hour, or on a date, either."

His smile broadened. "Don't trade opportunities for good times with friends and loved ones for a few more hours at the office. All it'll get you is more work, fewer friends, shallow relationships, and less happiness."

His softly delivered comment settled inside her like a burr. Since she began the new job, she felt she had to choose between proving her worth by spending long hours at work and having a life that included spending time with friends. For the most part, she had chosen work. As a result, she felt tired, guilty, deprived, and sexually frustrated. "I'd argue that I'm not doing that, but you'd know I was lying because you're still in the office when I leave. If you think about it, it's your fault since I'm only taking your lead."

He laughed. "Yeah, but I'm the auditor. There is no rest for me until the job's done."

"And when the job's done, you'll leave." The sudden reality of that fact struck Dani hard.

The look in his eyes said he realized it, too. "Yes."

"Do you have an idea when might that be?"

"We're farther ahead than I thought we'd be at this point, thanks in part to your work. I'd say November, maybe December. Hard to know."

Praise coming from him would normally make her beam with pride, but she couldn't smile about the fact he had just put a timeframe to any relationship they might have and started the stopwatch.

"No one expects you to put in the number of hours you've been logging," he said, obviously shifting away from the conversation about his leaving. "When the occasion calls for it, certainly, but not to the exclusion of everything else that makes life worth living."

"I'll remind you of your advice when you're still at the office as late as I am," she said.

He laughed, and she allowed herself to join him, pleased that she had made him laugh.

"Matt? Dani? I thought that was you two."

Karen stood before them, introducing her husband, Walt. Matt stood to shake hands, and Dani, though she could barely comprehend the words for the fog in her mind, somehow remembered to smile and say the right things as she was introduced.

"Join us for a glass of wine?" Matt offered.

"Thanks, but tonight's our anniversary, and my thoughtful husband has more surprises for me at home," Karen said.

"Looks like you two have some special plans of your own in the works." Walt smiled and winked at the younger couple.

Matt looked at Dani, and she looked at him, neither sure of the best response, but both made one, one on top of the other.

"She took pity on me so I wouldn't have to eat dinner alone."

"We're discussing our project."

Matt eased the awkward silence that followed by extending his hand. "It was good meeting you, Walt. Karen, enjoy your weekend."

"Happy anniversary," Dani added with a smile she didn't feel.

Before her boss left the restaurant, Dani saw her turn back and take a long hard look at her and Matt, as if she suspected something was going on between the two of them. Or maybe it was her own guilty conscience that made her attribute the look to suspicion and displeasure. Regardless, having witnesses to nonwork interactions between her and Matt added a layer of complexity Dani didn't want or need.

The waiter appeared, asking their preferences for dessert and coffee. Matt looked at Dani, his eyes willing her to order something more, but she silently refused.

"Nothing more," he said, and the waiter laid the padded leather portfolio on the corner of the table and walked away.

"Weren't you the one who said no dinner was complete without a decadent chocolate concoction?"

She'd said many things to him...in Vegas. But this wasn't Vegas. "I appreciate dinner and the advice, but I'll pass on anything else." Dani grabbed her wallet from her purse.

"Dinner's on me," he said, tucking cash into the portfolio and putting his wallet back into his pocket. "We could go somewhere else for a drink if you like, or—"

"Thanks, but I just want to go home to bed."

The shine in his eyes and smile on his face told her that was his preference, too, with them doing it together, of course. "Yours or mine?" he whispered.

"You know what I meant," she said.

"I know what you *want*," he said, eyes on hers as her face went hot.

He chuckled and moved to pull her chair out for her. She stood, and with his hand at her back, they left the restaurant.

"Thanks for dinner," she said when they reached her car. Wasting no time, she immediately turned toward her door. "Goodnight."

Before she could climb in to safety, he grabbed her hand. "Have dessert with me somewhere."

She pulled away. "Everything's closed this late."

"There's a fast-food drive-through open somewhere."

"You don't like fast-food places."

"But I do like spending time with you."

She turned again to her car. "No thanks."

"Are you afraid to be alone with me?"

"No, I'm not afraid. I'm tired. I have an ogre for a boss." She tried to smile at her good-natured jab, but she couldn't fake it. He didn't crack a smile, either.

"You're afraid because you know what'll happen if we're alone." He slowly ran his hand up her arm.

Did he hear her breath catch in her throat? Feel the goosebumps rise beneath his palm? See her nipples punctuate her blouse?

His hand went to her other arm, repeated the movement, and got the same results. Spurred by her response, he slid his hands low on her hips. And from there, it was a small matter to shift their bodies closer to touching.

"Matt." His name left her mouth on a sigh.

"Dani."

"Friends don't...don't do this. Our agreement...." Why was her voice shaking? Why was her mouth so dry? Why was her pulse jumping in her throat?

"To hell with our agreement." His low, smooth voice vibrated through her. "This is what we should have agreed to in Vegas before you left our bed."

He lowered his head and claimed her lips. The kiss wasn't a soft, sweet, tentative first kiss couples new to each other shared. It was a kiss borne of a man and woman's intimate knowledge of each other, of a passion too-long denied. She tasted the wine on his tongue, the heat of his desire, and it threatened her ability to hold at bay her own desire. His hands cupped her ass and pulled her closer. Feeling him hard against her made her acknowledge the truth. She wanted this man as much as she always had.

Instead of pulling him closer like she wanted, she pushed him away. But he didn't let her go. "Matt. Please."

"Please, yes?"

"It would be a mistake. For so many reasons."

He claimed her lips again in a kiss that tipped her head back, filled her lungs with his breath, molded her breasts against his chest, weakened her knees. She almost fell when he released her abruptly. "The mistake is us wasting time when we could be making love to each other every night instead of just wishing we were."

Dani watched him stride away to his car, wishing she had the courage to call him back to fix the mistake. Instead, she got into her car and drove home to an empty condo.

Chapter Nine

"Meganlin's numbers are too high for us. Which is what I told Gibson when he approached me about bidding on my North Valley spa." Reina Rivera, owner of the area's premier real estate company by the same name, was living up to her reputation for being a hardass. She reclined in the plush corporate box seat at the baseball game, one booted foot propped on the back of the seat in front of her.

Matt shifted in his seat to mirror her posture. "You're saying you told him no?"

"That's exactly what I'm saying."

Matt's eyes darted to Dani, who sat at his side.

Dani's request for a meeting with Reina had been denied again and again—her secretary's standard response being that she was unavailable. When Dani discovered, through her energetic network, that the queen herself was attending the game, she and Matt took advantage of the opportunity. For the past ten minutes he had flirted the information, bit by bit, from her, and so effortlessly that Dani could almost feel her brown eyes turning a wicked shade of green.

"We have Rivera contracts, invoices, and receipts that indicate your company is a client," Dani interjected.

The blonde's mouth twitched into a scowl directed toward Dani. "I don't care what you have. I'm telling you I didn't do business with Meganlin."

"Would you like to?" Matt's smooth voice broke through the charged air, and he threw in a charming smile for good measure.

Reina's blue eyes captured his like a hawk spying a rabbit for dinner, and a throaty laugh danced from her wide, full lips. "You get this little mess cleaned up, and maybe you and I can come to a mutually beneficial arrangement."

Matt held out his hand to Reina, who took it and held it long enough to draw Dani's jealousy full-blown to the surface.

"It's been a pleasure," he said.

"Yes, it has," Reina purred.

Matt stood, but Dani had one more question. "Ms. Rivera, are you one hundred percent sure it was Elliott Gibson you spoke to?"

Throughout the interview, the woman had all-but ignored Dani, staring either at Matt or into the field. But at Dani's last question, her head shot up, stabbing Dani with her gaze. "What are you suggesting?"

"I'm not suggesting anything. I'm simply asking whether you knew Elliott well enough to know it was him and not someone posing as him."

The woman looked dumbstruck for a few seconds then regained her composure and looked away. "He approached me at a charity function. I'd only met him once before, so I can't be absolutely sure."

"Can you describe him?"

"No. I can't."

Dani felt Matt tug on her arm, so she thanked the woman for her time. As she expected, her comment was ignored.

She made it out of the private box and into the cheap seats before releasing a string of hot slurs under her breath.

Matt chuckled. "I take it you don't care for the charming Ms. Rivera?"

"Women like that are part of the reason women have to fight so hard to get ahead."

"She acted that way because she was jealous of you." Instead of leaving the stadium, he sat on the hard bleachers.

She slid in next to him, brows furrowed, temper high in her cheeks. "Oh, please. She's an intelligent, shrewd businesswoman, almost as wealthy as Bill Gates. Why on earth would she be jealous of me?"

She felt his eyes on her and turned to him. His look was soft and open, full of humor. "Because you're beautiful, brilliant, young, and competition."

"Competition for what?"

"For a bigger piece of the business world and," he took her hand and linked their fingers, "for me."

Breath hitched in her chest at his touch. She scoffed dryly to try to ignore his heat slipping into her skin, igniting her cells. "Someone has a high opinion of himself."

"I know when a woman wants me, Dani."

"She wasn't exactly subtle about it."

His low laughter vibrated though her. "I didn't mean Reina."

She made the mistake of allowing her gaze to land on his mouth. That beautiful, clever mouth that had brought her so much pleasure. Her heart raced at the thought of giving in and kissing him, and she tried to turn away and stare instead at the game in play.

But looking away wouldn't stop the chills that marched down her back and lodged low and deep inside her stomach, fanning the fire always burning there. Wouldn't stop the fully formed actions being enacted in her mind of them fucking in every position he'd taught her. Wouldn't stop her desire for this man she feared would always be a part of her, like her dark eyes, her craving for chocolate and chile, the leaf-shaped birthmark on her right inner thigh he loved to trace with his tongue. Those feelings, those thoughts, those memories, those desires would still be there whether she looked away or not. So she kept her eyes on his. Just for the pleasure of it.

He lifted his hand, ran his fingers down her jaw, ending at her mouth, and rubbed his thumb softly across her lower lip. There was no denying the all-too-familiar feeling of her body wanting to fuse closer and deeper into his. Of the ever-glowing embers of passion fanning to life inside her. Of the quickening spiraling low in her stomach. Desire spread through her body, her skin tingling with anticipation, her breath evaporating in her lungs.

It was senseless to deny it. She couldn't react this way to his presence, his touch, and still maintain she didn't want him. He leaned in. She leaned in, ready to give in and fit her mouth fully over his, but a buzzing in his pants stopped her. She pulled back from the temptation swirling around them, but he kept his eyes locked on hers as he answered his phone.

After a brief moment listening to the caller, he responded, his tone brusque. "We're on our way in." He hung up but didn't make a move to rise from the bleachers. His silence and narrowed eyes worried her.

"Has something happened?" she asked.

He brushed his mouth over hers, not really a kiss, more of a caress. "A detective from the Albuquerque Police Department is in Karen's office…to talk to you."

Dani averted her eyes and swallowed the cold ball of fear that had risen from her stomach. APD knew about her affair with Elliott. And now Matt would know, too.

****

The silence in the SUV on the way back to their office lacerated Dani's heart. Matt was waiting for her to explain why the police wanted to talk to her about her former boss' death. Once he knew she'd had an affair with the man who was a suspected embezzler, he would suspect her, too.

She wasn't sure she could take seeing the disappointment and confusion that would cloud his face whenever he looked at her after that. He would probably insist she step down as his assistant, which would lead to her being asked to relinquish the assistant director position, and then having her relationship with the company—and with him—severed completely.

Yet, it would be better for him to hear the sordid details from her than from the cops. It would be tough, but she owed him that much.

Matt had pulled into the executive parking lot, shut off the engine, and unbuckled his seatbelt before Dani found the courage to speak.

"Matt." She shifted in the seat, turning toward him, and met his questioning eyes. "I have something to tell you before we go in."

He removed his hand from the door handle.

Her heart turned to ice in her chest and fell into her burning stomach. She'd rather have her teeth pulled than to see the disgust that would appear on his face after her confession. But she had no choice. "I had an affair with Elliott Gibson."

Yep. There it was. Something died in his eyes, like the night swallowing a shooting star. She'd ripped a hole in his soul that was bleeding out. She could feel it, feel his affection for her leaking out through the growing gap between them.

****

Dani's words ripped a hole in Matt's gut. He tore his eyes from her and focused on the gray cement walls of the parking structure beyond the windshield. A loud buzzing like a nest of yellow jackets started in his head, and a fiery pain radiated from his chest. He hadn't felt this cut off at the knees since Jessica. He didn't trust himself to speak, so when he didn't respond, Dani filled the silence.

"It ended shortly after it started when he dumped me. It ended the night he died."

The air ripped from his lungs, leaving behind a raw burn. He felt trapped in the tight vehicle, and it was difficult to breathe, but he steeled his body—and his heart—against the next blow he knew was coming.

"The night I flew to Vegas. The night you and I…I learned about it when I got home."

Within the small space that separated seconds, Dani Parker had transformed from the woman he wanted a relationship with to one who was a suspected embezzler and murderer. His heart ceased to beat for an instant. How could he trust her now? How had he let himself trust her at all? She had left her lover and come to his bed hours later. Hadn't he learned his lesson well enough with Jessica to know women couldn't be trusted?

Hot words ready on his tongue, he twisted to face her. The liquid depths of her dark eyes showed the emotional toil her error in judgment was taking on her, the regret and pain eating away at her, and dissolved his damning words.

She didn't need him to blast her for making mistakes of the heart. Lord knows he had made plenty of his own. Besides, the Dani he knew could never kill anyone. Or embezzle money. He'd bet his life on it.

He swallowed the bitter taste of disillusionment caught in his throat. "I imagine that's what the detective wants to talk to you about. Let's get it over with so we can continue our investigation."

****

The detective stood at the wall of windows looking out of Karen's office, commenting to her on the view from the tenth floor, when Dani and Matt walked in.

Dani's stomach did a nose dive, but she held tightly to her composure. "I'm Dani Parker. I understand you're here to see me."

The man turned. "Ms. Parker. I'm Detective Rey Anaya with the Albuquerque Police Department." His gray eyes were as cold as the metal badge he flashed at her. "I have some questions about the death of Elliott Gibson." His gaze shifted to Matt, who stood like an angry bodyguard at her side, but his statement was directed at her. "Perhaps you'd prefer to discuss this matter in private?"

Dani shook her head. "Ask your questions."

Matt touched her arm but kept his eyes on Anaya. "Dani, it would be better to have a lawyer present during the detective's questioning."

"I don't need a lawyer. I haven't done anything

wrong."

Matt shifted his gaze to Karen, who wore the same worried look.

"Thank you, Ms. Parker," the detective jumped in. "I appreciate your cooperation in helping us solve the murder of your…" He opened a small notebook. "What was the deceased to you? Your boyfriend?"

"Elliott Gibson was the president of this company and, therefore, one of Dani's superiors," Karen answered before Dani could.

"Yes, of course. On the night Gibson died, you received a speeding ticket on I-25 south. Where were you going in such a hurry?"

She'd forgotten about the ticket, so the question surprised her, making her pause to recall the event and the answer to his question. "I was headed home from a conference in Santa Fe."

"Was the conference over?"

"It was for me."

"It was scheduled to last through the weekend. Why did you leave Friday night?"

"I…it wasn't as beneficial as I thought it would be."

"You knew that after one day?"

"Yes."

"Did you indeed go home?"

"Yes."

"Did you go anywhere else that night?" The tone in his voice told her he knew about her flight to Vegas.

"I needed a little R&R so I flew to Vegas."

He smiled. "Get in some blackjack? Some shows?"

She willed her gaze not to shift to Matt. "Actually, neither."

"Oh?" The detective's eyes cut to Matt and back to

her. "What did you do?"

"Rested. Relaxed."

He smiled again, but she could tell he was not amused by her response. "Getting back to the citation. The officer mentioned in his notes that you were upset."

Matt stepped forward. "Was the officer in question qualified to make judgments on a driver's mental condition with one quick glance in the dark?"

Detective Anaya shot a dark glare at Matt. "The officer in question noted that she was crying. I think anyone—especially a trained officer—would reasonably call that upset." He continued with his questioning before Matt could respond. "Do you recall telling the officer you'd had an argument with your boyfriend?"

Dani could see now why Matt had advised her to wait until a lawyer was present. Her answers to the questions were casting a wide net of suspicion around her. "I said I'd had a disagreement with my boss."

"Oh, my apologies. I must have misread my notes. Disagreement with *boss*," he said slowly, writing as he spoke. "That boss being Mr. Gibson?"

"Yes."

"Do you own a gun?"

The question surprised Dani, and it showed in her hesitant answer. "Um, no."

"You sound unsure, Ms. Parker."

"No, I don't own a gun."

"You and Gibson were at the conference together."

"Several Meganlin employees attended," Karen inserted. "I can get you their names if that would be helpful."

"Thank you, I've already spoken to them. Getting back to your," he referred to his notes again, "disagreement with your boss. What was the disagreement about?"

Nerves were building a skyscraper in her stomach as the realization sank in that the detective wasn't interested in anyone but her. "I questioned some decisions he'd made."

"What decisions?"

She shrugged. "Company business."

"This is an official murder investigation, Ms. Parker. Be more specific."

"She answered the question," Matt said, looking like he was about to body slam the man. "Move on."

Detective Anaya met Matt's challenging stare. "If Ms. Parker would prefer not to answer my questions, that's her choice. But unless she has retained you as her legal counsel, I'll ask you to stay out of my official investigation."

"Next question, please," Dani echoed Matt, feeling a headache coming on.

"Witnesses at the hotel recall seeing you and your boss together at the conference and at what one described as a 'cozy dinner' the night he died." He eyed Dani, waiting. For something.

"Is there a question in that she can respond to?" Matt asked.

The detective's gaze never left hers, and he spoke over Matt's question. "The day after you left the conference early, Gibson was found dead in his room, naked in bed, with a bullet in his heart and female DNA all over him and the room."

Tears burned the back of her eyes. She had assumed, of course, that Elliott had been shot, but to hear it confirmed was an affront, both as his former lover and as a human being. The image of him as she left him that night rushed to the forefront. It was embedded in her soul. So were the feelings of his loving her, of his hurting her. The intensity of her reaction told her she hadn't really faced it. Matt's love, or whatever it was, had saved her from having to.

"I ask you again, Ms. Parker, what was your relationship with the deceased? Were you lovers?"

Matt stepped between her and the detective. "That's enough."

The detective's stance stiffened and so did his lips. "I'm sure Ms. Parker wants to do all she can to help the police find the person who so brutally and heartlessly murdered her lover."

"Boss," Matt growled.

"She certainly does," Karen jumped in. "But she'll do it through her attorney. As is her right." She picked up the phone and asked her assistant, Noah, to come in.

"We're done here," Matt said.

The detective closed his notebook and put it and his pen in his overcoat pocket. He pulled out a slim plastic package. "I need a DNA sample from you before I go, Ms. Parker."

Her tears had stopped as quickly as they had started, but she was still shaken, her legs about to collapse, her heart pounding. If they took a DNA sample, they'd know it was her in Elliott's bed. And knowing was a heartbeat away from arresting her for his murder. She couldn't avoid it forever, but maybe she could put it off for a few days.

"Do you have a court order?" Matt's tight tone was sharp.

The detective ignored the question, keeping his gaze

tight on hers. "I can take it here or down at the station. Your choice."

Matt gripped her arm, his touch drawing her gaze to his. "You don't have to give him a swab unless he has a court order. If he doesn't have one, it's because he has no evidence to support it, and you're under no obligation to give him a sample." He kept his voice low, soft, just for her, comforting her with his touch, his words, his beautiful, caring eyes on hers. In that moment, she didn't care how the other people in the room might interpret the look of love in his eyes or in hers.

She smiled her thanks, her love, and turned to the detective. "I'll schedule a time to come downtown to give you a sample. And a full statement. With my lawyer."

"Very well." He slid the DNA kit back into his pocket. "I'll see you soon, Ms. Parker. Oh, and don't leave town."

"Noah, please escort Detective Anaya out of the building," Karen said to her assistant who came in just then, and she shut the door after they left.

Dani looked between Karen and Matt, her stomach lodged in her throat, her emotions racing just under her skin. "He thinks I did it."

"Preliminary questioning is an attempt to build a case against someone...anyone," Matt said. "They're hoping you'll incriminate yourself and make their job easier."

Karen laid her hand on Dani's shoulder. "Talk to Laurel." Dani knew the company lawyer, of course but had rarely needed to interact with her except on certain contract issues. She was a nice person, but the thought of talking to her in an official capacity set her on edge. "She can't represent you," Karen continued, "but she can provide you with some general guidelines on the best approach to responding to their questions so that they get the information they need while you protect your rights."

"I will. Now, if you'll both excuse me, I have work to do." Dani turned her back on her two protectors and walked out the door, walking as fast as was appropriate to her office.

Matt came to her a short time later as she was pouring through Elliott's files, looking for anything that could lead them to a motive by a third party. Feeling eyes on her, she glanced up from her computer, saw him staring at her, questions in his eyes, so many questions. She averted her gaze, not wanting to see the disappointment, the suspicion, the disgust. She didn't even want to see care and concern. Seeing either would rip away the bolsters that supported the dam holding back her tears.

"I made appointments with the next two businesses on the list…two for tomorrow morning and one—"

"Dani."

"—for tomorrow afternoon. I also talked to—"

"Dani." He walked to her desk, stopping at her side.

"—my contacts at the vigas supply company and the tile company, who assured me—"

He jerked her chair back from the computer and spun her toward him. Placing his hands on the armrests, he leaned in, his face inches from hers. "Enough!"

She wasn't ready for him, for the discussion that would follow, not when her emotions were clawing at the surface to be set free. Her only hope to avoid it was to get away. Fast.

She stood, pushed past his arms, and headed for the door. "Excuse me."

He grabbed her arm and pulled her to him. "Dani—"

"Not now." Keeping her gaze pinned on the wall behind his head, she felt her chin quivering, her eyes burning, but she gritted her teeth and blinked her eyes to stop the torrent hovering in the wings.

He cupped her face and brushed his thumb across something wet on her cheek. "Baby, look at me." His voice was a whisper, but it was also a command. One she couldn't ignore.

She shifted her gaze to his. And melted in the care shining in his eyes. The breath she pulled into her lungs was ragged and unfulfilling. She tried again but lost it half way through. She felt more wetness on her face, then Matt moved in, kissed her face, her eyes, her mouth.

With a mournful sigh, she wrapped her arms around him, her hands clutching him, and buried her head against his chest, releasing shaking sobs. His arms were tight around her, too, his heart beating in her ear, letting her lose control in the comfort and privacy of his warm, loving embrace.

"It'll be okay. I'm with you," he whispered into her hair, along with other soft nothings that did wonders to settle her heart and grief.

After she'd wiped her face with a couple of tissues he handed her, she looked up at him. "Thank you."

"For what?"

"For not asking me whether I killed him."

He kissed her softly on the mouth. "I didn't need to ask."

His reaction to her confession and to her breakdown warmed her insides. She had expected something different from him—disgust, disappointment, mistrust, anything but the understanding and tenderness he'd given her.

She stood in his embrace, enjoying the comfort it gave. Though they both wanted more than this from each other, for now, it was enough.

"When you go downtown to make your statement, I'm going with you."

"I appreciate it, but I doubt they'll let you go in with me."

"I'll go as your legal counsel."

"You're a lawyer?"

"Corporate, not criminal, but I know the law. I know when they're trying to railroad someone."

She wasn't sure she wanted Matt to hear all the sordid details of her failed relationship with Elliott, how stupid she'd been. But when she went into the station two days later, he was there by her side, listening to her recount every detail of that night. And she allowed the officer to do a cheek swab to analyze her DNA.

The police didn't have enough evidence to arrest her—yet—and she wasn't looking forward to future dealings with them, but knowing Matt was on her side— and at her side—gave her courage and energy to get through it.

Chapter Ten

"Dani, I have a personal matter to discuss with you."

Karen and Dani had a standing biweekly lunch, which landed a few days after the detective's questioning. Today's discussion was to cover her progress on the financial investigation, so she was taken aback by Karen's departure from topic. This was the first time in the five years she'd worked for her that she'd wanted to discuss a personal matter.

"Of course," she said, taking a sip of her ice tea.

"I urge you to end your relationship with Matt before things get even more complicated for you than they already are."

Dani couldn't stop the guilty heat that bloomed over her chest and up her face, the rapid beating of her heart, or the speed with which she went on the defensive. "My relationship with Matt is a professional one." That was true, but it also was quickly morphing into more.

Karen held up her hand. "I was suspicious of you two from the day he arrived. The way you two interacted, the way you looked at each other, spoke to each other, as if you already knew each other…and very well. Since you've been working together, well, it's become even more obvious there's something between you. His protectiveness of you during the police questioning capped it. And there's been gossip."

She opened her mouth to refute Karen's accusation, but nothing came out.

Karen put her hand on hers. "I shouldn't disclose this information, but I think you need to know, to protect yourself. Matt Collins has the power to make your life very difficult, both as the auditor and as...the owner of the company."

Dani struggled to pick her jaw off the table. "The owner? The owner is—was Geoffrey Linton."

"Matt's full name is Matthew Collins Linton. He dropped his father's last name in college, apparently wanting to make his own way in the world without riding the Linton name. When his father died recently, Matt was put in charge of the Linton business holdings. He came to Meganlin to investigate the financial irregularities, fix the problems, and get the business back on sound footing so he can sell it. Once that's accomplished, he'll go back to his more lucrative businesses, of which there are many."

Karen watched her as the information sink in. "So, you see, it would be a mistake for you to get involved with a man who is here only temporarily. One who may come to see you as a liability to the company's bottom line. Scandal could kill any profitable deal he attempts to negotiate."

Dani tried to swallow the lump of *déjà vu* in her throat, but it was too big.

Elliott assured her she had the assistant director position but had given it to Nathan. Elliott had assured her she was the love of his life, but he used her and dumped her.

Matt said he wanted a relationship with her, all the

while knowing it couldn't happen because he was leaving when the job was done.

As Dani drove back to the office after lunch, she was more determined than ever to guard her heart—and her body—from Matt Collins.

****

Their hearts pumping as fast as their legs, Dani told Liz, through thin breaths, Karen's news. "Matt isn't just...the auditor. He *owns*...the company."

"No way!"

"Yes, way. After the...investigation...is done...he's selling."

"C'mon ladies! If you're yapping, you're not pumping! Move those legs!" The instructor, a tall Amazonian blonde who went by the exotic name *Ahhn-yah*, didn't condone talking in her spin class and made sure offenders paid dearly.

Liz rolled her eyes at Dani but stood on her pedals and pumped faster, giving *Ahhn-yah* no chance to inflict additional punishment.

After class, they showered in the locker room, dressed, and headed to dinner at one of the Nob Hill area restaurants.

Dani got a reprieve from Liz's questions while they ordered dinner and wine, but as soon as the waiter poured their first glass of riesling and left the carafe on their table, the barrage started.

"What else did Karen say?" Liz asked.

"She suggested my career could suffer if I continued my involvement with him."

"Did she say it like, 'I'm going to fire you if you don't stay away from him'?"

"No. It sounded more like concern for me and my

career."

"I hope you didn't agree to stay away from him."

"I was so shocked to learn Matt was the owner *and* that Karen suspected he and I were involved, that I never actually agreed to anything. But I do agree it's the best thing."

"Wrong!" Liz downed her wine and refilled her glass.

"Why would I invest time and energy getting involved with a man who's leaving in a few months? Why would I do that to myself?"

"It didn't stop you last time."

"What?"

"Your Vegas fling wasn't permanent, and you decided to 'invest in' Matt anyway. What's the difference between then and now?"

"He and I weren't working together. He wasn't my boss. The relationship has changed. In Vegas, it was temporary and we both knew it. Now…well, now, the expectations are different. At least on my part. I don't want a sex-only relationship with him. And I'm pretty sure that's all he wants with me."

An undignified scoff huffed from Liz's mouth. "You can't have a sexual relationship with a man you're crazy about? You do know what century this is?"

"I can't have one with *him*. You and I both know how things worked out with Elliott. I agree with Karen. Being with Matt could seriously hinder my career."

"That's a load of crap, and you know it."

Dani grabbed her glass. "Then tell me, Liz. What do I do when he's gone? After my heart's broken because he's dumped me and moved on? I'm not willing to risk everything again for an affair I know from day one has no chance of being anything but temporary. What don't you get about this?" She downed the remaining pool of crisp peach nectar and reached for the bottle to refill her glass, wanting to defuse Liz's words and her own doubts.

"Here's what *you* don't get, Dani. You have to grab every chance at happiness when it comes, because if you don't, it will pass you by and go to the next person on the list. You have to fully live your life, so when it's your time to leave this world, you'll slide into home with your heart bursting with remembered bliss, instead of empty with regrets from all the should-have, wish-I-had, if-only moments you missed out on."

Dani stared at her friend with a mixture of awe and humor in her eyes. "How did you get to be such a sage woman?"

"With age comes wisdom."

"You're only six months older than I am."

"Yeah, but I've stuffed a lot of life into those months."

"I'll give you that." Dani clinked Liz's glass with her own in toast. "But I'm afraid you're wrong about it working for Matt and me."

"I'm never wrong. Don't you know that by now?"

****

Matt and Dani sat in the outer office of Big W Construction owner Earl J. Wallner. Their appointment was for nine, but the clock on the wall showed nine-fifteen, and Big W still hadn't shown.

Dani stood and walked to the secretary's desk. "Excuse me. If Mr. Wallner's going to be delayed much longer, perhaps we should reschedule with him."

The woman's fingers ceased the tap-tapping on the keyboard and turned to Dani. "One moment please." She picked up the phone and pushed a button. "Mr. Wallner, shall I reschedule your nine o'clock appointment?...Yes, sir." She hung up, stood, and walked to the double door, then turned back to Dani and Matt. "Mr. Wallner will see you now."

She opened the door and shut it after they'd entered the office.

Big W came out from behind a massive wooden desk that looked like it was two hundred years old. The man had come by his name honestly. He was big. Not overweight but tall. Six-five or -six, if Dani's guess was correct.

His gaze fell first to Dani, but he extended his hand to Matt. "Matthew, I knew your father. Sorry to hear about his passing. Are you here to take me up on my long-standing offer to buy Meganlin?"

Matt's face went tight, but he didn't pause in shaking the offered hand.

"Thanks for your condolences. This is Dani Parker, assistant director of construction for Meganlin and my partner in an investigation we're conducting."

Dani held out her hand. Big W's face beamed with a smile, and he took her hand between his and held it like a rare orchid. "Ms. Parker, it's a real pleasure to finally meet you. You've got quite the reputation in this field, but I had no idea you were so young and pretty."

Dani returned his smile. "A reputation for what, might I ask?" she asked, curious about what she'd hear.

"For being one of the best in the business. A real ball-buster if you'll forgive the vulgarity."

"I take my business seriously."

131

"And your pleasure, too, if I'm not mistaken." The man was a player. She could see it in his sparkling blue eyes, ear-to-ear grin, and charm oozing from every pore of his ruddy face.

"We appreciate your meeting with us," Matt cut in, pulling them back to the business at hand, and, she noticed, gritting his teeth at some irritation—the fact that Big W had brought up his father, which he probably didn't want her to know, or the fact that her hand was still encased in the man's big grip?

"Have a seat." Big W led them to a couch and chair grouping, he taking the large padded chair at the head of the arrangement, leaving Matt and Dani to take the couch. "My girl just made fresh coffee. Would you care for some, Ms. Parker, before we get started?"

His use of the term *my girl* grated on her nerves, and she bit her tongue to keep from commenting on it. "No, thank you."

He settled back in his chair and propped his elbows on the armrests, tenting his fingers. "Now what can I do for you two?" His gaze had returned to Matt, all softness gone from his voice.

It didn't escape Dani's notice that the courtesies were directed to her while the business matters were directed to Matt. If she had a reputation for being a *ballbuster*, it was because it seemed to be the only way a woman could compete in the male-dominated field she'd chosen. But she loved every minute of it and would keep fighting to retain her spot on the rung and advance to the next.

Matt leaned forward toward the table, opened the folder they'd brought with them. "Have you done business with Meganlin in the past five years?"

Big W crossed one booted foot on his knee. "No."

"Have you had any dealings with Elliott Gibson?"

"No."

"But you know him?" Dani asked.

"I know of him. Everybody in this business gets to know all the players eventually."

Matt flipped to the next page in the file. "You never ordered talavera tiles through Meganlin for your museum project last year? Or iron grill work for the restaurant you built two years ago in the downtown area?"

The man's face turned as red as the chunk of coral in his bolo tie. "I said I hadn't done business with Meganlin, and I meant it. If that's what you came to ask, the question's been answered." He stood, prepared to haul them out if they didn't go, it seemed to Dani.

Matt stood, too. "We have documents suggesting that you had several business dealings with Meganlin over the past year."

"I don't care what documents you have," Big W said. "I told you I didn't do business with Meganlin." He turned and stormed toward those double doors. "I have another appointment, so I'm going to ask you to leave."

"Mr. Wallner, Elliott Gibson was murdered," Dani said.

Big W stopped in his tracks. Turned to face her. Shock or some other strong emotion erased the ruddiness from his face. "If you're suggesting I had something to do with—"

"No, of course not," she said. "After he died, we found some irregularities in his files that we believe might hold clues as to why he was killed. We're contacting everyone listed in those files to determine the veracity of that information. And now that you've confirmed you had no dealings with him or with our company, we'll leave you to your next appointment." She extracted a card from her jacket pocket and handed it to him. "But please call me if you remember anything that might help our investigation."

He took the card.

"Thanks for your time." She nodded goodbye and turned to go. "We'll show ourselves out."

Matt followed Dani out.

****

"When's our next appointment?" Matt asked when they got back to the SUV, agitation still riding his body from the meeting with Big W. Arrogant SOB was a card-carrying member of the good ol' boys club that kept out everyone but rich white men. A man just like his own father. He'd heard the rumors that he went by Collins instead of Linton because he wanted to make it on his own, without his father's name to open doors, and that was true to a certain extent.

The primary reason was that he and his father had never seen eye-to-eye on what made good business. And a good business person. Now that he was in charge, things were going to change. He was going to pull the Linton business holdings into the twenty-first century, kicking and screaming if necessary. He'd let Meganlin crash to the ground before he'd sell to Big W...or anyone like him. He thought Dani was going to come up out of her chair at Big W calling his assistant his girl, but she had kept it together to get the job done. Remembering the red in her cheeks and the spark in her eyes when her gaze found his after the comment lifted his mood.

Dani checked her list. "Ten-thirty, with Bee Jensen of Bee Homes."

Matt glanced at his watch. "By the time we get back to the office, it'll be time to head to the appointment. Let's grab some coffee."

He pulled into the parking lot of a local coffee shop. After getting their drinks, they went outside to one of the tables. He steeled himself for her questions about Big W's comment regarding his father and selling the business, but they never came. She just sat there, thumbing through the file of their next appointment.

"Bee Homes apparently ordered cabinet pulls, thousands of them," she said. "But it's odd because—"

"Dani." He took her hand and caressed her skin with his thumb. "About what Big W said... About my selling the business and about my father..."

"Yeah?"

"You didn't blink an eye."

Her only response was a raised eyebrow.

"You knew I'm the owner of Meganlin."

She nodded.

Shit. She knew. How? How long had she known? Since Vegas? What had she really been doing in Vegas that weekend? She'd never told him the reason, other than a vague getting away from reality that said nothing at the time. She'd confirmed that she wasn't a Sin City kind of woman, yet there she was, and she'd wrapped him around her so quickly and effortlessly he would have done anything to fuck her and keep fucking her...like he wanted to fuck her now.

Fuck! He hadn't fallen this hard and this fast...ever. He scratched his fingers through his hair, digging into his skull for some control. He was being ridiculous and suspicious for no reason. She had been in Vegas to get over Elliott's betrayal. Nothing more. "How long have you known?"

"Just after I was assigned to work with you," she said, retracting her hand from his. "I just wish you had told me."

He wanted to touch her, but obviously she didn't want that, so he let it go. For now. "You know why I couldn't."

"No, I don't."

"Dani—"

"I know why you'd want to keep it secret from the employees. Things are already shaky because of the financial investigation. Revealing you're the owner and you've come to sell the company would only cause more upset. The good people would start leaving and the not-so-good would do even less work. The company could fall apart and wouldn't be as valuable an asset to a buyer. Business principles 101. I get that. But you and I are…"

He leaned in close, close enough to smell the perfume of the sun heating her skin, to feel her breath on his lips, to see her pupils dilate in her toffee brown eyes. "Are what? What are we, Dani?"

"We're…working together." Her voice was a breathy whisper that begged him to kiss her. "Closely." She swallowed whatever emotion was pinking her cheeks. "You could have trusted me with the truth, Matt. I would never betray you or your confidences."

The words "I do trust you" formed on his tongue, but for some reason he held them in. He leaned back in his chair, out of reach of her tempting mouth. "The fewer people who knew, the better. I'm trying to avoid complications."

"Complications like me?"

This was the part he'd been dreading. The part that

would make him look like a complete asshole. He jabbed his tongue against the back of his teeth, trying to avoid the yes. "My motive was to keep a piece of sensitive information secret to protect the company."

"And it had nothing to do with your not wanting to tell me because I might not sleep with you again?"

"I want to make love to you again, but my position in the company plays no part in it."

She shook her head, and a brusque snort left her mouth, a sound that said she was no stranger to being lied to by men who wanted to sleep with her. "Withholding information is lying."

"You didn't tell me about you and Elliott until the cops showed up. Was that lying or just protecting information that had no bearing on the issue?" He saw the hurt in her eyes before her gaze left his and dropped to the folder in her hand.

"That's hardly the same," she said, jabbing her thumb into a corner of the folder.

Dammit! He had hurt her, and he felt like the biggest piece of shit for it. What had possessed him to bring that up? He had to explain, had to get her to see his reasons for keeping secrets.

"I know you feel like I deceived you, and I'm sorry. I promise you I had no motive other than keeping the business together during this difficult time. I'll be more forthcoming from here on out about business matters when I can."

"Don't feel like you have to. It's certainly not like we're confidants. Or anything."

Her emphasis on *or anything* stung. He thought he'd been making progress with her, getting her to remember how good they were together. His big mouth had just lost him ground. "We're more than co-workers, Dani."

Her phone rang, saving her from having to respond. "It's Big W."

Jealousy punched him in the gut. He knew she wasn't interested in Wallner, but the thought that *he* was interested in her pissed him off. "Probably calling to ask you for a fucking date." It also pissed him off that a small grin lifted her mouth, as if she saw his jealousy and was happy about it.

"Dani Parker... Hello, Mr. Wal—okay, Big W... We'll meet you there... Okay, *I'll* meet you there... Eleven-thirty."

"You're not going anywhere with him alone," Matt said the second she'd ended the call.

"Why not?"

Why not? Let me count the fucking reasons, he wanted to say. The truth was, the thought that another man was going to be sitting with her, enjoying her company, seeing her smile, hearing her laugh, ate through him like acid. Even though Big W was twenty years her senior and married, the man was obviously enthralled by her.

And rightly so.

She was a gorgeous, sexy, intelligent, interesting woman that most men would give their left nut to be with. Him included. But she was his, goddammit. Whether she acknowledged it or not. Whether he spoke the words aloud or not. And he would not allow any man to take her from him.

Everything inside him wanted to order her not to go, but that kind of archaic behavior would go over like a lead balloon. She'd laugh in his face. Or punch him. The thought of Dani pounding his chest with her fists, of having to subdue her, with his hands, his mouth, his body, lifted his cock until it was punching hard against his boxers. "I don't trust the guy."

"It's lunch. At a public place. What's he going to do? Kidnap me? Slip poison into my salsa? Shoot me under the table? Besides, it's my job. And I'm damn good at it." The more she talked, the madder she got and the more beautiful she became, her face flushed, eyes burning, voice low but stretched with passion. "Furthermore, I don't need you to hover over me to make sure I don't fuck things up. I've done a superior job at Meganlin before you came, and I'll do just as well after you leave."

She stood and picked up her folder and gripped it tightly in her hands as she tossed her cup into the trash and stormed to the SUV.

He couldn't hold back a proud grin at her feistiness. She was a formidable woman, a good match for him. No, a perfect match. A perfect partner to help him turn the culture in his businesses, elevate the standards of operation. She'd keep him on his toes, keep his heart and mind fully engaged, and he'd do the same for her. He swallowed the last bit of coffee in his cup, stood, and three-pointed it into the trashcan, then joined her in the SUV.

They sat in silence for a moment, her glaring out the windshield, him staring at her. He took her hand, brought it to his mouth, and kissed it. "The reason I want to go with you has nothing to do with doubting your ability to do the job and everything to do with not wanting to leave you alone with a man who looks at you like he wants to tear your clothes off and eat you for lunch."

His words drew her gaze and a raised eyebrow. "I

can take care of myself."

He smiled. "I know you can. That's not the point."

"What is the point?"

"I don't like men looking at my woman like that." *My woman.* Okay. Maybe he was as unevolved as Big W and his own father. But she *was* his. He took advantage of her stunned silence to lean in and kiss her. His mouth smoothing over hers, his hand cupped the back of her head, and he kissed her more firmly. Her mouth opened to his tongue, letting her low moan tremble into his mouth. He tasted the sharpness of her coffee and the iciness of the mints she'd popped into her mouth to counter it. Her hand cupped his face, and she slanted her head to take his tongue deeper.

Way too soon she turned her head, breaking the kiss. "We should go." Her voice was breathy and low, making it clear the kiss had affected her.

Smiling, he started the SUV and drove to their appointment. He was growing on her. He would keep reminding her how good they were together. And no matter what argument she posed, no way in hell was she going to that lunch alone.

****

Their meeting with Bee Homes revealed a similar story. They bought their cabinet pulls from a competitor because Meganlin's prices were too high. Afterward, they drove to the Nob Hill restaurant where she was to meet Big W.

She flipped down the visor and looked into the mirror as she applied lipstick.

"You know it's not a date," Matt said, his voice almost a snarl.

She smiled. It had been like pulling teeth, but she

finally convinced him to sit in the car during her lunch. "You know you're acting jealous." She was surprised at the power and satisfaction rushing warm through her body at hearing his jealous growl. So he didn't like her being with another man? Good. But what did that mean? He really did want more than just sex? He really did want her as his woman? The rush she felt turned cold when she realized it didn't matter what it meant because it would end when he left in a few months. She relaxed her mouth out of the soft grin and focused on applying her lipstick.

He made a sound through his teeth. "I'm concerned you're walking into something—"

She turned to face him. "Dangerous?"

"Something that will require me to step in and save you." The corners of his mouth lifted into a sexy grin. "Like in Vegas."

"I'm just positive I won't be facing that same situation with Big W, so you can relax, hero."

"I wouldn't mind rescuing you again. Turned out pretty well for me last time."

The air-conditioning of the SUV did nothing to lower the rising heat of her body at the thought of Vegas, at the memory of his kiss in the coffee shop parking lot. Sweat beaded on her forehead, and her heart raced. Her gaze lowered to his mouth, and she could almost taste his kiss again.

He leaned across the seat, and she shifted away until her body hit the door. He kept coming.

"I better get in there," she said and reached behind her to open the door.

"Chicken." His whispered taunt grazed across her mouth, making her shiver with wanting. Then he closed the gap between them. He kissed her, not nearly long

Sophia Ryan

enough, then was back in his own seat.

She climbed out of the SUV on shaky legs. Before she closed the door, he called out, "be careful," the teasing in his tone absent.

"Wipe the lipstick from your mouth," she teased. "Melon's not your color."

She closed the door on his chuckling. Turning away, she yanked on the hem of her jacket, trying to pull herself together before entering the restaurant.

Scanning the tables, she spied Big W at one in the back corner. Her heart was still fluttering so much from Matt's kiss she wasn't sure her legs could carry her to the table where Big W sat smiling widely at her. But they did, and she took the seat across from the big man with the strawberry-blond hair and blue eyes who, according to Matt, wanted to eat her for lunch. She smiled at the thought, probably giving Big W the idea that the warm smile was for him.

They engaged in small talk for a few minutes, ordered food, then Dani got down to business. "You said you had information for me?"

"You don't waste time, do you gal?"

"I hear directness is a characteristic you appreciate."

He chuckled. "You've done your homework." He eyed her appreciatively. "I usually do mine, but I admit I slipped up about Gibson. When you and *Junior* left my office today, I pulled up some information on Gibson, just to refresh my memory."

Matt would hate that he'd called him *Junior*. She'd make sure to tell him. "And you found something," Dani prompted and opened her notebook and grabbed her pen.

"Two things. A man calling himself Elliott Gibson approached me at a fundraiser several months ago. Said he'd like to do business with me and would beat any price we were currently getting. I told him I was happy with my current dance partners. He slipped me his card and said if I changed my mind, he'd make it worth my while."

Her heart racing, she wrote down the information that might help uncover who murdered Elliott...and get the police off her back. "Did you ever call him?"

He shook his head. "No. Like I said, I wasn't looking for a change."

She licked her lips. "And the second thing?"

"I dug up the newspaper article on Gibson's death. The picture with the story wasn't the man who talked to me at that party."

Chapter Eleven

"What did he look like? The man you talked to?" Dani leaned forward to make sure she heard every bit of Big W's response in the noisy restaurant.

"Youngish fella, late twenties, dirty blond hair cut short, dark eyes, medium build but on the soft side like he'd never done a day of physical work in his life, scruff on the chin that made his face look as if he'd been playing in the dirt. That's about all I recall. I didn't talk to him but for a couple of seconds and pretty quickly dismissed him as unimportant. But I know for a fact, the man who came up to me wasn't the man in the newspaper photograph. There was a similarity, but not enough for me to mistake one for the other."

Elliott had blond hair, but it was more of a golden blond and longer. His eyes were more of a hazel. He was six feet tall, but then Big W was well over six feet, so to him most people would be of medium build. Elliott had a runner's build, which could be considered lean, but he had well-defined muscles. No. In her mind, Elliott was not the man Big W met at the fundraiser. Who could it have been? A competitor? Someone within Meganlin trying to make deals on the side?

"You have quite a memory, Mr. Wallner," Dani said, writing down every detail. "Maybe you remember whether he had a small dark spot here?" Dani pointed to a spot above her upper lip. Elliott had accidentally been stabbed with a just-sharpened lead pencil in grade school, which had left him with a lasting and distinguishing mark.

"Nope. But he did have a damn shiny earring in his ear. And, before you ask, I don't recall which ear."

The waitress delivered their food, and Big W dug in. Dani set down her notes and took a few bites of her salad. "Did the man talk to anyone else in the room?"

"He circulated, but I didn't notice anyone in particular he spoke to. Like I said, I wasn't interested in what he was selling, so I didn't pay him any mind after we parted ways."

Dani was about to ask another question when Big W held up his hand. "I have a rule. No talking business while eating."

The way he was scarfing down his food, she wondered whether any talking at all was advisable, but she didn't say so. "How's your oldest daughter doing in volleyball at Trinity this year?" she said instead, earning another wide smile from her companion.

"I swan, little lady, you sure do your homework."

They spent the next fifteen minutes in friendly but decidedly one-sided chit-chat, then Big W got a phone call and cut their lunch short.

The two walked out of the restaurant side by side, his large hand at her back. She smiled when she saw Matt leaning against the SUV, arms crossed, waiting for her, right in front of the restaurant.

Big W chuckled when he saw him. "Looks like Junior's got his panties in a bunch again." He let his gaze crawl over her face. "But if you were my woman, I'd be the same way."

She wasn't sure how to respond to his overtly sexual

tone and mistaken opinion about her and Matt's relationship. "Thanks for the information." She held out her hand.

He took it, not shaking it, but holding it. "You know, there is one other thing, which may be nothing at all. I remember how white and perfect his teeth looked. Too perfect to be—"

An old primer-gray low-rider, speakers blaring, the bass turned all the way up, rumbled past them at a crawl. The noise drowned out the tail end of Big W's sentence. Distracted for an instant, Dani turned toward the noise. Matt turned his head toward the car, too. A man with a black bandana on his head and wrap-around black shades extended his arm out of the window, a gun in his hand, the barrel pointed directly at her and Big W.

Matt immediately spun back to her. Her eyes locked on his, his wide with distress. Her name on his lips, he rushed toward her, waving his arm and shouting, "Down! Get down!"

Motion slowed as Matt grabbed her by the waist and pulled her to the sidewalk, covering her body with his. A crack sounded in the air, then everything around her muted, as if it was being smothered by a loud, high-pitched ringing.

Though Matt covered her body, her eyes saw clearly.

His big hand stretched out toward her, his big blue eyes wide on her, Big W fell to the cement, blood oozing from a bullet hole in his head.

The sounds of screams from all around broke through the silence plugging her ears. The loudest sound of all was that of Matt's heart pounding against hers, his voice in her ear. "Oh, God, Dani. Tell me you're okay. Talk to me."

She threw her arms around his neck to show she was okay. She held on tight to show she was glad he was, too.

He tightened his hold. "I got you, baby. Fuck, I got you."

The police arrived minutes later, took their statements, and cleared them to go. Matt helped her into the SUV, climbed in the driver's side, and pulled out into traffic.

"I need a drink," he growled. "It's not every day I watch a man shot to death."

Dani tried to respond but found her throat clogged. She turned toward the window to hide her face, but nothing could hide or stop the scene playing out behind her eyes.

She felt Matt's hand on her thigh, and she grabbed it. She'd never been so glad to have someone with her, beside her. Someone who could take charge, see to her needs when she could barely breathe on her own. For once, she didn't have to be strong and tough all by herself. It felt good. Really, really good. Mostly, she was glad he was the one with her.

He pulled into the left lane to turn toward Dani's condo and caught the red light. "I'm taking you home."

She turned toward him to argue, to say she was okay to go back to work. But then she found his gaze on her, and in that moment she knew—she needed him. Beside her. Inside her. Where he belonged. Home was exactly where she wanted to go. As fast as he could get there. "Stay with me?"

His hand cupping her neck, he nodded and held onto her gaze as if he were afraid he'd lose her if he looked away. He leaned in, kissed her until the car behind them honked, then he floored it.

Minutes later, Matt pulled into the condo parking area and came around to her side of the car to help her out. He put his arms around her and pulled her into his hard frame, as if he wanted to take another moment to make sure she was whole and well and alive. Dani clung to him, the feel of his body against hers slowly replenishing the strength she'd lost on that bloody sidewalk.

He kissed her gently on the mouth, one hand at the small of her back, the other at the back of her head. Dani felt herself open to the feelings he was building inside her. She had waited for this for too long. What had she been waiting for? If that bullet had found her or him instead of Big W, Matt would have been gone from her forever. As she took his hand in hers and walked with him up the stairs, she knew this was the right thing to do.

At her door, she dug her keys from her purse. Matt leaned in against the door and it swung open. Dani's head snapped around to Matt's. "I never forget to lock my door."

He moved her behind him. "Go back downstairs and call the police." Slowly, he opened the door wider and moved into the room. She was right behind him, on the phone.

Couches and chairs were overturned, the cushions sliced open. Her DVD collection littered the floor like big, three-hole-punch dots. Pictures were off the walls, some even out of their frames. Kitchen cabinets and drawers were wide open, dishes broken on the floor. Dishwasher and microwave doors stood open.

Dani headed to the bedroom and got as far as the door when a man dressed all in black, including a full-face ski mask, rushed out at her and shoved her backward. Matt rushed toward the man but stopped when he saw the gun pointed at Dani's chest.

"Get back," the man growled, his voice low and rough.

Matt reached a hand toward Dani, grabbed her, and pulled her behind him, shielding her with his body.

The man made his way to the front door, giving Matt and Dani a wide berth.

"Into the bedroom," he said, waving the gun toward the room. Keeping Dani behind him, Matt backed into the room.

"Close the door."

Matt closed it. "Did you call the police?" he asked Dani.

"Yes."

"Good. Stay here and lock the door."

"Wait," she said but he ran out of the bedroom. She ran out after him, but he was already headed down the stairs in pursuit.

Matt returned a minute later, said the man must have taken off on foot because he hadn't seen a car speeding away.

Dani surveyed the destruction in the bedroom. Nothing appeared to be missing, but she couldn't be sure until she'd sorted everything out. Her jewelry box had been upended onto the floor, the jewelry spread out like the burglar had examined each piece before moving on to the next...and not taking any of it. Odd thief, one who didn't steal anything even semivaluable.

A lone police officer came by to take their statement. She knew by his responses he didn't seem to catch the possible connection between the break in and the earlier murder, and neither she nor Matt reminded him. "If you have another place to stay for a couple of days, I recommend it," he told her.

"Is that really necessary?"

"It's up to you, of course, but if he broke in once, he could do it again. Especially if he didn't find what he was looking for before you interrupted him and decides to question you personally."

The officer left, with a promise to follow up with her if they found the guy. Matt stormed into the bedroom, Dani behind him. He had grabbed her suitcase from the closet shelf, laid it open on the bed, and was pulling clothing from her dresser drawers and tossing it in.

"What are you doing?" she asked.

"Packing you a bag. You're staying with me until we find out what the fuck's going on."

"I don't think—"

He held up his hand. "Right this minute I don't give a damn what you think. Your life is in danger, and I'm not leaving you alone. And I'm not arguing with you."

His face was red, his green eyes on fire. She smiled. Then giggled. It only exaggerated his angry features.

"What's so goddamned funny?" he asked, slamming a balled pair of socks into the suitcase so hard they jumped out and rolled across the floor.

"As I was trying to tell you, I don't think I'll need twelve bras and all those socks. Throw in a few pairs of panties, for God's sake."

He glared into the suitcase he'd been packing, then shook his head, his scowl fading, and he chuckled.

She laughed, too. Then the laughter turned to tears, and her body began to shake. Matt picked her up, laid her on the stripped and gouged mattress, and held her.

****

150

One of Matt's contacts at a security company had come by to outfit her door with new locks, and next week they would put in a security system, but still Matt insisted that she go with him.

"Is this all you're bringing?" He stared at the two suitcases and one overnight bag neatly stacked in the living room. "I know you didn't fit all your shoes and entire wardrobe in those suitcases."

Dani zipped her toiletries bag into the side pocket of the suitcase. "I'm only bringing what I'll need until the alarm system is installed."

"You shouldn't be here at all until they catch the guy who broke in."

"That could be a long time...never even."

He pulled her into his arms. "That would be okay with me."

Before she could respond, he brushed his thumb across her mouth. "Promise me you won't come back here without me."

"You're being overprotective."

"And you're being reckless," he said but released her. "In the last few hours, you were shot at, a man died right in front of you, your house was broken into, and a maniac waved a gun in your face."

"And, man, am I hungry." She had changed into jean shorts and a T-shirt earlier, so she slipped into her leather flip-flops where they sat at the door, then grabbed one suitcase and the overnighter. "Let's get home before I starve to death."

She hadn't meant to say *home*, but it felt right. Not waiting for him, she headed toward the door. She looked back in time to see him shake his head and grumble some choice words about hardheaded women before grabbing the other suitcase, pulling the door closed behind him, locking every lock, and rushing downstairs to catch up with her.

Matt drove through downtown and turned into the Country Club neighborhood, site of many of the city's oldest and most unique luxury homes. The 1930s adobe home he was staying in sat back from the street on a large corner lot, snoozing in the shade of majestic, old cottonwoods protecting it from the heat of the autumn sun.

They entered the covered brick patio through a wrought iron gate built into the side of a thick adobe wall. An old wooden bench near the massive wooden front door showed weatherworn slashes of teal and tan. Scattered here and there were large terracotta planters filled to overflowing with colorful flowers in pinks, reds, and oranges. Just off center stood a stately cottonwood tree, its craggy bark crawling with smooth green ivy that had also found footing on the beams and posts comprising the patio cover.

Matt opened the front door and led the way inside. The open, light room was saved from being cavernous by the sparse but colorful furnishings and rugs that decorated it. A *kiva* fireplace commanded quiet attention from the corner of the room, with several *nichos* displaying an assortment of local artwork.

The doorways into other rooms were wide and arched, showing the ancient adobe walls to be over a foot thick. Equally thick vigas spanned the ceiling, wall to wall, and were repeated in every room.

She couldn't hold back her appreciation. "This is what people envision when they think of a classic New Mexican adobe house. It's gorgeous."

"The owner is a friend of my mother's, who, fortunately for me, is spending three months on Padre Island and another three with her daughter and new grandchild in Atlanta," he said. "I get a place to stay, and she gets someone to look after her house and the jungle she has growing from every corner."

He set her luggage down in the living room. "I'll change clothes, then be back to start cooking," he said. "Have a seat, either on the patio or in the living room."

The last thing she wanted was to sit and think about what happened. "I don't cook, but I'd like to do something other than sit." And think.

"How are your chopping skills?"

"Excellent."

He took her hand and led the way into the kitchen, which was a blend of traditional and contemporary, with solid pine cabinets alongside brushed stainless appliances. He pulled vegetables out of the refrigerator and set them on the Mexican-tile island, a knife from the drawer, and a bowl from the cabinet. "Have at it. I'll be right back." He kissed her and left her standing in a pool of sunlight on the tiled floor. She washed her hands and began washing and chopping.

When Matt returned five minutes later, barefoot, wearing baggy khaki shorts and a T-shirt, she had a chunky pile of red and orange peppers, yellow squash, mushrooms, and cherry tomatoes ready to be skewered and grilled. He poured a little olive oil on the veggies, sprinkled them with salt, pepper, lime, and cilantro and tossed them with his hands.

Chatting and laughing, they threaded veggies on skewers and chunks of steak on others and soon had a platter filled with more food than they could possibly consume in one sitting. He carried the platter out while she carried plates, silverware, napkins, and two bottles of beer with a wedge of lime perched in each lip.

The back porch was similar to that in the front but extended wider and deeper. Set into the corner of the low adobe wall was a built-in wood-burning fireplace and, to the side, a built-in gas grill with a patio furniture grouping surrounding it. Matt laid several skewers across the already prepped grate.

"I forgot the platter," he said. "Watch the kabobs?" He tried to hand her the long-handled tongs, but she held up her hands and backed away like he was trying to hand her a stick of lit dynamite.

"Nooo. I'll get the platter. I don't want my lousy cooking skills to be responsible for turning our meal into a burnt offering. Where is it?" She was already jogging toward the door.

He laughed. "In one of the cabinets. A huge white platter with slashes of colors."

Dani found the platter and was pulling it down when the phone rang. "The phone's ringing," she called out to him.

"Let the machine get it," he called back.

She nearly dropped the platter when she heard a woman's sweet-tea accented voice come on the line.

"Matthew? Matthew, pick up." An irritated sigh followed the silence. "It's Arienne. I ran into Natalia yesterday. She said you were probably bored out of your mind and that I should give you a call. But I forgot your new number, and Brenda was being her usual obstinate self and wouldn't give it to me. You really need to get a new assistant. Her people skills are just frightful and will hurt your business." Her tirade ended, and she chuckled, a low sexy sound meant to tease a man's cock to attention. "But I didn't call to tell you all that. I called to say, come home, lover. I miss the taste of you in my mouth."

Chapter Twelve

Dani went cold all over except for the fireball burning in the pit of her stomach. So this was Matt's *real* lover. Arienne. Even the name sounded sexy, luscious, and familiar.

The woman moaned the way Dani did when Matt's tongue played between her legs.

"Come home, darlin'," she said. "My body craves yours." She giggled again in that sexy, husky way. "Gawd, I hope no one's there with you, listening to me go on about how wet I am for you. Maybe I should speak French." The voice mumbled a string of melodic words in French that Dani didn't understand but had a good idea of the meaning from the erotic sounds alone.

After Arienne hung up, with a kissing sound, of course, Dani stared at the phone, unable to move from the quagmire of quicksand she'd been thrown into. The thought of Matt with another woman hurt like a dagger shoved into her heart. He'd been jealous today when she went to lunch with Big W, and now she knew exactly how he'd felt. But nothing about exclusivity had come up when he had discussed wanting a relationship with her. Yes, he had implied it, but if he had wanted it, he would have mentioned it specifically. But he hadn't.

Making her feet move, she left the kitchen and rejoined Matt on the patio. Her mind was never far from the phone call as she and Matt enjoyed their first co-created meal.

Don't get crazy. Don't let your jealousy and suspicion take that one message and build it into Shakespeare's entire body of tragedies. If you want to know about Arienne, just ask him. Get it out from between you so you can enjoy him. If Arienne were that important to him, she'd have his cell number. Yeah. That's it. She's just an old girlfriend looking for a way back into his life.

Though her mind didn't quite believe that version of the story, it was the version her heart chose to cling to. She had Matt now, and she would keep him. Even if it meant ignoring that little red flashing light in the back of her eyes that warned of danger ahead.

****

They avoided talking about the day's unfortunate events until they'd eaten and put everything away. Then they sat together on the patio, enjoying the lazy, quiet afternoon.

"He was in the middle of his sentence when he died," she said, rubbing her forehead. The ache that had begun shortly after she did the body slam onto the concrete sidewalk had grown in intensity despite the good food and excellent company.

"Did he say anything useful before he…"

"Actually, our entire conversation may have been useful. He said Elliott approached him at a social function months ago, asked him to do business with Meganlin, but he brushed him off and thought no more of it. After you and I left his office today, he did a little research on Elliott, found the newspaper article about his murder. Get this—he said the photo with the article wasn't the man who tried to get his business at that function."

"Could he describe him?"

Dani nodded, sipped her beer, which was doing its part to warm her blood, relax her muscles, ease her doubts. "What's odd is that the description he gave is close to Elliott, but it was *off*."

"Faulty memory coming into play?"

"It's possible. He admitted to quickly dismissing the man and the conversation, but I don't think so. The man, he said, had blond hair, but it was dirty blond, not golden blond like Elliott's, and it was cropped short, not longer like Elliott's. The man was thin and of medium build while Elliott was six-feet with a strong build, and the man Big W talked to didn't have a black mark on his—"

"While Elliott did."

"Exactly. And if you remember, Reina Rivera suggested that the man who claimed to be Elliott may not have been."

They were quiet for a moment, digesting everything.

"I wonder if the man impersonating Elliott was the one who broke into my house. He was pretty well disguised, but he had the slim build and medium height Big W described."

"What I wonder is what he was after in your house. You said nothing was missing."

She rubbed her head again, trying to sooth the ache. "I don't know."

Matt stood, moved behind her, massaged her shoulders. At his touch, her eyes fluttered closed, and she luxuriated in the sensations rolling through her like thick, warm syrup. Tense muscles unknotted, releasing the brake on too-long-caged feelings and desires.

"We won't figure it all out today." He moved to her

side, took her hand, and helped her to her feet. "You should rest." Before she could tell him she wasn't that tired, he bent and picked her up in his arms.

"Matt, I'm not an invalid. I can walk."

He ignored her protests and carried her into the house and into a bedroom and laid her across the bed. "The guest bed isn't made up yet, so you'll have to sleep in my bed."

"That's convenient," she said with a little smile.

He leaned down and kissed her on the forehead. "I'll be in the living room. Call out if you need something."

When he stood and would have headed toward the door, she grabbed his hand. "I need something."

One look in her eyes, and he knew what she was asking for. "Baby, you had a rough day."

"No, I had a really shitty day. But I don't need a nap. I need you."

He brought her hand to his mouth. Kissed it. "Are you sure?"

God, yes, she was sure. She wanted—needed—Matt's passion filling her, mingling with her own. Matt's weight on her body. Matt's mouth and hands branding her skin. Matt's cock inside her, connecting them, merging them body and soul. Matt. "Make love to me, make me feel whole again, like you did in Vegas."

He lay on the bed next to her, and she went into his arms. Where she had wanted to be since she left their bed in Vegas. His hand caressed her cheek. His eyes captured hers. His lips touched hers. And in that small moment, she became his again.

Wanting to touch him, feel the heat of his skin

against hers, she removed his shirt and ran her hands over his back, his chest.

She bowed up, and he easily removed her T-shirt. He lowered his head and kissed her, leaving warm little tattoos on her cheek, her neck, across her shoulders, her breasts. She melted in delight. His hand palmed her breast, his thumbs flicking the nipple into a hard bud. He licked around her nipple and sucked it into his mouth, biting it, then gave the other the same treatment until pleasure had stolen her breath and blurred the day's horrific images in her mind.

His kisses and nibbles down her stomach had her tingling. He peeled her shorts from her body and tossed them to the floor next to her shirt. He hooked his fingers on the waistband of her panties and slid them down and off.

She unfastened his shorts, tugged them and his boxers down and off, and pulled him back on top of her. Slipping her hand between them, she gripped his erection, thick in her palm, and a thrill trembled through her.

A low groan rumbled in his chest as she touched him, slowly, tip to base, her fingers dancing up and down his rod in a light, silky touch. She wrapped her hand around him, feeling his heat, his strength, his heart beating in her hand. Her thumb circled the tip, smearing the pre-cum, her hand slicking down over the swollen shaft.

He slid his hand between her legs. He palmed her mound, teased with his finger the damp lips hidden behind the tiny triangle of curls. She opened herself to his exploring hand. A finger dipped deep, igniting her while the knuckle of another rolled her clit to accelerate the blaze. She closed her eyes, slipping into the velvety tunnel of pleasure he built for her. A long way off, as if in a dream, she heard him call her name. "Dani."

She opened her eyes and caught his eyes, sparkling with naked passion. For her.

"Tell me what you want."

Her throat was dry, as if all the moisture in her body was at that heated juncture where his hand toyed. Her tongue snaked across her lips, and she managed to utter the words that would quench her thirst, her hunger, the wildfire of need burning out of control. "What I've wanted since the minute we met. You inside me."

He grabbed a condom from the bedside table and rolled it on, and was back on her, plunging deep, filling her steamy depths. She squeezed her eyes shut at the sublime feel of having him sheathed so tightly and fully in her pussy again. His belly warm against hers. His chest brushing her nipples into tight, sensitive peaks. His mouth feeding on hers. His heart beating as one with hers. She was home.

Later they'd fuck in every position they knew, but for now, she wanted him heart to heart, mouth to mouth, sex to sex.

"Oh, God!" she cried as he pressed his body against hers, into hers, every inch of them touching. "I shouldn't have waited for this."

He grinned. "That's what I kept telling you."

Her answer was to wrap her legs around his waist and squeeze. "Shut up and fuck me. You can be right later."

His lips found hers again, and he kissed her deeply, pulling his cock almost all the way out before plunging it back inside, in an easy, smooth rhythm that had her crying in pleasure every time he hit her G-spot. The deeper he kissed her, the faster and harder his strokes became.

Their flesh slapping against each other was like music. She could feel the head of his cock swelling inside her and knew he was close. She wanted to come with him. "Don't hold back, baby," she said. "Come with me."

His growl vibrated against her breasts. The sensations of this suspended fraction in time—of his body moving against her, her nipples pressed against his chest, his mouth wet and hungry on hers, her pussy clenching his cock with every thrust—was pushing her toward oblivion.

Wanting to see the sublime moment pleasure took him, she concentrated on his face. His eyes were unfocused and bright and filled with love. For her. She could see it. Feel it. Knowing it pushed her over. She cried out his name in joy, in love, in pleasure, and rocked against him, her whole self opening up to him as the flood of love and pleasure swept through her. As soon as hers started, he called out her name in a long groan, then his eyes squeezed close, his lips parted, and he rode to the end with her.

****

Hours crawled by as they lay together in bed, Dani snuggled against him, his hand lightly caressing the silky strip of skin from her hip to her breast. Soft whispers in the fading light the only sound as even their heartbeats had slowed to almost nothing in the aftermath of their lovemaking. He could stay here forever, just like this, with her. This was what he'd wanted since finding her again—her in his arms, in his heart, in his bed. Nothing would tear them apart again. He'd make sure of it.

"Matt?"

"Hmm?"

"Who's Arienne?"

Ah, shit. He tensed, and his hand stilled. The name sent shockwaves through him. How in the hell did she know about Arienne? "Arienne?"

"Yeah. She's the one who called today when I was in the kitchen looking for the platter."

Dammit! She must have talked to Natalia. How else could she have gotten the number. "What did she say?"

"I don't quite have the drawl down, but her exact words were 'Come home, darlin'. I miss the taste of you in my mouth.'"

He mumbled a low curse. "Arienne and I had—past tense—a sex-only arrangement. We broke up six months ago."

"Why sex only?"

"Neither one of us wanted the complications and frustrations of a relationship. We agreed to no ties, no commitments, no pretenses of what we were about. But lately, she wanted more. I didn't, so we ended it."

"What am I? A complication or a frustration?"

He propped his head on his hand and looked into her eyes. "You're the woman I want in my life. The one I want a relationship with." Addressing the doubts in her eyes, he continued. "Since the night I met you, I've wanted no one else. I've been with no one else."

His hand crawled across her stomach. "I was kicking myself for letting you go in Vegas before getting your number. I had decided that as soon as I got settled in Albuquerque, I was going to use company resources to find you. The moment I saw you again was the happiest I've been since Vegas. I've been trying to get you back in my life—not just my bed—since." He rolled on top of her. "And you know it."

He kissed her mouth, deep, wet, his cock between her legs, so close to her pussy that if he shifted a bit, he'd be inside her again. And he would. Just as soon as he knew she was ready.

Right now, her mind was working on something, and nothing could spoil the mood like a bunch of hairy questions. He'd work on getting her ready, and he'd start with the breasts he loved so much. He palmed one, played with the nipple, then drew it into his mouth, swirling his tongue over it.

"You don't want a sex-only relationship with me?" she said.

His mouth left her nipple and kissed her mouth. "No. I want more."

She roped her legs around his waist. "I want more, too."

"Do I hear a 'but' in your voice?"

"How long were you and Arienne together?"

He brushed his thumb over her cheek. "Let's not bring another woman into bed with us. I told you who she is and who's she's not."

"I want to know what kind of woman you allowed to play such a significant role in your life."

A sigh, heavy with irritation, eased from his mouth. He rolled off her and onto his back, leaned his head back into his pillow, and put one arm behind his head. His cock jutted slick and strong into the air, disappointed as hell he wasn't already going for his third run around the bases. "She satisfied me sexually, sometimes accompanied me to social events. She was a friend. That's the only role she played."

She leaned up on her elbow, and he felt her questioning gaze burning into him. "And that's what I don't understand. You're handsome, intelligent, fun, interesting, successful, sexy as sin, a talented lover—a great catch. A man like you doesn't have to have arrangements. Why aren't you in a serious relationship?"

He met her gaze. "I am. Her name is Danielle Parker."

Her answering smile was warm. "Good save, Collins." She lay across his chest, her ear at his heart, and was quiet for a moment or two, as if trying to form her next question in a way he couldn't dodge with a clever remark. "Why her?"

"We'd known each other for years, ran in the same circles, and she was okay with my boundaries."

"What was going on in your life at that time that you needed that type of relationship?" she asked quietly. "Were you too busy working to develop something more...substantial?"

He stared at the ceiling, trying to come up with the best way to answer her question. The truth might very well hurt her, but he wouldn't lie to spare her feelings. He didn't want lies between them. Lies ate holes in the fabric of relationships until they were too threadbare to survive. He wouldn't let that happen with him and Dani. He sighed and swallowed to clear his throat. This was one truth that could destroy him as much as it could set him free.

Chapter Thirteen

At Matt's protracted silence, Dani lifted her head from his chest and looked at him, waiting expectantly for his response. He kept his eyes glued to the ceiling, but she could see in their depths the shadow of the dark secret chained inside his heart.

"Matt?" she asked softly, prompting him, her chest going tight at what his hesitation meant, instinctively knowing she wouldn't like his answer.

He glanced at her, then right back at the ceiling. "My family had fallen apart, and I wasn't capable of or interested in pursuing anything substantial."

Dani didn't break the silence that followed his brief, vague answer, hoping he'd say more. When he didn't, she prompted him with the answer she hoped she'd hear him give. "By family, you mean your parents? Siblings?" She thought she'd read that Geoffrey Linton had two children.

Matt pulled in a deep breath and released it. "No."

She didn't *want* to know the truth, she *had* to. Their relationship was already too tentative, too fragile. Lies would weaken it even more. Lies destroyed relationships.

"A wife. A child," she suggested and held her breath on his response.

His slow, short nod spoke volumes.

Her heart stopped, frozen in her chest, but she

moved into his arms and hugged him to show she cared about him, to show he could talk to her. "If you want to talk about it, I want to hear it." After a long pause he began.

"Jessica and I married right out of college because she was pregnant. We loved each other, I guess, but..." She heard him swallow and felt his heart pounding against her chest. Was the truth that thorny? "Months later, I was in law school and had a good job, we had a healthy son, and Jessica was fulfilling her dream of being a wife and mom. After a couple of years, she grew restless, resented the hours I was gone, in school and at work to support her in the lifestyle she wanted, resented being left alone all day with an energetic toddler. She said she wanted a career. To support her in that goal, I hired the best nanny money could buy and found her a good job in one of my father's businesses. In less than a month, she'd quit, saying she'd made a mistake in leaving our son in someone else's care. I just wanted her to be happy, so I supported her decision. I thought things were improving, but six months later, I found her in bed with her best friend's husband. She blamed me, said that being a wife and mom had sucked the joy from her life. Said she didn't want to do either anymore."

Anger surged through Dani at the careless actions of the woman and the anguish that it caused him, the anguish that had frozen his face into a mask of grief since he started talking about her. "But she had choices. You never forced her into a role."

Her eyes never left his, but he wouldn't meet her gaze. He was too focused on the memories flashing through him. "She didn't see it that way. She said she was filing for divorce and sole custody of our son."

"Even after she made it clear she didn't want to be a mother?"

He nodded.

"What did you say?"

"I told her I'd never let her raise Justin alone. We argued all night about it, but in the end, we agreed to see a counselor before either of us saw a lawyer. Running on no sleep, coffee, and raw emotion, I drove to work, relieved I had saved my family. Minutes after I hung up from making a counseling appointment for us, I got a call."

He stopped there, and oh, God, she knew why. She knew what was coming. And it was bad. Soul-crushing bad. Pain oozed from every pore of his body and triggered the same response in hers. She'd rather take it all on herself than to have him hurt one more second, but she couldn't. Maybe talking about it might help exorcise it a bit, to where it no longer roared inside him.

"She ran with him?" she said softly, gently urging him to continue.

"It was raining hard that day. The roads were slick, making traffic worse than usual. The cop who called me said she'd been going too fast for conditions, so when she slammed on the brakes, she spun out on the bridge. Four cars ran into her, then a semi. It hit her so hard it knocked the car through the barrier and off the bridge into the river."

"Oh, God," she exclaimed in a harsh whisper, and her hand flew to her mouth, chills exploding in her body. "Justin?"

His lips thinned over his teeth, his nostrils flared, and his eyes clouded, as if it took every bit of strength he possessed not to break. "They found him still buckled in his car seat." His voice broke along with Dani's heart. He shook his head, as if trying to dislodge the memory.

Her throat tightened, and she swallowed against the shock and sadness blocking it. Seeing the same agony in his face, she draped herself across his body and wrapped around him, trying to ease the pain she felt pulsing from every cell in his body. "Baby, I'm sorry."

He accepted her embrace, clung to her. She was content to let the rest of the story go, almost sorry she'd even broached the subject, but he had a final comment that answered her original question.

"I lost them, and for a long time, I lost myself. When Arienne offered me her body and expected nothing in return, I... She was a crutch that allowed me to limp through the life forced on me until I was strong enough to walk on my own. She—and work—kept me alive."

For the first time since he'd begun his story, he looked into her eyes and ran his palm over her head in a soft caress. "I appreciate her, what she did for me, but I'm not now nor have I ever been in love with her."

She nodded and kissed him, gently. As they lay together in their welded embrace, his story replayed in her head, giving her a better picture of the man she loved. He might not be in love with Arienne, but she was in love with him and wanted more than sex. The voice on the answering machine said it clearly. But she'd let that go for now. Now all she wanted was to wrap around her man and sooth his wounds with her love.

****

Dani drifted off to sleep an hour or so before sunrise, but Matt lay awake beside her warm body, listening to her soft, even breathing.

He had been stunned to hear the words come out of his mouth about Jessica and Justin and Arienne. He'd tried to stop the outpouring of words and feelings, but once he'd started, he was compelled to keep going until it was all out. That he had unlocked his vault of secrets and shared the biggest ones with Dani told him something about the depth of his feelings for her.

He loved her.

The realization was overwhelming, filling him inside and out with a mixture of joy and fear. No woman since Jessica had meant this much to him. The pressure to do what was right, not to fuck up, was strong. So strong it frightened him.

He loved Dani, wanted her in his life, but he wasn't sure he could give her everything she wanted and deserved. Though they'd never had *that* conversation, like most women he knew, she probably wanted marriage and kids. A bone-numbing chill ran through him at the thought.

Marriage? Never again. He didn't have it in him to make himself that vulnerable again. No matter how much he loved her.

Kids? Another no. The pain of losing Justin nearly killed him, for a long time made him wish he'd died in that icy river with him. He never wanted to feel that kind of pain again. The only way to avoid it was not to put himself in a situation where he could be hurt that much.

And if Dani's dreams and desires conflicted with his? What would he have to give up or take on to keep her in his life? More importantly, could he do it?

The first muted rays of golden light slanted through the window, lighting Dani's face and burning away the confusion that had gripped him all night. He saw things clearly now. He loved her. He would do everything in his power to keep her in his life and to make her happy. Everything but marry her or give her a child. His love would have to be enough.

He pressed his mouth to her forehead in a lingering kiss before leaving her slumbering peacefully in their bed.

****

The smell of bacon and coffee wafting through the air gently teased Dani awake. She was alone in Matt's bed, the sounds coming from the direction of the kitchen telling her he was nearby. A happy grin spread across her mouth as she remembered last night. She stretched and ran a hand across one naked breast, feeling her nipple bead at her touch. He'd kissed and sucked that nipple, and the other one, and her pussy, and every other part of her body, several times in the night. She'd never felt so satiated and happy.

The smile faded when she thought back to his story of his wife and child. It broke her heart. She'd have done anything to ease his pain. Maybe the love they'd shared last night had helped. From now on, she would love him every day as if it were their last day.

She climbed from bed and washed up, then pulled on one of Matt's T-shirts instead of going to find her suitcase. Following her nose, she found him at the kitchen counter in his boxers, spooning scrambled eggs onto a plate alongside rashers of bacon, triangles of buttered toast, and a cluster of grapes.

She didn't announce her presence, but instead stood behind him, watching his domesticity in bloom, listening to him sing, off key, to some Country song she didn't know. When he did a little dance, rocked on his air guitar, she swallowed a chuckle, but he heard her and spun around. The smile on his face lit up her heart with love. And it was like the story was out and all was well again between them.

He took her into his arms and danced her around the kitchen. When the song ended, he dipped her low, then claimed her mouth. Her heart swelled when she realized she had never felt love like this before, never even believed it was possible.

"Whatever you put in your coffee this morning, give me a double shot," she said. "Someone kept me up way past my bedtime last night, and I'm in need of some go-juice this morning."

"If you get sleepy today at work, you can join me on the couch in my office for a pick-me-up." This was the Matt she had come to know, teasing and playful and completely different from the man who last night had revealed his horror story and cried silent tears in her arms.

"Are you propositioning me, Mr. Collins? That suggestion is way outside the boundaries of our agreement."

With the grin still firmly in place, he set her upright but kept her in his arms and kissed her. "Sorry, lover, you breached the contract when you fucked my brains out last night, rendering it void."

She chuckled. "Fine by me."

He kissed her again. "Cream, no sugar, right?"

"Right."

Letting her go, he poured her a cup of coffee, stirred in a liberal dose of cream, then handed it to her and watched her take a sip as if he wanted to make sure it was the way she liked it.

"Mmm. Perfect."

"You hungry?"

Actually she was. She'd been too upset to eat much yesterday. That and the vigorous sex last night had left her in need of food. "Starved."

He led her to the patio, where the table was laid with two placemats, cloth napkins, and silverware. "Have a seat. I'll get breakfast."

Her stomach growling, she sat and placed her napkin in her lap while Matt ran back inside for their food.

"You're spoiling me," she called out to him.

"Pampering, not spoiling," he said, placing a steaming plate before her and one on his mat.

"If this tastes half as good as it looks and smells I'm going to be a happy woman." Lifting the fork, she speared a bite of eggs and brought it to her mouth.

"Shit. Hold up." Matt jumped up from the table, and she held the fork still.

He came back to the table with a little bowl and placed it beside her plate. "I know how you like green chile on everything."

She laughed. "Ah! A man who understands the importance of spice in life. You're a keeper." She mixed some of the warm, diced chile into her eggs and lifted the fork to her mouth. She moaned her approval. "This is fresh roasted. Where did you get it?"

"Natalia had some in her freezer. The bags are labeled as last year's crop, but the mmm sounds you're making tells me it's still good."

"*Delicioso!*"

He smiled and picked up his fork and joined her in relishing the meal.

Matt insisted on doing clean-up duty, so Dani, realizing it wasn't a fight she wanted to win, gave in and relaxed in the lounge chair, head back, eyes closed, legs exposed to the warm morning sun. A short time later, a shadow passed between her and the sun, and she cracked open one eye to see what it was.

Matt stood at her side. His gaze on her legs.

Looking down, she realized the shirt she wore revealed more than legs. She kept her lids to thin slits she could peer out of unnoticed and tried not to smile. Keeping watch on his face, she bent one knee up and let the shirt rise even more.

His breathing changed, his tongue darted out to wet his lips, and he swallowed hard.

Raising her arms over her head, she felt the material rise up even higher. Knowing he was watching her made her nipples pucker, made her go wet between her legs. She stretched slightly and released a contented sigh.

A low growl came from his direction. "You know you're driving me crazy, don't you?"

Her smile grew, and she slowly opened her eyes to half-mast. "Am I?"

The heat and desire emanating from him was visible and palpable, and it ignited her own. She lifted her leg and placed her foot on his crotch, pressing against him, wiggling her toes, feeling the bulge grow and harden as he pressed his hips forward.

It was a good beginning but limited. She lowered

her leg and sat up, her face even with his bulge. She hooked her fingers on the lip of his boxers and slowly pulled them down, over his hips, down his legs. His cock sprang forth, fully erect, fully ready to serve, give, receive, his chest rising and falling in a broken rhythm.

Burying her face in his crotch, she inhaled the scent of him. She traced his cock with her tongue, from the base to the swollen head, slid her tongue along the length, up and down, letting her teeth gently scrape the ridge of the tip, and he watched her every move through dazed eyes.

She took him fully into her mouth, and he groaned, his hands diving into her hair, holding her head closer as he savored every lick, every stroke. It thrilled her that her touch could do that.

"Dani." Her name shuddering from his lips accelerated her desire. She wanted him. Now.

She pulled him down to the lounge chair on top of her, his weight pressing her deeper into the cushion. She raised her legs, opening herself up to him. With her hands, she guided his engorged member into her wet opening.

He pulled back a bit. "I'm not wearing a condom."

"I'm still clean. Are you?"

"Yes. Still on the pill?"

"Yes."

His hips plunged forward, and she savored the feel of her body stretching to accommodate him, feeling him without the barrier between them, as if that were the last barrier keeping them from fully being together.

They began to move, each stroke building on the one before it. He held himself over her, supported by his hands on the back of the chair, and lowered his head to bite one of her nipples through the shirt.

She arched her back and grabbed his hips with her hands, pulling him in closer.

His mouth moved to her lips, his tongue plunging between them, fully connecting them physically, both lost in desire, lost in each other.

Her climax hit, and she held him tight, fingernails raking his back as she shuddered.

He was right behind her, thrusting hard, fast, shooting hot cum into her with every groan.

They lay together, breathing hard, flesh throbbing with satisfaction. He raised his head from her shoulder. "I'm going to spoil you more often."

She chuckled. "Pamper, not spoil."

"Let's go in. I want to pamper you again in the shower before work." The kiss he gave her was long and passionate and full of promises for more delights.

Chapter Fourteen

Dani frowned at the screen in front of her, then at the files beside her, frustration gnawing at her brain at the inconsistencies in the basement archives where she was researching some of the data on Elliott's list. Some of the companies and representative names didn't seem to exist.

Nathan sauntered in, plopped down into one of the chairs and propped his feet on the table on top of her files.

Not even bothering to look up from the screen, she cut him short with a curt response. "Go away. I'm busy."

"You're a lot more savvy than I gave you credit for. Snagging the promotion, then the boss. Or was it the other way around? Whatever. You win the big prize."

As he had intended, the comment got her attention. How in the hell had he found out about her and Matt? They hadn't told anyone they were together. And they were careful to keep it professional in the office, with no touching, no kissing, no overly long quiet talks in the corner. Well, almost none. Lisa, of course, suspected because she'd seen too much. Had she gossiped about it? Liz knew, but she wouldn't say a word. Had people felt the vibe between them and assumed? Karen had said there'd been gossip.

"Leave now, or I'll call security." She shot him a poisonous look that matched her tone.

A wicked grin lifted his mouth. "You've grown some big-ass balls as assistant director. Or maybe your new lover is letting you borrow his."

She grabbed the phone. He jumped up and leaned in, slapping his hand down on hers so she couldn't call.

"He's selling the company, you know," he said, his face in hers. "And word is he'll have say in choosing a new president. I plan to be on the shortlist for that job, no matter what I have to do. And when I take over, I'll be ready for you." He put his hand at the base of her neck and gripped her hard. "In my bed. I know you only fuck bosses."

She pushed hard against him and jumped up. "You'll never be boss, and I'll never be in your bed. You disgust me."

She had taken two steps toward the door when he grabbed her by the arm and shoved her up against the wall, his hands trapping her arms on either side of her head, his body trapping the rest of her. His face was red, from stubbly chin to stubbly scalp. His eyes were chips of obsidian that shot into her with a wild, out-of-control look that said he wanted to do her harm. His breath was hot on her face and smelled like something left too long in the sun, and she turned her head to avoid the stench. In the midst of his anger, he seemed to be turned on because he was grinding his erection into her.

"Enjoy the ride, bitch," he growled into her cheek, his disgusting wet lips on her skin like bugs crawling on her. "Because it's coming to an end real soon." He lowered his head to kiss her, but she headbutted his mouth, splitting his lip and making it bleed. The surprise move stunned him for a moment, allowing her to slip free of his hold, but before she could get away fully, his hand grabbed her hair and yanked her back to him, again trapping her against the wall.

"Let me go!" she yelled, hoping someone might hear her. Knowing they were alone down here and she couldn't count on any help to get out of this, she delivered the tried-and-true knee-to-the-groin move, but he was ready for it and twisted just enough so that her knee dug into his thigh instead of his crotch. It had to hurt, but unfortunately not enough to secure her release. All it accomplished was to increase his anger and his desire to do her harm.

"I'm going to enjoy seeing you fall," he said, his voice a harsh whisper, every word a slap of hatred. His mouth was on its way down to hers again when the voice of Security Officer Arliss Brown boomed from the doorway.

"Take your hands off the lady. Now."

Nathan glanced behind him, then let her go and backed away, holding up his hands to the bigger man to show he wasn't a threat. "No problems here, man. We were just having a friendly chat. Go back to your jelly donuts and coffee."

Nathan moved toward the door, but officer Brown halted his progress with his brick-house of a body, his beefy paw, and his low voice. "Did he hurt you, Ms. Parker?"

The red grip marks on her arms ached, her scalp stung, and her stomach churned. "Your timing was perfect."

"Do you want to file assault charges against Mr.

Gerber?"

She eyed Nathan. What she wanted was for him to leave her alone. If that could be accomplished with a verbal warning, that's what she'd do. "No. But I would like it formally known that I am extremely uncomfortable in his presence and request that he stay away from me."

"I'll escort Mr. Gerber to HR so he can be reminded of the company's harassment policies. If he so much as looks cross-eyed at you again, you let *me* know, and I'll take care of…the problem."

"Thank you," she said.

Officer Brown escorted Nathan out, leaving Dani trembling. But as fear and disgust spun into anger, she felt like breaking something—Nathan's pearly whites, for starters. Instead, she channeled her emotions down another path. The path to the executive offices.

Matt was on the phone, staring out the floor-to-ceiling windows, when she strode into his office. He turned upon hearing the door shut and ended the call upon seeing her lock the door. She rushed to him, pushing her body into his, fitting her mouth over his in a demanding kiss while walking him backward. The two of them fell against the window, his back solid against the unyielding surface. She unfastened his belt and pants and was reaching inside his boxer briefs when a loud rap sounded on the door.

"Matt? Security Officer Brown is on the phone."

"I'll call him back," he said in a rough voice.

"He said it's urgent." Lisa's tone said she was growing impatient with having to have conversations through the door whenever Dani was in there with him.

Dani stepped away, and he retucked his shirt and

fastened his pants. She knew the instant he saw the marks on her arms. His eyes grew hard.

"Matt?" Lisa said again.

"Put him through."

Dani walked to his door and unlocked it. She was in her office, at her desk, when he stormed in minutes later.

"The son-of-a-bitch attacked you? Were you going to tell me?"

"No."

"Why the hell not?"

This was the second angry man she'd faced today, and it was more than she wanted to deal with. "Why do you think? I don't want you getting in trouble over someone like him. Plus, he's more bark than bite."

Matt ran his fingers lightly over the marks on Dani's upper arm. "I swear I'll kill the fucker if he touches you again."

"I don't think that'll be a problem. Officer Brown put the fear of, well, Officer Brown in him."

"Tell me the truth...did he do anything else?"

Other than creep her out? "No." She shook her head to add weight to her response, but she couldn't stop the shiver as she remembered his hands and breath on her.

Matt put his arms around her waist and moved into her, hugging her gently, kissing the top of her head, uncaring who might be there to witness the tender and inappropriate scene.

She breathed him in, felt her body drawing his warmth and love inside her, healing her, soothing her.

"Baby, if you weren't going to tell me about Nathan, why did you come into my office?"

"For this." She hugged him tighter.

He maintained contact for another moment, before stepping back and putting proper business distance between them. "If this happens again, you need to tell me. Immediately."

His jaw worked, as if he were still chewing on the tasty idea of beating Nathan to a pulp. She didn't like the idea of him fighting, but knowing that he would do it for her made her feel protected. Loved. If she needed more evidence of his feelings, it was there in his gaze. Surely that was love twining with the anger firing in his eyes. She couldn't resist a small smile.

"Immediately," he said again at her grin, as if he thought she wasn't taking it seriously.

"I'm sure he won't risk it again." At least she hoped not.

"Promise me."

"I promise."

He kissed her and went back into his office. Only later did Dani wonder why Officer Brown called Matt instead of Karen. Did the officer know Matt was the owner of the company? Or was it something else? How was it that he had arrived just at the right moment? Had he been asked to watch her? However it had come to pass, she was grateful for his timely arrival.

****

"I'm hearing rumors that you're living with Matt." Karen said days later at their biweekly lunch meeting. "I seriously questioned the veracity of those rumors as you and I had just recently discussed the risks inherent in such a relationship."

Not one to dance around an issue, Karen dropped her bomb right after the server brought them their ice tea and left to fill their food order. Taken aback by Karen's directness, Dani nearly choked on her drink. Holding her head high and facing her boss eye to eye, her voice steady and sure, she gave the only answer she could. "I'm in love with him."

Karen stared intently at her, as if looking for signs of other truths hidden in a blink of her eye, the twitch of her mouth, a raising of an eyebrow, the twisting of her hands. Whatever she saw—or didn't see—turned the corners of her mouth down into a slight grimace. "I can count on one hand the times in my entire twenty-five-year career I felt a need to pry into the private lives of my co-workers or employees. I'm about to add to that number. But only because I'm fond of you, and I want the best for you, personally and professionally."

Dani would have rather crawled under the table and licked the chewed gum stuck there than listen to the coming sex lecture from her supervisor, but she faced Karen with head high.

"Does he return your level of affection?"

"Yes, of course. Or I wouldn't be with him."

The look on Karen's face spoke the doubts her mouth did not. "If you have doubts—any at all—now would be the time to raise them, before the two of you get in any deeper." She put her hand on Dani's arm. "And before you get hurt."

Again. Karen didn't say it, but the word was out there nonetheless. Like Dani needed a reminder about the disaster of a mistake she'd made with Elliott. But then, maybe she did need a reminder. Had she been completely honest with Karen, her answer would have been slightly different. Matt had never actually said he loved her. Had never talked about the future and how

Sophia Ryan

they, as a couple, fit into it. In truth, she didn't know whether they had a future beyond living together for the next few months as he was cleaning up the business to sell it.

Dani nodded in response to the warning. "Thank you for your concern, but he and I are good and are committed to keeping our personal and professional lives separate."

Karen leaned back in her chair, and it was as if she had switched masks, transforming back into Ms. Professional. "Where are you on the investigation?"

As Dani filled her boss in on her progress, she wasn't as engaged as she wanted to be. Under the table, her hands twisted the life out of the napkin in her lap and her mind fidgeted on the question about Matt's level of commitment.

Chapter Fifteen

Movement and giggles and a chorus of "Trick or Treat!" out on the front porch caught Dani's attention, and she jumped up from the couch where she and Matt sat eating popcorn and watching a horror movie. She peered out the window. In the stark light of a full, almost dripping moon was a vampire, fangs as blood red as his silky cape and slicked-back hair as dark as his midnight black sweatsuit, a three-foot tall ghost draped in white with exaggerated blackened holes for eyes, a taller green-faced witch in a black dress, green and black striped socks, and a pointed hat with a rhinestone tiara sitting on her head, and a full-grown Frankenstein hanging back.

Grabbing the plastic orange pumpkin nearly overflowing with candy, she opened the door to a another chorus of "Trick or Treat." The breeze carried a whiff of fireplace smoke, flurries of amber and brown leaves, and something else...children's joy and innocence.

"Oh, you guys are scary," she said, her faked fear an award-worthy performance.

The witch, who had no front teeth, cackled in response and clawed at the air with her long black fake nails. The vampire bared his fangs with a menacing hiss and tried not to smile. The ghost delivered a "Booo!" that was more funny than frightening.

"Hey, I'll make a deal with you guys. If you don't bite me," she pointed to Drac, "or hex me with one of your magic spells," to the witch, "or haunt me," to the ghost, "I'll give you each three pieces of candy. Deal?"

"Deal!" the trio whole-heartedly agreed and stuck out bags already heavy with loot.

"Count with me to make sure I give you the right number." One by one, Dani dropped three mini-sized candies into each bag, counting along with the kids as she did so.

"All right! I got gum!" the vampire said, peering into his bag.

"And I got some chocolate. That's just for me, Daddy," the witch yelled over her shoulder to Frankenstein.

The ghost pulled a sucker from his bag and held it out to Frank. "Daddy, can I have this one now?"

"What do say to the nice lady?" prompted Frank as he unwrapped the ghost's sucker.

"Thank you!" the trio said in unison.

"You're welcome," she said. "Happy Halloween!"

The dad picked up the ghost and found the hole in his sheet that matched his mouth and popped in the red sucker, then the gang left the porch through the side gate she had decked out in Halloween decor the week prior. With a reminder from Frank for the vampire and witch not to run, they headed to the next house.

At watching the kids enjoying themselves with their father, she couldn't help letting her mind build a scene of Matt running up and down the streets with their kids on a crisp Halloween night, wearing a silly mask to join in the fun, and stealing their candy on the trek home. Bathed in thoughts of the fairy tale future she was spinning for the two of them and their two-point-five kids, she melted when his arms slid around her waist.

"That little blood sucker was eyeing your very lovely neck," he said, *eyeing your very lovely neck* sounding like a bad imitation of a Transylvanian accent from the old Dracula film they'd been watching. His bite on her neck, however, sent delightful shivers to her core and made her want to swoon like the women Dracula feasted on.

"What he was eyeing was my lovely bowl of candy." Dani tipped her head back to look up at Matt, and he dropped a kiss on her smiling mouth.

"I don't blame him. I want some of your candy, too." He kissed her again, then slid his hand behind the pumpkin and fondled her breasts until her nipples were as hard as pieces of candy corn against her shirt. "When is Halloween duty over for the night?" He kissed her again.

Her eyes closing against the sensations he brought to life inside her, she struggled to speak. "You do realize we're standing in the front door, making out, while your neighbors are in the streets with their kids?"

"They get treats, why shouldn't I?"

"Kids are coming this way," she said, turning to face him. "Why don't you handle this one so I can go prepare special treats just for you?" She pressed the pumpkin to his chest.

He raised his hands in refusal. "Can't we just leave the pumpkin on the porch and let them help themselves?"

"Sure, if you want spend tomorrow morning scrubbing egg off the house and picking toilet paper off the trees."

He sighed and took the pumpkin. "I'm cutting the little monsters off at eight."

"I'll have your treats ready by then." She kissed him. "You just make sure to have your tricks ready." She caressed the bulge slightly tenting the front of his sweats.

He tried to kiss her again, but she moved out of his reach as kids walked through the gate hollering "Trick or Treat!"

She left him alone at the door but couldn't resist standing just beyond that to listen to his exchange with the three mid-schoolers wearing dead slutty-cheerleader costumes.

"Dead cheerleaders?" he asked wryly as he dropped a fist full of candy into each of their pillowcase bags.

The girls, clearly gaga over the hottie at the door, giggled their response.

"Yeah. We had a dead football player with us, you know, like for the whole look, but he kept grabbing our candy and yelling 'and the beast scores again,' so we dumped him."

"You're smart to dump the beasts, especially the ones who steal your candy."

"Totally!" The girls giggled. "Thankyousomuch!" they said in sing-songy unison before waving and moving aside so the next kids in line could get candy.

Dani's heart swelled in her chest as she watched him with the next round of kids, younger ones of about four or five, with their parents.

Tonight, she would give him treats befitting the wonderful man he was and the exceptional father he would be.

****

At eight on the dot, as promised, Matt handed out candy to the last trick-or-treaters and when they were gone, closed the gate, placed the nearly empty pumpkin on the table in the foyer, turned off the porch light, and locked the front door. Stopping in the kitchen for a drink of water, he noticed that Dani wasn't about. Figuring she was in the bedroom, he checked the house to make sure all was locked up tight, then padded down the hallway toward the bedroom.

The door was slightly ajar. He pushed it open slowly and peered into the dim room. The drapes were open, and moonlight spilled into the room through the opening. Near the settee, the lamp was switched on low, with a thin scarf of some kind over it, making the room shimmer softly in pink. Dani rose from his bed, wearing one of his white T-shirts, severely altered. Fun-sized candies covered the shirt, and black hand-drawn lettering appeared on the front that said *Matt's Candy*. A deep V-cut sliced the shirt from her neck to mid breast, and the hem skimmed the top of her sweet candy patch.

She strolled toward him, hips swaying provocatively, eyes pinning him in place, her smiling mouth ripe with promises of a better-than-a-handful-of-chocolate-minis night of sweet ecstasy.

"I hear you like yummy treats," she said, stopping in front of him.

The sex in her voice made him drool. "I do."

"See anything you like?" She slowly turned, giving him a tantalizing view of her treats.

His grin—and his dick—grew as he contemplated

the many ways he'd enjoy the sweets being offered. "I like everything I see."

"Unwrap your favorite."

He lifted the wrapper over her head, his eyes touching every inch of her delicious body. He ran his hands down her arms, around her hips, and gripped her ass as her hands slid up his chest. He took her mouth, and she pressed her lips onto his. He opened his mouth wider on hers, and his tongue found hers. They kissed, deep and slow, hands exploring, caressing, pleasing.

She slid her hand between them and grabbed his cock through his sweats, stroked it, pinching the thick head. "Tell me what you want, Matt. Tonight's about you. I'll do anything you want, because I want to make you as happy as you make me."

He grinned and took her hands in his. "Anything?"

"Anything."

"And what if what I want is to shave your sweet little pussy?" The thought of it tugged at his balls, and his heart was suddenly pounding in his chest. He liked her little tuft of hair. He just wanted to see and touch and taste all of her.

A smile hovered at her mouth, and she lifted an eyebrow. "After you shave me, what would you do?"

The images flooded his mind. First, he'd run his hand over all that silky bare skin, tugging her pussy lips, then he'd spread her lips and massage her clit, fuck her with his fingers, until she was wet and squirming for him. He'd push her legs wide and bury his face in her pussy, draw her scent into him. His tongue would get a turn next, lapping and licking the smooth, tasty filet until she came in his mouth, and still he'd eat her until she came again, flooding his mouth with her juice.

Then, ah fuck, then he'd slide his dick right up through her all her tasty cream and pound her until she came again, her inner walls gripping his cock until he spewed his own cream inside her.

His face was hot, his heart was jackhammering, and it was all he could do to stop himself from yanking off his sweats and taking her now. But he held back and managed to answer her question. "Eat you and fuck you until you come so much you can't breathe."

Her lids lowered and her wet lips parted, telling him she'd like that too. "Would that bring you pleasure?" she asked, her voice husky. He could smell her, knew their conversation was a turn on to her as much as it was to him.

He was almost beyond turned on. If there was such a thing. Blood surged into his rod, and pre-cum leaked from the tip. "Making you come? Fuck, yeah, that brings me pleasure." And he wasn't lying. Nothing made him feel more satisfied, more powerful, more heroic than feeling her body spasm around his finger, his tongue, his cock as he made her come.

"Fine. But just don't cut off anything important while you're at it, like my clit. I'd like to keep my clit."

He chuckled, loving how game she was. "I like your clit, too." He pulled off his shirt, then turned her around and delivered a little spank and a push to her ass. "Into the bathroom." He made her lead the way so he could watch every wiggle of her luscious ass, his cock rubbing against his leg the whole way.

Once there, he laid a towel on the top of the toilet tank, and patted it. "Have a seat."

She did while he gathered scissors, her razor, his shave cream, and washcloths and set them on the counter. He sat facing her on the toilet seat. She spread her legs, bringing her pussy into full view, making him want to go down on her and forget the shave. He ran his hand across her mound, reveling in the feel of her hair against his palm. She gasped as his finger brushed her clit. He leaned in and kissed it, buried his nose in it. The scent of her made his cock jump against his boxers. He couldn't fucking stop smiling.

"Ready?" he asked as he sat back.

"Ready."

He spread her legs as wide as they would comfortably go, then grabbed the scissors. He trimmed away most of the hair, then traded the scissors for the can of shaving cream. He shook it good and hard.

"You're good at that motion," she said. "Have you been practicing when I'm not around."

He laughed. "Not lately."

He squirted shaving cream in his hand and slowly spread it across her mound.

She jumped. "It's cold."

"Now you know how I feel every morning."

"You're used to it. This is a first for me."

Matt looked up at her. "Spread a little wider?"

She did, and his dick stiffened even more, seeing her pussy open to him. *Concentrate, Collins, or you'll shoot your load in your boxers like a virgin.*

After she was lathered up, he picked up the razor, then stopped and gave her his most serious face. "Dani, before I begin, I want you to know…I'll love you, with or without a clit."

She laughed and bopped his shoulder.

"Hey, hey, none of that. I need a steady hand for this. Artist at work." He dipped his head to view her full-on. "Here goes."

The soft sound of the razor scraping against her mound scraped all along his hard cock. He couldn't wait to bury it inside her bare pussy. Now and then, he used his fingers to move her flesh to shave it. Every time he did, she moaned. As he rinsed the razor, he glanced at her face. Her eyes were intent on him, and she was smiling.

She put her hand on his head and ran her fingers through his hair. "You're so fucking hot."

He grinned. "Glad you think so." He turned his attention back to his work.

"Know what else is fucking hot?"

"What?"

"That hard-on in your pants."

His grin grew bigger. "You do remember I have a razor in my hand?"

"Am I breaking your concentration?"

"Big time." He rose and kissed her mouth. "But I'm getting used to it. I can't concentrate on anything if you're within fifty feet."

"Glad to know it."

"Quiet, you." He wiped her off with a towel and used his fingers to check for areas that still needed work. Her delicate lips were hot and moist under his fingers as he spread her, and his touch made her gasp and her body twitch. The scent of her arousal made his mouth water.

"How about you take off your pants and let me see what I'm getting when you're done with this pussyscaping."

"If you don't behave, you're not getting anything but a spanking."

"Tease."

He continued on, running his fingertips along her pussy lips, feeling for missed hairs, until he was satisfied all the hair was gone. Then he took a washcloth and wet it with warm water. He wiped her off, slowly and thoroughly, making sure to get all the shaving cream. After rinsing a few times, he washed the razor and his hands, then sat back down.

"Now. To inspect my masterpiece." He looked at her beautiful pussy, wet, bare, swollen, aching for him to pleasure her. He brushed the tip of his finger along her slit.

She moaned, her breath ragged. Her face was flushed, and the spark in her eyes spoke of barely controlled excitement. She squirmed, and he knew she might be feeling vulnerable.

He withdrew his touch. "Baby, how do you feel right now?"

"Excited. Vulnerable. Eager. Horny as hell. How about you, lover? I can see your hard-on from here. You can put it in my mouth if you want. I won't bite. Hard."

He chuckled. He was supposed to be running this show and already she was jumping in, making him want to forget the routine he had in mind and just bury his cock between her spread legs now and fuck her 'til they both came, screaming the roof down.

"You'll suck my cock when I'm ready for you to."

He looked at her bare pussy, and the hard-on she'd mentioned grew. She was trickling moisture between her lips, telling him that the shave, his touches, their sex talk had turned her on. As he'd hoped.

"Well?" she asked. "Is it everything you hoped for

and more?"

"Much more." He stood between her legs, and she ground her pussy against him, as if trying to find relief. He grabbed her wrists, raised them over her head, and kissed her deep, twirling his tongue with hers, tasting her. She had eaten a few of the chocolate candies tonight, and he could taste the sweetness, reminding him that she was his candy. His sweetness. His treat.

"Grab the towel bar with your hands," he said. She did, and he pulled the decorative tieback from the shower curtain and tied it around her wrists and then the bar. "Don't let go. For any reason."

She nodded, licking her lips.

She'd told him in Vegas she wasn't into BDSM. He wasn't either, preferring his women to be eager participants, giving as good as they got, and the idea of spanking or whipping or clamping any part of her sweet flesh turned him cold. But light bondage play, like this and that they'd done in Vegas, was meant to tease, entice, enhance, and prolong the experience. His dick was hard and leaking from anticipation. At this point, tying her hands was to keep them from him. If she touched him, he'd come.

He dipped his head and met her gaze. "If this makes you uncomfortable in any way, say stop and I'll stop and untie you."

She nodded again. "I trust you, Matt. Completely."

She trusted him. Her words ran through him like wildfire, making him feel like an all-powerful being. He'd never break that trust with her.

He kissed her again and inched his hands slowly down her arms to the sides of her breasts. She shivered, inhaling a sharp breath, and he saw goosebumps roll across her body, her nipples puckering into a tight bead, drawing his touch. She jerked when he cupped her big tits in his hands and brushed his thumbs against her hard nipples.

"You like that?" he asked.

"Yes. I like your mouth on me, too."

"Glad to hear it because I'm going to suck these beautiful tits."

He leaned in and licked around one nipple, making her moan and arch against his mouth. He took it as eagerly as she gave it and sucked deep. Her arms jerked on the tether, as if she wanted to take his head in her hands to hold his mouth closer. She arched higher, showing her frustration, which thrust her breasts up, full and pointy. His core heat flamed.

"Don't let go of the bar," he reminded her.

"I'm not," she moaned.

A quick glance up showed her hands had a death grip on the bar. Matt drew her other nipple into his mouth, swirling his tongue over it, sucking it hard like she liked. He purposefully kept his body from touching hers. He wanted her to feel his hands and his mouth, to intensify every touch, every lick, every suck. But that hadn't stopped her from rolling her hips back and forth toward him, reaching for his body with hers. His slow, calculated touches were driving her wild. Which is what he'd wanted. When he finally got to her pussy, she'd explode and he'd drink every last drop of her cum. In automatic reflex, his hips ground into her, and they both moaned.

"You like my tits," she said.

"I fucking love your tits." Maybe he was the one being driven crazy by her, her movements, her panty little breaths, her groans, her voice, her body. He could smell her arousal, knew she wanted him.

He kissed down her stomach, licking until he was at her shaved mound. He kissed, laved, and sucked his mark into the silky flesh but didn't touch her pussy lips or beyond. Her legs trembled, and moisture trickled from her slit, showing how turned on she was. He thought about burying his face in her now, not making either one of them wait any longer, but he wanted her to dance on that edge just a little longer. It would make the fall all that more pleasurable.

He lifted her leg and set her foot against his chest by his shoulder and nudged her knee outward to open her wider. He kissed up her thigh, slowly, deliberately. When he got to her pussy, he opened his mouth over it, not touching, and breathed on it. A long, low ahhh left her mouth.

He placed her other leg similarly. Both legs splayed, opening her even more. He kissed up her other thigh, and this time, when he reached her pussy, he nibbled her swollen, wet lips and sucked them into his mouth. She jerked hard against the wall and the bar, and the sound that came from her squeezed his cock in a tight grip. The scent of her, taste of her, ramped up his desire and seemed to have sent hers off the chart from the way she was moving and moaning.

Unable to wait any longer, he dove into her pussy, using his lips and tongue to cover every bit of her flesh, lapping her, sucking her, thrusting into her, tasting her sweet juice. He teased between her folds with his tongue, parting them gently with his fingers so he could find the tiny, swollen head. He circled her clit, making it harder. A few strokes from his tongue inside her tunnel triggered her climax.

Her whole body tensed, then jerked, her pussy thrusting against his mouth. He pressed harder so she wouldn't fall off her perch on the toilet, which was shaking. He drank her, softly lapping while he watched the joy explode on her face as her orgasm hit. God, he loved watching her come, knowing he'd done that for her. If he could bring her such pleasure, she'd never leave him.

"Was that good, baby?" he asked as her climax ebbed.

"Yes," she whimpered. "Yes."

"You ready for more?"

"Yes."

He inserted two fingers into her still spasming pussy and stroked her, rocked it in and out of her wetness while the tip of his tongue brushed across her sensitive clit in a steady pattern, wanting to give her another orgasm before he had his.

"Come for me again. I want more of your cum." His words, his hand movements, his mouth on hers shot her right back to the top, and her pussy squeezed his fingers as she came again. He drank her deep as she arched up into his mouth, crying out, the breath shuddering from her lungs. His lips softened against her, helping her ride it out, her body shaking to the core from the pleasure throbbing through her. This was his treat.

When she'd calmed, he stood and gently kissed her mouth. His hands went to the bar and untied her restraint. The second her hands were free, she wrapped her arms around his neck and pulled his mouth to hers and kissed him with a passion that showed how much she'd enjoyed what he'd done to her. And how much she wanted him again.

He wrapped her legs around his waist and lifted her from the toilet.

"You ready for my cock?"

"I'm dying for your cock."

He grinned and carried her out of the bathroom. At the bed she unwrapped her legs from him, then her arms, and slid to the floor in front of him. Her hands went to his sweats, hurriedly pushing them down.

"Tonight is about what you want. Please tell me you want me to suck your cock." She pushed down his boxers and grabbed his swollen rod. Her touch. Fuck, her touch. It gave him life. He needed to hold on a bit longer.

Stepping out of his sweats and boxers, he put his hands on her shoulders and pressed gently. "On your knees for me. Don't use your hands. I'll move your mouth to where I want it." They'd done this in Vegas, but that time her hands had been tied behind her back.

She dropped to her knees, put her hands behind her back, and leaned in, licking the pre-cum from his slit. A sharp groan left his mouth and he held her head between his hands.

"Open your mouth," he said, his voice a hoarse whisper.

Her mouth opened wide for him and he guided himself between her lush lips.

"Suck me," he said.

She sucked him, hard, twirled her tongue over his head, and licked around his shaft as he disappeared deep inside her. He held her head still and pumped into her mouth, fucking her mouth, the feel of the wet tightness on his shaft sending him out of his mind. He stopped just short of shooting his cum in her mouth because what he wanted even more was to be inside her shaved pussy, making her come again.

He gently pushed her head back, away from his cock, and lifted her to her feet. He drew her close and kissed her deep. The taste of her, the taste of him, in her mouth and in his... He'd crave it forever. He picked her up and lay her on the bed, settled on her between her legs, kissing her, rubbing his cock against her wet, wet pussy. His lips moved to her breast, rolled his tongue over it, and she moaned. He sucked her nipple into his mouth and she writhed on the bed. He moved to the other and got the same reaction.

The way her body was moving and arching up to his mouth was sending white, hot desire through him. He started kissing down her stomach, but she stopped him, held his head."Oh, God, Matt. Please. Fuck me." She was bucking her hips, begging for his cock. And it thrilled him that she wanted him so much. Him. His love. He would give her what she wanted.

He almost came at her pleading, harsh words. He needed to be inside her, too. He slid his cock into her pussy.

She gasped at their union, and so did he. Her hips rose against him, as if wanting to feel it all. His eyes locked on the spot where they were connected. The sight of his cock disappearing into her bare, wet, gripping pussy increased his speed. She continued to arch up into his thrusts, and the only sounds were their slapping flesh and their sharp pants for air.

After only a few strokes, her head dropped back, her mouth open, and her throat arched in a silent cry before a wild groan broke through. She trembled beneath him, her pussy squeezing his cock. At the height of her release, he found his. He clenched her tighter, thrust harder, hitting the top of her again and again. He released a long, low, growled fuck as he shot into her. One last deep push, and he stilled, his breath ragged in his heaving chest. His body trembling on hers. Husky joyous laughter bubbled up from deep in his soul, and she joined him.

When he could breath again, he kissed her mouth, tenderly, lovingly. Kissed her eyes. Her forehead. Her mouth. Stared into her eyes.

"I never thought it would be that...I don't know...intense," she said. "All the sensations were intensified."

It had been that intense for him, too. "Glad you enjoyed it." He kissed her again. He had never felt so connected to another person. Never felt so loved. He had waited a lifetime for someone like her, and he never wanted it to end. He would work harder than he'd ever worked at any job, at any relationship, to keep her with him.

They lay there wrapped around each other for a few steadying moments, moments he wished could last forever.

"So what do you think? Is Halloween your new favorite holiday?" she asked.

"I have to admit I was dreading Halloween, with all the kids and candy and hoopla involved in it. Not my favorite holiday."

But it had been one of his favorites. He'd enjoyed walking through the neighborhood with Justin, teaching him how to say the magic words that would get the best treats. He remembered the first year Jessica had dressed him in an orange footy pajama thing and painted his face to look like a jack-o'-lantern, complete with a green cap. The second year he'd been a vampire. There hadn't been a third.

He'd never forgotten his memories of his son, and he never would. But he'd worked damn hard over the years to keep them caged where they could do no harm. Talking to Dani about Justin seemed to have released them from their carefully guarded prison, and they were still on the loose.

"And now?" she prompted.

Now? Well, now, because of Dani, he could have new memories of Halloween, memories that didn't end in tragedy. "We should have Halloween every month."

"Might cost a fortune in candy." She ran her hand over his dick.

He had made her come three times, with his mouth, his hand, and his dick, but the look on her face, the way she arched into him, stroked him, told him she wanted more. And he'd give it to her, all she wanted, tonight, tomorrow, forever, to make up for what he couldn't give her—a Halloween with her own children.

"We can leave the candy and the candy-gobbling monsters part out," he said.

"You were great with them, by the way."

At her remark, he rolled onto his back, leaving her arms. He chanced a glance at her. The expression on her face told him she was confused by his action. He pulled her into his arms, but he stared up at the ceiling, not at her.

"Me and kids—like vegans and sirloin. I never know what to say to them. They stare at you and methodically strip away who you think you are to who you really are, then, while you're standing there exposed, they're analyzing whether you're any damn good."

She trailed her fingers over his chest. "That's the great thing about kids. They're the real thing, before layers of fear and mistrust get plastered over them. After watching you with them tonight, I know you'll be a great dad."

The look on her face as she smiled at him was borne of pure internal radiance and joy.

He, on the other hand, felt like he'd been punched in the nuts.

At first, he couldn't breathe, much less speak to correct her misconception that he would ever wear the daddy moniker again. One look at her face, and he knew that what he had to say would hurt her, but it had to be said.

"Dani." He grabbed the hand caressing his chest and squeezed, looked her in the eyes, and spoke the truth gently but firmly. "I don't want children again."

He knew the second the implications of his words sank in. The smile vanished from her face, a shadow crossed her eyes, and she took her hand from his.

"Oh." Her voice broke as if her throat was suddenly too dry to say more.

"I thought you knew."

"How would I? We've never discussed kids before."

"No, not in so many words, but I thought you knew enough about me—about what happened to my son—to realize that children aren't a part of my life plans."

"I thought that eventually you'd want to marry

again, start a family."

He put his hand low on her stomach and caressed her skin. "No. To both."

"Oh." It was a painfilled syllable.

He rolled toward her and leaned up on one elbow, looking down into her face. She wouldn't meet his eyes, but even in the moonlight he could see that her face had gone as pale as the fake cobwebs she had strung on the patio gate to help enhance the Halloween experience for the kids.

"And when I say I don't want to get married or have kids, it's not a statement suggesting that I don't want these things with you. It means I don't want them with anyone." When she didn't speak, he did. "You know how I feel about you."

"I thought I did, but I wasn't even in the right universe regarding your feelings on marriage and kids. So, I'm a bit unsure about everything at the moment."

"Then let me clarify. What I want with you is what I have with you—a committed, loving relationship. I'm committed to us, Dani."

"For how long? A relationship—even a supposedly committed one—can be broken at any time for any reason. Marriage brings with it a golden cord that binds couples together, insisting they try harder when life threatens that bond."

"Don't be naïve. What makes a relationship last is the commitment the couple brings to it, not the marriage ceremony or the ring or the mythical cord knotting them together in good times and bad, sickness and health, wealth and poverty."

She glared at him. "Don't call me naïve just because we have differing beliefs regarding the importance of marriage and family."

"I didn't mean it that way," he said. "Look…" He rammed his fingers across his skull. "This isn't coming out right." Fucking understatement. What had possessed him to call her naive, suggesting her way was wrong? This was not going well. He was as cool and collected as a marble statue in the boardroom, but none of that experience was helping him in this bed, in this situation. His heart was racing, and his throat was tight. He was in full-blown panic mode. Too many more wrong word choices, and she'd leave. He'd lose her. He cupped her face. "Dani, I'm committed to this relationship for as long as the two of us are committed to keeping it healthy and alive."

She shrugged away from his touch and sat up.

Fuck. Bad to worse.

"What does that look like?" she said, her voice tight. "You wake up one day, decide the hot woman coming on to you is what you'd rather have, and boom, our relationship has died and I'm out on my ass? There are all kinds of temptations out there. As your lover, I can't control who comes on to you or your reaction to those come-ons. I can't influence anything you do."

He sat up, too, and gripped her shoulders. "Of course you can. You're Danielle Parker. The woman I'm totally, completely, and utterly in love with. I have no need for another woman when I have you. Don't you see that? Don't you see how much I love you?"

She put the safety on her fully loaded tirade and stared at him, eyes wide, lips parted. Then her body softened, relaxed a bit, the fire inside her seeming to flip off. Had he finally found the right words? He hoped to God he had.

****

I love you. The words lifted her heart into her throat where it expanded with joy. It was the first time he'd said those words. Not only I love you, but also I'm in love with you, which everyone knew was two very different things. At his words, her anger, panic and tension diminished, and all she could do was stare at him in shock, in love, for a few sizzling moments when she thought she'd explode, sending joy all over her, him, and the room.

"You love me?" she whispered.

He smoothed his hands over her shoulders. "I love you, Dani. You fill me up—mentally, physically, emotionally, sexually, in every possible way. You make me want to do everything within my power to please you so you'll *choose* to stay with me. I don't want you to stay with me because the laws of marriage demand it. I want you to stay with me because you want to. Isn't that how you feel about me?"

"Yes." She wasn't lying. She did agree. With everything he said.

"All I'm saying is that we don't need to sign a paper and stand up in front of friends and family and a preacher in a church and vow to them that we'll love and cherish each other for us to last as a couple. I'd rather we make that vow to each other, then stand by it. And that's what I'm doing. Right now." He took her hands in his. "I'm yours. For eternity if you want it. I promise you, it's what I want. You give my life meaning."

His words swirled like a whirlpool in her head. They filled her heart to bursting with their deep and rational ardor. He loved her. She loved him. But was it was enough?

"I love you, too," she said, "and I see a lot of sense in what you're saying."

"I hear a *but* coming."

How did she explain to him why the *but* was there and so strong? How did she tell him about her promise to never put herself in the position of loving a man who wouldn't commit to her in marriage? She had to tell him. She would tell him. But, oh God, not yet. Not tonight. Not when her emotions were already stretched thin. "When I envisioned my future, it was always career and married with children."

His eyebrows lowered into a slight frown, and a look of panic fixed on his face again. "So what does that mean for us?"

"It means I love you, and I want a future with you, but that I need time to sort out everything you've said and decide whether it's even possible for me to give up my dreams to live within the boundaries of your conditions for our love. Can you understand that?"

He nodded. "I do, but—"

She put her hand to his face and kissed him, gently, softly. "Goodnight, Matt." She rolled onto her side, away from him.

"Would it disturb your sorting if I hugged you?"

She smiled into her pillow. "Probably, but do it anyway."

He shifted closer, spooning her from behind, and she held onto his hand that snaked around her waist. She tucked herself back into him, feeling his satiated dick tucked against her ass.

He soon fell asleep, like he always did after sex, but she tossed and turned for hours, eyes staring into the darkness as memories rushed forward, memories of her promise and the day she'd made it, of a past that led her to this moment.

****

Her mother had been in a funk for days, ever since her dad left again to spend time in another woman's bed. She had come out of her funk long enough to fly into a rage that made the air in the house spark with intensity when Dani—or as she was known back then, Dancing Star, Danci for short, because apparently that's the first thing her father saw outside on the night she was born—told her she was meeting Kai at the river.

"Stay away from that boy." Her mother's command struck like a rattler.

Shocked by the violence behind her command, Dani's own vehement response surged straight from the raw part of her gut, not stopping to question what had prompted the unusual reaction to a boy she'd known her whole life.

"No, I won't," she yelled. "I love him, and he loves me."

"Love?" her mom said. "Men say they love you, then they use you and rip your heart out, leaving you wishing for death to make the pain go away." She grabbed Dani's arms. "Don't let any man do that to you."

"Kai's not like that," Dani shot back.

"Don't be foolish. They're all like that, and you need to protect yourself. Never believe them when they say they love you. If they want you, they need to commit to you in marriage. Promise me," she yelled each word and shook Dani as if that would make them sink in.

She winced at her mother's work-roughened fingers digging into her flesh and jerked away from the punishing grip. Anger and fear sharpened her tongue. "If your man goes off to fuck other women and treats you like dirt, don't blame love. That's your fault. You don't even try to make him stay. You just let him go."

Her mother recoiled as if the words had delivered a physical blow. Ignoring the pain contorting her mother's face, Dani backed away.

"Promise me," her mom yelled, her blue eyes as wild as her blonde hair, her body trembling.

Not wanting to decipher the crazy look in her mom's glassy eyes, Dani raced out the door.

Kai, whose name meant willow, was waiting for her at the river, and she ran into his arms, let him pull her into the deep water and into a deep kiss. In his arms, she was able to push aside her mother's bouts of darkness that sucked all the fun out of being alive. She buried herself in the strange and hot feelings his touches and kisses built inside her, and she stayed there in that bliss for long sweet moments before reality in the form of her annoying little sister intruded.

"You gotta come home," Bunny yelled from the shore. "Something's wrong with Mom!"

Dani didn't spare her a glance, but her mouth left Kai's for a split second to respond, "She's in one of her moods," before they were back on them, sucking, biting, kissing.

"She…she won't wake up!"

Bunny's pitiful whine pulled Dani out of her bliss, and she twisted in Kai's embrace to find her sister. Tears made trails across her dirty cheeks and dropped off her quivering chin, and her watery blue eyes were as wide as her moon face, the skin so pale it hid the freckles that usually dusted her nose and cheeks.

Beneath the water Kai teased the curls at her private area, and she grabbed his hand to stop him.

"What do you mean, she won't wake up?" she asked Bunny.

"I shook her and shook her and called her name bunches of times, but she won't wake up. Her face looks like a trout belly."

At the last sentence, the soft tingles of desire Kai had built inside her twisted into sharp thorns of fear. "I'll be back," she said as she left his arms. He protested, but she ignored him and swam the short distance to shore, pulled on her dress, and grabbed Bunny's hand. The two raced home.

The one-room adobe house that had been her home since birth was dark, still, and hot when she entered. A sickly sweet odor she knew but couldn't place stabbed her nose. A teapot sat on the table at her mother's spot, and the cup next to it held an inch of midnight black liquid, not the amber brew her mother preferred. She stuck the tip of her finger into the liquid. It was warm.

Feeling her insides pull in on themselves, her squeezed lungs unable to take a full breath, she knew something wasn't right. "Go get Andela," she said quietly but firmly to her sister.

Bunny was frozen to her side, her thin chest rising and falling rapidly, her fingers curled into the side of Dani's wet dress.

"Bunny," she said, louder and more insistent. "Go!"

The girl jerked, as if being awakened from a trance. On long, skinny legs she raced out the door to find the commune's *curandera*—healer.

Dani crept forward, deeper into the room, feeling like she was trudging through thick mud. She paused at the faded patchwork quilts that hung like curtains over a rope strung across the back part of the room. The quilts separated her parents' sleeping space from the space she and Bunny shared and from the rest of the room.

Her breath caught in her lungs and burned there, alarm gripping her heart, but she forced herself to part the material with the back of one hand.

Her mother lay on the bed. Face up. Still. Sleeping. Just sleeping.

Bunny was right. Her face did look like a trout's belly—pale, bloated, unreal.

Dani's stomach swirled, and she felt her breakfast wanting to come up. Putting her hands to her stomach to still the churning, she forced herself to shuffle closer. When she stood a foot from her mother, she called out, softly, "Mom."

Her mother made no response.

"Mom," she said again, a little louder.

Nothing.

Dani swallowed, but the sour taste that had filled her mouth since stepping through the door wouldn't leave. She moved closer and knelt next to her mother, slowly stretched out her hand and placed it on her cheek. The skin beneath her palm was cold. She jerked back her hand but then gathered her courage and grabbed her mom's arms and shook her, lightly at first, then more urgently when she didn't get an immediate response.

"Momma!" she said, over and over again, even

though a part of her knew her mother wouldn't respond.

She didn't feel the hot tears streaming down her face until Andela pulled her away from her mother's body and pushed her into her father's arms.

Rafael Montenegro pulled her to his chest to comfort her. She smelled lavender sage spice on his open shirt, on the sun-browned skin at his neck and chest, knew he'd been lying with the *curandera* while his woman lay dying.

Dani looked up into his glassy, toffee brown eyes, so much like her own, and was overcome by a tornado of fury twisting in her heart.

"You did this!" She hurled the accusation at her father and shoved him so hard in the chest he teetered backward.

Tears pooled in his eyes. "*Querida!* I didn't kill her." He tried to grab her arms, but she flung him away.

"Yes, you did. Every time you left her to fuck another woman, a little more of her died. If you'd have stayed faithful, if you'd married her, she'd still be alive. Her death is on you, *cabròn!*"

She ran out of the house, back to the river, to Kai, her body craving his touch, needing him to somehow help her put her life back in balance, to find her place again.

Kai, her love, was there with Rain, his arms holding her, his mouth kissing hers, his hips thrusting against hers.

Her entire body shaking, her very soul wailing, Dani hid behind the tree and cried. She'd lost her mother, her place in the world, and her belief in love in one swoop.

The small circle of mourners for Delilah Parker

drifted away, and Rafael carried away a sobbing Bunny. The diggers stood at a respectful distance, giving Dani a final few moments alone with her mother.

"I won't be like you," she whispered, refusing to let the pain inside her be eased by shedding more tears. "I won't love a man who won't commit to me in marriage. And once he does, I won't allow him to go to another woman. I won't be like you, Momma. I promise you that."

She picked up a handful of rich, brown dirt and let it sift through her fingers onto the wooden box that was her mother's final resting place. Then she picked up her backpack and turned, not toward home, but toward town. The sounds of the earth hitting her mother's coffin serenaded her down the dirt path that would take her away from the commune that had been her only home and into a future that would be far removed from the life her mother had lived.

****

Dani turned into her pillow and cried tears for the old pain she thought had healed. Cried tears as she replayed and evaluated all that had been said between her and Matt tonight. The decisions she made now would determine whether they would be walking different and separate paths tomorrow. Would determine whether she would walk the path her mother had chosen or whether she would demand the commitment of marriage from the man who loved her, from the man who enjoyed her body, her mind, her love.

She kept coming back to the words Matt had spoken: *You make me happy. I love you. You give my life meaning. I'm committed to you and to us—for eternity.*

Looking at those characteristics alone—passion, commitment, happiness, love, respect, a partnership— she had to admit they were the very things she wanted. He was offering her all of it. He just wasn't granting it the permanence that making it legal through marriage could bring. There would be no engagement, no wedding ceremony, no matching bands. No filling out his name in the Spouse line of sundry forms. And no soft, sweet-smelling, heart-capturing children, or grandchildren.

Not that she had been pining for kids. She hadn't given them a lot of thought before Matt came into her life. But the deeper in love she fell with him, the stronger the idea became, filling her mind with the heady thoughts of feeling his child growing under her heart, having it suckle from her breasts, sleep in her arms, holding its hand while it took its first steps, being a part of each miraculous phase of its life.

Would their very real, very strong love for each other be consuming enough to fill the space in her heart meant for a child? And if she were to become pregnant, would he leave her? Ask her to abort it?

She turned everything over to her dreams to ponder as sleep finally claimed her. When she awoke just before dawn, her first thought was of Matt. He had turned over in the night, faced away from her, and her body felt cold and alone without him against her. She wanted him. Not just sex. Him. Everything he was offering. Sometimes you couldn't have all the information you needed to make a sound decision. Sometimes the only option was to take a leap of faith. She hoped she was strong enough to make that spacious leap.

Dani curled herself around his backside, her arm around his waist. He sleepily turned toward her and opened his arms to her. She went into his warm comfort and held him close.

He made her heart beat and her breath flow. How could she give him up? She didn't know whether she could fully accept his conditions, but she knew one thing. She would stay with him, enjoy him, love him, even while knowing that when he went home to Dallas, it might be without her.

Never had she better understood her mother. Never had she been more afraid of the future that lay ahead of her.

Chapter Sixteen

Matt slumped heavily in the sumptuous overstuffed leather chair, propped his elbows on the desk cluttered with audit reports submitted an hour ago by his team, dropped his head heavily into his hands and uttered a heartfelt *fuck!*

Figures didn't lie, at least not those compiled by his people. They were well educated and well trained, all experts in their field. They didn't make mistakes. And dammit, figures didn't lie.

He stared at the two names emblazoned on the synopsis page, trying to will them away. The same two names that appeared prominently in the body of the paperwork before him. The same two names that were the sources of the money discrepancies amounting to losses in the hundreds of thousands. Two names. Elliott Gibson and Danielle Parker.

He felt as if he'd been kicked in the gut. The woman whose very essence satisfied him like no other, the one who fulfilled his every need, the woman he loved, the one he could not conceive of living without. Dani. His Dani. A thief.

Christ. He groaned. He'd rather rip out his heart than take the next step. Calling her and Karen into his office and accusing her would hurt her, hurt him, and destroy their relationship.

There had to be a mistake. The Dani he knew

wouldn't steal a paperclip, much less hundreds of thousands of dollars. But the so-called proof was there, in black and white. Fuck!

He picked up the phone.

****

Dani was in the basement up to her elbows in the archived records researching the names on Elliott's lists when Karen called, summoning her to Matt's office. Karen was already in Matt's office when Dani arrived.

Her lover sat behind his desk, his face a cold mask. Her mentor looked upset as she patted the arm of the chair next to her, where Dani's purse and coat sat.

The tension in the room set her stomach rolling. She didn't know what this was about, but she knew it wasn't good. She walked the few steps across the room and sat, trying to catch Matt's eye. But his gaze remained downward, on the report in front of him.

"Karen said you have something?"

For the first time since she'd entered the room, Matt looked up and caught her gaze. She saw pain in his eyes, anger in his stiff mouth. He picked up the report, opened it to a specific page, plunked it down in front of her on the desk, and went back to avoiding her gaze.

She leaned forward to skim the highlighted words, and her eyes snagged on two names. The words blurred. She blinked her eyes and looked closer, sure she wasn't seeing it correctly. But there it was, in black and white, the names of the suspected embezzlers. Elliott's and hers. Her stomach pitched, and she thought she was going to lose her lunch.

Her eyes darted from Matt's to Karen's. The look on their faces was tied to the contents of the report.

"I don't care what this report says," she said, "I didn't steal anything from this company."

"Dani," Karen said, "you should know Matt's team recovered an email from some of Elliott's deleted files where he confessed to embezzling money to pay you off. He said he knew it was wrong but you threatened to tell his wife about your affair if he didn't."

Dani shot up out of her chair. "That's not true. I never did that. Someone is setting me up." She looked at Matt. "Have you talked to Nathan? You know he threatened me, threatened to do whatever he could to make me lose everything."

"Elliott's email was on the thumb drive with his other deleted files well before then," Karen said.

Deleted files? There were deleted files? She looked at Matt. "Why didn't you tell me about the deleted files?" At his silence, her mind filled in the only possible answer—he didn't trust her.

"Until this matter is settled, you're on unpaid leave from the company." Karen spoke but Dani couldn't take her eyes from Matt's stone-cold face. "You won't be allowed back into the building unless you're cleared of all charges, so if you have any personal items at your desk you want or need, you should take them now."

"There's nothing here I want or need," Dani said, and Matt's eyes finally met hers.

Officer Brown entered Matt's office. Karen stood. "Officer, please escort Ms. Parker to her car."

Officer Brown looked at Dani, then at Matt, then back at Karen, his wide eyes showing his confusion by the request. Then he shook his head and held out his arm, his hand pointing toward the door. "Ms. Parker."

She took a last look at the man she loved. "You

know I didn't do this."

He said nothing. And the silence hollowed out her heart.

Feeling like hundred pound weights were attached to her, she turned and let Officer Brown lead her out the door, down the long hall to the elevator, and out the front door of the building where she'd worked for five years, of the company she'd given her time, energy, and sweat to.

It was over for her.

She would go to jail for something she didn't do.

She would lose the career and professional credibility she had worked so hard for.

She would lose the love and respect of the man she loved.

As Officer Brown walked her out of the building and to her car, she felt her soul drain out of her. By the time she pulled out of the parking lot, she was an empty hull.

Being accused looked bad, but hopefully a good lawyer could come up with a strong enough case to exonerate her. What turned her insides to dust was Matt. His reaction...or lack of one. He believed the report. He believed she was a liar and a thief...and, most likely, a murderer.

****

She couldn't go to her condo and sit alone with nothing but her thoughts for the rest of the day and long, lonely night. She headed for the drivethrough of the nearest golden arches and ordered a cola and a large order of fries—her go-to down-in-the-dumps junk food—and just drove around town.

Traffic started to pick up, and she realized she was

on the cusp of rush-hour, so she headed for home. Her home. Not his. His home had too many memories. Too many…ah, shit. She should have been at his house packing her clothes while he was at work instead of cramming her face with fries and driving aimlessly. Dammit. Too late now. Although he worked late every night, she didn't want to chance running into him if he decided to knock off early today to celebrate the conclusion of the investigation.

She climbed the stairs to her condo, her body heavy with angst and junk food. Matt was waiting at her door. Her heart tripped all over itself in her chest, but she ignored the draw of his body, his eyes, her mind focusing instead on unlocking the over-the-top security locks on her door and getting inside, away from him.

"Dani…" He reached out to her, and she jerked away.

"Don't touch me." One lock down, two to go.

"I know you didn't do it. I just don't know how to prove it yet."

"Lucky for me that's not your problem." One more lock, and she could barricade herself from him and release the death grip on her emotions. Hopefully her heart held out that long. It was pounding so hard she half expected it to punch through her chest.

"Let me come in. We'll put our heads together and come up with a plan."

"My lawyer has advised me not to discuss my case with anyone." That wasn't totally true. She didn't have a lawyer yet. But Laurel had advised not to discuss Elliott's murder case with anyone, so she felt safe saying the advice would be the same for the embezzlement case.

The lock refused to turn. She removed the key and tried again. And again. Still it wouldn't budge.

"Dammit," she mewed, yanking out the key and pounding the lock, as if that would help.

Matt took the keys from her hand, and she saw that she had been trying to put the key to his house into the lock. He saw it, too, and found the right one, inserted it smoothly into the lock. In his hands, the key and lock worked together as they were supposed to. Like she and Matt were supposed to.

He opened the door and handed her the keys, his fingers brushing her palm as he did. She slid his house key from her ring and handed it to him. He didn't take it, just shook his head, so she dropped it into his jacket pocket. Then she fisted her hand over the keys, letting the teeth bite in to her flesh to destroy the tingling his light touch had set off.

"If you wouldn't mind packing my clothes and bringing them to me. I'll need my suits for court." She went inside, turned off the alarm, and closed the door behind her, making sure to secure every lock on the door, locking him out of her house, out of her life.

****

Liz dropped by the next day. When Dani saw her friend, she practically jumped into her arms, so happy to see a friendly face.

"So, is it all over the company that Elliott and I embezzled money from the company?" she snarked as she handed Liz a goblet of wine and sat on the couch next to her.

"There are a few folks in building maintenance who haven't heard." Liz smiled, but like a snowball thrown on a hot skillet, it didn't hold for long. The tip of her nose reddened and her eyes blinked rapidly, trying to stop the tears. She yanked a tissue from the box sitting on the coffee table and dabbed at her eyes.

"Dammit, I swore I wouldn't cry. I'm just so pissed off. Those charges are asinine. No one who knows you believes you could do anything like this."

Matt believed it. And he knew her better than anyone. "I appreciate your support, but you might be better off distancing yourself from me. You don't want our friendship to give them a reason to suspect you were in on it with me."

"Someone set you up, and my money's on Nathan. He's such a snake."

Dani shivered. Just hearing his name made her want to vomit. "I thought so, too, but to be honest, I don't think he's smart enough to mastermind a phone call."

Liz made a face. "He walks around with a smug smile that makes me want to rip it off his face. But I know something about him that might make you feel better."

"Please!"

"Well, you know how I've been dating Jon, the new guy in legal? A couple of weekends ago, he booked us a suite at the casino. Nathan was there, throwing money around like he'd just won the lottery."

"The sleaze has money to burn and that makes me feel better how?"

"Let me finish. I know for a fact he had to sell his car a year and a half ago and was riding the bus to work. His paychecks were being garnished for not paying his student loans. Then a few months ago, the loans are paid off, he's sporting shiny white veneers, driving a new car, and gambling the big-stakes tables at the casino. My point is, where'd he get that infusion of cash?"

Dani felt a sparkle of hope dawn inside her, but she tapped it down, afraid to let it grow. "I know where you're going, but it's possible he got it from an inheritance or something."

"Or he could have helped Elliott embezzle it from the company. Or done it alone." Liz shifted toward Dani. "We should tell Matt about this."

Dani grabbed the wine bottle and refilled their glasses. "I'm not telling Matt anything. And neither are you."

"Why not?"

Her face heated from the hurt and anger that flared to life whenever she thought of what happened. The look on his face. His stone-cold silence. "He believed the report. He didn't stand up for me. He didn't say, 'There's been a mistake, and I'm not going to rest until I find out the truth.' He had security escort me from the building. No. I don't want him to know anything about my life."

"I know it hurt when he didn't discount the report in front of you and Karen, but look at it from his point of view."

"Are you kidding me?" Dani snapped.

"Just listen. He's the lead auditor investigating crimes against the company—his company—and his hotshot team reported their findings after a thorough review. He doesn't have the luxury of letting his personal feelings come into play, especially when his lover is the one accused. He has to go by the book, or it will do you more harm than good. It will make it look like he's trying to get you off. He doesn't want that. You don't want that. There can't be any question about your innocence at the end of this fiasco. I bet you anything he hasn't closed the book on this investigation or given the so-called evidence to the police to charge you. If I know him, he's continuing to dig, trying to find evidence to disprove it and get you off."

Liz's words sunk in, tamping the flames eating at her, putting her in a calmer frame of mind. "He *was* waiting at my door when I got home, wanting to help."

"I bet he even said he knew you were innocent."

Dani nodded. "He did."

She stood, grabbed her purse. "Okay then. Let's go tell him what I just told you. He'll know what to do to follow up. Get the cops to look into Nathan's bank accounts or something."

"I guess it couldn't hurt." Her heart lighter than it had been in days, she grabbed her purse, slipped into her shoes, and opened the door. Her heart sank at seeing Detective Anaya standing there, finger poised at the doorbell, two uniformed cops beside him. Had Matt called them after all?

"Danielle Parker. You're under arrest for the murder of Elliott Gibson."

****

Dani spent the night in an APD holding cell and the next morning was arraigned. The judge set bail, but it was an insanely high amount, so she didn't imagine she'd see home again for a while. She was surprised when, a few hours later, she was released on bond, and Matt was waiting there to take her home. Later, she'd thank Liz for calling him.

He pulled her into a hug. "Let's get you the fuck

out of here."

She signed for a large manila envelope that held the items she'd had in her purse and on her person when she arrived at APD, another that held her purse, then climbed into Matt's SUV.

He didn't take her to her condo but to his house. She didn't argue. She didn't have the spirit to fight anything at the moment.

****

While Dani showered, Matt dumped the contents of her envelope onto the table. His gaze took in the items that represented Dani's daily life—her phone, her wallet, a lipstick, a lip balm, lotion, hand sanitizer, mints, gum, a book of matches from their Vegas hotel room, a notebook, several pens, a hair clip, birth control pills, two condoms, three tampons, neatly folded receipts in a ziplock bag, another ziplock bag of almonds, a travel-sized pack of tissues, a half-eaten dark chocolate candy bar, and a thin, silver rectangular box. He opened the box.

A silver locket topped with a chunk of turquoise sat in the box. It didn't appear she had ever removed it, because the chain was still pinned in place. He removed the pins and lifted the necklace from its velvet bed. He tried opening the locket, curious about whose picture he'd see there, but it wouldn't open.

He pulled his knife from his pocket and used the tip of the blade to pry it open. It finally popped open, flinging what looked like a miniature memory card onto the table. Matt picked it up and examined it. Something about it was familiar.

He pulled out his phone, called his tech expert. "Hey, Dina. Remember those minicams you used on that job in San Fran a few months back?"

"The museum gig?"

"Yeah. The memory cards used…how do I play it if I don't have a reader?"

"Plug them into any phone, tablet, or laptop charger."

"Okay. Great."

"You bet. Call me if you can't figure it out."

"Will do. Thanks." Matt hung up and plugged it into his laptop.

Nathan Gerber's grinning face appeared on the screen. "What are you freaking out about today?" he said, clearly annoyed at whoever he was talking to on the other end of the camera.

"I've given it more thought," the man behind the spy cam said, "and I've decided I'm not breaking up with Dani."

The words ripped away Nathan's smirk, leaving behind a face that burned red with rage.

The voice continued. "The only reason I helped you embezzle money from the company was to pay off Candace so she'd give me a divorce and I could marry Dani. I love Dani and don't want to break up with her. I won't hurt her like that. I promise you, she's not a threat. She knows nothing about what we did, and I want to keep it that way."

"I know you," Nathan said, eyes narrowed as he shook his head in disgust. "Your guilt will chew on you and chew on you until one night, after sex, you'll break down and tell her what we did. The high and mighty Dani Parker will run straight to the cops, and you and I will be in jail before the day dawns."

"No. I'll keep our secret, because I want to keep

Dani. You think I want her knowing I'm the kind of scumbag who does what we did?"

"No," Nathan said, shaking his head. "It's too risky. Break it off."

"I won't do it!"

"Don't fuck with me, Elliott," Nathan yelled. The man looked like he was on the verge of coming unglued. "Break it off, or I'll implicate your bitch in our scheme." He blinked a few times, then stepped away from Elliott, a wicked grin lifting his mouth, as if the idea of implicating Dani made perfect sense. "Wouldn't that be fun, watching her twist on the hook for masterminding it all while you and I go scot free."

The spy device must have dropped because the picture dropped, showing a view of the sidewalk. Matt heard scuffling and then Elliott's voice again.

"If you so much as think about disrupting her life in any way, I'll go to the cops myself and tell them everything. I swear I will."

"Fine," Nathan said after a moment. "She's off limits. To both of us. Agreed?" At Elliott's silence, Nathan continued. "Look at this from another angle. Leaving her is for her benefit. If what you and I did is ever discovered, and the cops come looking for you, and she's with you, she'll be implicated regardless. Is that what you want for her? To go through the embarrassment of accusation, a trial, possible jail time when she's innocent?"

"No."

"Then do her a favor and break it off. The sooner the better."

"All right," Elliott spat out the word in anger as if it had a bitter taste.

"When?"

"At the builders conference in Santa Fe. End of next week."

"Make sure to fuck her a few times before you tell her. You certainly won't get a chance afterward."

"God, you're a sick bastard. How I got such a heartless dick for a brother, I'll never know."

"And how I got such a pussy for a brother, I'll never know."

Nathan must have handed Elliott his dropped device, probably a pen, because the picture zoomed upward and focused on Elliott's face. The man was a picture of grief, remorse, and anger. The signal went black after he took it and slipped it into his pocket.

Stunned, Matt sat in front of the laptop, staring at the blank, silent screen as relief flooded over him. She was free. Of both crimes. With this one selfless act, Elliott had saved her.

He heard a soft sound behind him and turned to see Dani leaning against the wall, a towel around her body, her wet hair loose around her shoulders, her hand over her mouth, tears streaming down her face. She'd seen the video, or at least heard it.

"It's the proof we needed," he said softly. "You're free."

She inhaled a shaky breath, released it as if she had been released from a heavy burden. "He loved me," she said. "Elliott loved me." She wiped her tears. "When he broke it off that night, I was devastated. All I could think about was what a fool I'd been. I ran away to Vegas feeling worthless, unlovable, and stupid."

Matt went to her and ran his hand up and down her back. More than anything he wanted to pull her to him, hold her, kiss her, but hearing how much she'd loved Gibson held him back.

Had it worked out, she never would have gone to Vegas and met him, and he'd still be living the life he'd found he could no longer stomach, the life of surface relationships that demanded nothing of him but a fat bank account and a talented cock. Of a life filled with work and more work to keep his mind off what he'd lost and what he really wanted.

Dani would probably be married by now, with a child on the way. With his criminal actions, Gibson hadn't just cheated the company, he had cheated Dani out of the life he promised her, the life she wanted...and deserved. Wasn't he doing the same by withholding marriage and motherhood from her?

"I'm sorry your plans didn't work out the way you wanted," he said.

Her eyes flew to his. "I hate what he did, and I'm sorry he died. But I'm not sorry he dumped me. If he hadn't, I never would have met you." Her hands went to his chest. "Because of you, I know what real love feels like. I love you, Matt. So much. And I'm so glad you're in my life. I'd choose you over Elliott, over anyone, every time."

Relief flooded him. Not just that the investigation was over and Dani was free. That she loved him. That they could move forward with their lives now. He wrapped his arms around her, held her tight, and she clutched the back of his shirt like she never wanted to let him go.

He breathed her in. "Baby, I love you, too."

****

They took the evidence to Detective Anaya, and an

APB was put out on Nathan Gerber, aka Nathaniel Gibson.

After the traumatic day, neither Matt nor Dani felt like cooking dinner, so he went for takeout. She was in her robe making a salad to go with whatever he brought home when the doorbell rang. Matt wouldn't ring the bell, and no one they knew would drop by this late without calling first.

She went to the door and peered out the peep hole. Seeing no one, she looked out the window and saw a brown delivery truck driving down the street. Thinking the driver might have left something on the doorstep, she opened the door.

Nathan filled the doorway, one arm above his head and leaning against the door frame, the other at his side with a gun in his hand, pointed in her direction. She tried to slam the door, but he blocked it and pushed it open. She stumbled back as he rushed in, slammed the door, and advanced on her, the gun pointed at the floor.

"Get out, now, or I'll call the cops," she said, her voice firmer than she'd imagined it would be when she was facing down a murderer.

"If I were you, Dani, I'd be nicer. I might find the need to use this gun."

Fear, disgust, and fury swirled like a tornado inside her. "What do you want?"

"What I've always wanted." He grabbed her, pulled her to him. "You."

His mouth tried to burn kisses across her neck and face. She struggled to get away, but he was strong. Stronger than he looked. She got off a lucky shot with her knee to his groin. He blocked the brunt of it, but it delivered enough pain to cause him to loosen his grip.

She ran for her phone and grabbed it, but he knocked it from her hands and it shattered on the floor.

Capturing her from behind, Nathan wrapped his arms around her, pinning her arms at her sides. He yanked at the belt to her robe. She felt cool air on her exposed skin, felt the ridge of his hard cock pressing against her ass.

It seemed like her struggles were only serving to excite him, so she stopped struggling and went completely limp, dropping to the floor between his arms. It caught him off guard and broke his hold. She quickly rolled away, jumped up, and ran to the door. He grabbed her by the hair and yanked back until she thought her neck would break. He took her down to hands and knees on the floor, roughly flipped her onto her back, and straddled her hips, his knees trapping her legs and her arms. Ripping open her robe, he leered at her naked body and leaned over to bite her breast.

She kicked her legs and bucked her body, all the while screaming for him to stop.

Headlights flashed across the window pane. Nathan, who was too occupied with trying to rape her, didn't see it.

Please be Matt. Please! Hope soared in her heart, knowing she was seconds from safety.

The door opened, and Matt came in, his shocked gaze finding her on the floor with Nathan straddling her. "Get your fucking hands off her," he bellowed, dropping the food and charging forward.

"Think before you take another step." Nathan jerked her upright and held her in front of his body, arm around her neck, the gun pointed at her head. "I've killed before." He stood, dragging her up with him.

"Think her life matters more to me than my own brother's? Turn around and get the fuck out of here. Dani and I have a lot to discuss. Don't we, bae." He licked her cheek, making her want to vomit.

Her eyes met Matt's. Pain crashed against pain, fear against fear, anger against anger.

The arm around her neck released as his hand slid down to grope her breast, just to antagonize Matt and show his power over her. Feeling the change in his weight against her, she thrust back against him, making him shuffle backward a bit. Matt took the opportunity to charge at him. Startled, Nathan reared back. A gunshot cracked the tense air, and Matt twisted and stumbled back against the wall.

"Matt!" she cried out and started to run to him, but Nathan grabbed her again.

Matt stared in surprise at the blood blossoming on his shirt at his shoulder. His eyes found hers.

For the longest seconds of her life, fear paralyzed her, squeezed her heart so viciously she thought she would pass out. She wanted to run to him, help him, be with him, die with him if it was to be.

"Fuck, Dani. This is the second lover of yours I've had to pop off," Nathan said with an evil grimace, his arm choking her so tight she was struggling to breathe. "I'm beginning to think you're something of a slut." He raised the gun and took aim at Matt. "Say goodbye to your lover."

She was going to lose the man she loved if she didn't do something and fast. Gathering the fear-induced energy and adrenalin pumping through her body, she blocked out everything but her self-defense instructor's voice running through the steps for disarming a gunman. Then she made her move.

Ignoring the pain of Nathan's arm across her neck, she twisted in his hold and positioned her body in line with Matt's, in front of Nathan's gun hand, right in the path of the bullet. Grabbing his wrist with her right hand and the barrel of the gun with her left hand, she pushed his hand toward his chest, rolling the gun against his thumb, the weakest part of the hand. His wrist twisted inward as she'd hoped, which brought the gun toward his chest and away from Matt. She continued rolling the handle of the gun against Nathan's thumb, and in the next moment, it was out of his hand and into hers.

Shocked to her toes that it had actually worked, she quickly stepped back and, holding the gun in both hands, pointed it at the widest part of Nathan's body. The seconds-long maneuver had required very little effort, but she was out of breath, her heart racing as she yelled at Nathan. "Get on the floor, face down, hands out."

He didn't move but stood stark still, staring at her, his mouth open in shock.

"Now, you son-of-a-bitch, before I pull the fucking trigger," she yelled.

Keeping his eyes on her every second, he did as she instructed.

She was afraid to let her gaze leave him, so she called out. "Matt. Are you still with me?"

"Baby, I'm starting to believe you didn't need my help in Vegas at all," came his rough, slightly shaky, but teasing reply.

"Well, I really need your help now. You need to call the cops before I accidently shoot Nathan in the head. The gun's getting pretty heavy."

Nathan dropped his forehead into the carpet as Matt made the call.

The scene was a buzz of activity minutes later, with the arrival of the cops, paramedics, and news media. The paramedics cleaned and bandaged Matt's flesh wound, which was painful but not serious, and the cops hauled Nathan to jail. Getting no other facts other than it was a break-in with a single shot fired, the media left to pursue grittier fodder.

The next day, Detective Anaya showed up on their doorstep with news that Nathan had confessed everything—embezzling funds with his brother, murdering Elliott with the gun he shot Matt with, hiring someone to kill Big W while he broke into Dani's condo. He'd been looking for the evidence Elliott said he left with someone. He'd planted false evidence to set Dani up to take the fall for embezzlement in order to get revenge on her for spurning his advances and instead choosing his brother. Elliott was motivated to help him because he needed to pay off his wife so she'd give him a divorce and he could marry Dani. It sickened her that she was the clench pin around which the wicked little plan revolved.

"Not that it matters now," the detective said to Matt, "but as Ms. Parker's legal counsel, you might like to see this." He handed him a folder.

Matt opened it, read the contents, smiled.

"What is it?" she asked.

He looked at her. "It's a final autopsy report that puts Elliott's time of death at between eleven o'clock Friday night to three o'clock Saturday morning."

When the implications hit her, she smiled. "That

means—"

"Even if we hadn't found Elliott's recording and Nathan hadn't confessed, you'd still be off the hook for the murder, because from ten p.m. and on that night…baby, you were with me."

She laughed, and he hugged her with his uninjured arm.

"What are the odds, Ms. Parker, that your Sin City fling would turn out to be your alibi?" Detective Anaya said, taking the file from Matt.

"Guess I got lucky," she said, still grinning.

He studied her face, then shook his head slowly. "No, Ms. Parker. I'd say your alibi was the lucky one."

As he ambled out the door, the meaning of his words sank into Dani's brain, and she chuckled, shaking her head at the only compliment the man had ever given her.

Matt drew her close. "He's right. I'm the lucky one."

"Because homicide detectives are never wrong," she said and laughed.

Chapter Seventeen

The party to celebrate the resolution of the embezzlement case, the impending sale of the company, and the upcoming Thanksgiving holiday was in full swing. Many of the celebrants were already toasted, but Dani sat with Liz and other co-workers on the large sofa, happily buzzed and reveling in gossip, laughter, and quality girlfriend time. But even friendship shifted to the back burner when Laura Williams, director of the IT department, exited the elevator and walked into the room with her husband, Phil, and their new baby boy, Carl.

Phil kissed his wife and son and made a beeline for the bar where several men crowded around the football game on the big-screen TV while Laura joined the women on the couch. She answered all the baby questions the group tossed at her. Dani laughed at the appropriate places, asked questions and listened to the answers, but in reality she was mesmerized by baby Carl, who was bundled in a candy red all-in-one and carried his little pink thumb in his constantly sucking bow mouth.

She could barely drag her gaze away from his pudgy face, his tiny hands, his dewy soft hair, or that sweet smell of angel's breath that still clung to him. Her hands itched to touch him and her arms ached to hold him.

"Dani, would you like to hold Carl?" Laura seemed to recognize the look of longing on Dani's face as she watched him kick and coo. A look that was quickly replaced by one of trepidation when the offer came.

"Oh, no, I couldn't. I don't think I know how." She laughed off her hesitation to inexperience, but what she really feared was that holding the little one in her arms would shatter the carefully erected but fragile wall barricading her longing for a child with Matt.

"I hate to beg, but I'd love to go to the bathroom by myself for a change." Laura laughed and stood to pass Carl to Dani.

The babe was warmer and heavier and softer than she had imagined. The solid weight in her arms felt right, and he fit perfectly, his little head resting at the crook of her arm, his little bottom cupped in her hand, the side of his body secure along her front.

When his blue eyes zeroed in on her dark ones, the joy that flooded her cells was like nothing she'd ever known. It was like the blood flowing in her veins had become filled with rainbows, causing a warm tingling sensation to radiate all along the pathways.

It was exactly as Matt had said. With their innocent eyes, they strip the veil from who you pretend to be and see you as you are, then demand your truths.

To minimize the emotions she was feeling, she turned to her friends. "One wail from him and you guys are taking over."

They all laughed, and with one backward glance and a smile, Laura strolled across the room and took the long way to the bathroom.

****

Matt heard the music blaring even before the

elevator arrived at the floor. He glanced at his watch, calculating that he was an hour and a half late. He'd hoped the festivities would be winding down by now so he could carry Dani off to their bed and make love with her for the rest of the night. Hell, he'd even take her on the conference room table if no one was there to watch. With his long hours at the office, it had been a couple of days for them, and he was as edgy as a caged tiger.

Since he and Dani had moved in together, he'd been perfectly content to rush home in the evenings after work to spend the time surrounded by her body and her love, but instead, he was, more often than not, stuck in damned meetings with lawyers, buyers, and the board.

The noise level of the celebration masked the sound of the door opening and Matt walking into the large conference room. He scoured the room for a glimpse of Dani. His eyes caught on Liz's wild blonde updo, and figuring she'd know where Dani was, he made his way over to her. A few steps closer and he spotted Dani, in her sexy, ruby-red dress, sitting on the couch, holding a blond cherub in her arms, a look of radiant bliss on her face.

His heart dove into his stomach and landed at the bottom with a sickening thud. She held the babe like she was born to it. Smiling down into the infant's face, babytalk noises slipping from her luscious lips, her eyes lighting up when the baby responded with a coo or a bubble or a crooked, toothless grin that one of the women looking on insisted was just him passing gas.

The baby seemed mesmerized by Dani's dark eyes, by her calm movements, her smell, her voice, her touch. He didn't blame the child. So was he.

When the babe reached out a hand for Dani's breast, Matt groaned inwardly as he watched the silk-covered nipple pucker into a shape that would perfectly fit the baby's mouth, as if it knew instinctively what was required of it. In a sudden stab of jealousy, he realized he wanted to be the only one to have her breast in his mouth.

As if sensing Matt's presence, Dani looked up and caught his gaze. She shot him a million-watt smile, her eyes shining with love.

Which of them—him or the child—had put that look on her face?

Turning her attention back to the babe in her arms, she leaned over and kissed its forehead, taking a moment to brush her nose against its downy head and inhale its baby smell before gently handing it to Liz, who waved her hands in a no-way sign. Another woman, Teri he thought, held out her arms and took the bundle. Dani said something to the women and extracted herself from their midst.

Matt couldn't keep his eyes off her as she strolled toward him, a warm, welcoming smile on her mouth. She was as stunning as usual, but something was different about her this night. The glow of holding a child in her arms?

"Glad you made it," she said. "I was about to send out a search party."

He nodded toward the door, and they stepped out of the room. As soon as the door closed, he hugged her to him, hard, drawing her warmth and love into his numb, tired body, running his hands along her back and down her ass, wanting, needing, to feel all of her. She wrapped her arms around him.

"Baby, you don't know how glad I am to see you," he whispered against her neck.

"Rough meeting?" Her fingers slid into his hair, caressing him.

"Yeah," he said.

She pulled back to look at him. "How about a drink? Some food?"

"All I want right now is you."

She put her hands on either side of his face and kissed his lips. "Are you all right?" she said, a tinge of worry coloring her tone.

He released a sigh. "Do you think anyone would notice that the boss arrived an hour and a half late to the party, stayed all of four minutes, then left without saying so much as a hello to anyone?"

"Who cares? I'll get my coat."

They pulled into the driveway twenty minutes later and walked to the house.

"It's good to have you home," she said. "I've missed you."

Matt stopped under the portico and pulled her into his arms. He kissed her hair, inhaling her exotic scent that never failed to send a thrill through him. A heavy, hungry need roared inside him suddenly. A need to take her, to make her his. Seeing her with that baby had flipped on some innate jealousy and need to prove she was his and only his. If it wasn't so fucking cold, he'd flip up that hot dress of hers and fuck her against the door just to prove it.

Christ. Jealous of a baby. It was irrational and crazy and an all-time low for him, but he couldn't help it. What made him so good in business was his ability to spot the enemy and disable its attempts to take what was his. Babies were his enemy now, because they could lure Dani away from him. They didn't discuss it, but he knew she wasn't fully on board with his no marriage and no babies conditions. She was trying because she loved him. Any time spent in the company of babies might have her rethinking things, might make her decide she couldn't live without children and a husband.

He kissed her, long and hard, as if he were grasping—for energy, for breath, for love, for whatever would allow him to keep her. His hand slipped inside her coat and found her breast, the same breast the baby had found so intriguing. Cupping it in his palm, his thumb brushed her nipple and received an immediate response.

"I need you, Dani. I need to feel you naked against me."

Smiling, she took the keys from his hand. Sliding the key into the lock, she opened the door, drew him inside, and shut the door. She pulled off her coat and hung it up in the hall closet, then reached out for his and hung it up while he shrugged out of his suit jacket. Then she took his hand. He thought she was leading him to their bedroom, but instead she pushed him up against the closed door. He dropped his suit jacket when she yanked his shirt out from his pants, grabbed the hem, and ripped it open so hard that buttons popped off like popcorn.

She shoved aside the material and ran her fingernails down his chest, making his nipples pucker. Her nails skated on down his stomach, making it clench when she traced the slim line of hair running into the waistband of his pants. His breathing hitched in his throat when her hands attacked his belt, unbuckling it. Then she undid his pants and yanked them down far enough to wrench his cock from his boxers.

His knees went weak when she dropped to her knees in front of him, her hands gripping his ass, and enveloped his cock in her sweet, red mouth. His hands moved to her head, his fingers tightening in her hair as he watched his swollen wet pole disappear into her mouth. She sucked him hard and deep, her tongue licking around and around his head and up and down his shaft, again and again, until he was gulping air into his lungs.

Low growls rumbled up from his chest and from between his slack mouth. Unable to stop himself, he pumped his hips against her giving mouth. He stopped himself just short of coming. He wanted to feel her pussy wrapped around his cock, squeezing it, coming on it as he shot into her.

He pulled out of her mouth and gripped her arms to quickly lift her to her feet. Smashing his body into hers, his cock against her pussy, he kissed her, his mouth sucking, his teeth nipping. His hand dove under her dress, urgent to plunge into the wetness he knew he'd find there. His dick grew harder and longer, and he groaned when he realized she wore no panties. He thrust two fingers inside her slick, tight channel, using his thumb to rub her clit into a tight peak of pleasure.

She thrust her hips against his hand, her mouth matching his hunger. "Fuck me," she groaned, then nipped at his mouth. "From the back."

He spun her around and made her face the door, him tight behind her. He stuffed his knee between her legs and spread them. Placing her hands on the door, she spread wide. He dropped to his knees to eat her pussy, to get her ready for him. She was already ready, wet and juicy and throbbing, but he sucked her, licked her, and tongued her deep.

"I need your hard cock, not your teasing tongue." Her breathless but demanding words were almost enough to make him come right then.

He stood and flipped her dress up around her back, revealing her tight round ass, tilted up and arching so that her pussy opened even more to him. Bending his knees, he rammed the head of his cock into her slick pussy and fucked her, hard, fast, her ass thrusting back against his balls to his rhythm.

The sounds of their slapping flesh, the feel of him so tight inside her heat, the scent of her, his grunts, her low moans were sending him there already. She hadn't come yet, but fuck, he couldn't hold on any longer. He gripped her hips with both hands, his fingers digging into her flesh, and pounded her pussy in a steady hard and fast rhythm that would save his life.

She cried out, and her pussy tightened around his cock, clenched him, and he let go, too, shooting his cum deep inside her in hot, thick jets. His orgasm went on and on, his vision and mind dark, until he, empty and exhausted, fell against her. She was gasping, too, her face plastered against the door. They both stayed put, trying to breathe and come down from the haze.

He stayed glued to her until his dick slid out of her pussy, then he unzipped her dress, letting it fall to the floor. He bent over and kissed and bit her ass cheeks, then slowly turned her to face him, her back against the door to hold her up.

She slid her hands down his arm to his cuff and

unbuttoned it, then the other one, and removed his shirt, letting it drop next to her dress. The whole time, her eyes were half open and shining, her wet full lips curved into a soft, satisfied smile, pleasure flushing her cheeks. That look told him how much she enjoyed him. He gave her pleasure, that much was clear, but was it enough to fill the place in her heart she'd saved for a baby? Was it enough to keep her with him for a lifetime?

He stepped out of his pants, boxers, and shoes, then picked her up, carried her into the bedroom, and laid her in bed. He lay beside her, his hand caressing her face. He loved this woman. The very sight of her, the smell of her, the feel of her soft skin sent a strong thrust of desire and possession plowing through him. He didn't want to let her go. Ever. He would show her so much love she'd never want to give him up, even to have a baby with another man.

"You're so beautiful you take my breath away," he whispered, his eyes never leaving hers. "I've never loved anyone the way I love you, Dani Parker. I need you in my life."

She closed her eyes and turned her head to kiss the palm caressing her cheek. "I'm here, Matt. I'm with you."

Yes. But how much? And for how long? "Move to Dallas with me." His heart ached at seeing the panic roaring through her. "It can't be a surprise that I'd ask you."

"No, it's not."

"What's stopping you from saying yes?"

"A move like that will change my entire life."

He cupped her cheek. "I can't stay here. My work,

my life is in Dallas."

"Mine's here."

"I don't want to lose you."

"I don't want to lose you, either."

"I leave just after the new year. I want you with me. If that's not what you want, you need to tell me. Soon."

"I need a little more time to decide."

She wanted to be with him, he knew it. He wasn't a praying man, but damned if he didn't pray everyday she would give him the yes he needed. But even at this moment, this tender, loving moment, something was stopping her from saying it. Even as she assured him she was considering the move, the voice inside his head was warning him to prepare for the possibility that when he left here, he'd be leaving alone. Did that stem from his own insecurity about relationships? From knowing his conditions about marriage and babies troubled her? Or something more?

****

Even though it was a Saturday and Matt had worn her out last night—he'd awakened her twice in the night to make love—Dani awoke just past dawn. Instead of trying to get back to sleep, she slipped out of bed, threw on some leggings and a T-shirt, grabbed her mat, and moved into the living room to do a long yoga practice. She was in the final moments of corpse pose when she opened her eyes to see Matt leaning against the wall, arms crossed, watching her.

She rose into a seated pose and held out her hand to him. He joined her on the floor and took her hands in his.

"Hey, Sleeping Beauty." She kissed him. "How

Sophia Ryan

long have you been up?"

"A few minutes."

She crawled onto his lap, facing him, laced her legs around his hips and her arms around his neck. She loved that they still smelled like sex, like each other. "Did you sleep well?"

He grinned. "Best in a long time thanks to you."

She chuckled. "Good."

The house phone rang, shattering the moment and bringing the outside world in on them. Neither moved to get it, both silently agreeing to let the machine answer it.

"Matthew, since you refuse to come home, I'm coming to you. My assistant is making the reservations as we speak. I arrive...well, I'll let that part be a surprise. See you soon, lover."

A stinging buzzing began in her stomach that spiked right through her heart, climbed, and stuck in her throat. The air between them pulsed with negative emotion. She stared past him, into thin air, fighting with her emotions. Was Arienne just being stubborn and possessive about letting him go, or did she have no idea they were over?

"She and I are over. For good." His voice was soft and sincere.

"Have you told her that?"

"Not in those exact words, but we broke up—"

"Maybe you should tell her," she said, her eyes finally meeting his. "Using those exact words." She rose from his lap.

"She knows," he insisted, reaching out for her hand.

"If she did, she wouldn't be coming to surprise

246

you." She pulled her hand away, turned, and headed to the bedroom.

She climbed into the shower and let the hot water sluice over her. As she washed, she questioned whether she had been fooling herself that their relationship had a chance. What she didn't know, couldn't feel, was whether love would be enough, for either one of them.

The curtain slid back, and Matt stepped in behind her. His large, strong hands roamed slowly on her, up and down her spine, across muscles, over pockets of collected anger. They slid around her waist, and his fingers brushed through the rivulets of water flowing over her breasts, stomach, and between her legs. His fingers teased her pussy, parting her wet lips and manipulating the swelling, pink flesh, her clit, and finally deep inside the slick canal. His other hand stroked and kneaded her breasts, teasing her nipples hard with his thumb.

She was still upset, and it was almost shameless how quickly and easily her body responded to his touch. Desire surged through her, the entire throng of nerve endings on high alert. She groaned her appreciation for the wild pleasure swirling at her center just as fireworks lit up behind her closed eyes and spread through her, dissolving all tension, all anger, all doubt for one perfect moment. She turned into his arms and clung to him, and he held her, stroking her skin, her hair.

"I've broken up with Arienne before, several times, but I always went back to her. When I broke up with her this last time, I told her I wasn't coming back. I changed my phone numbers and gave my family, my friends, and my close work associates orders not to give them to anyone, especially her. I did everything I could to remove her from my life. I can see why she might not believe me, but I told her."

"Yet she's coming here."

"No. She's not." He dipped his head to look her in the eyes. "I called her just now and told her not to."

Warmth filled her chest. "What did you tell her?"

"The truth. That I'm with you. That I love you. That you're the woman I want in my life forever."

"Did she believe you?" she asked.

"I hope so. But even if she doesn't, it doesn't matter. It doesn't change anything about what I want and how I feel about you."

She would have felt better had his response been more concrete, but he couldn't help it if Arienne was psycho. "Thank you, Matt. It means everything to me that you did that."

He kissed her, and she kissed him back. She felt his love in every brush of his lips, every touch of his tongue, every caress of his hand on her body.

Chapter Eighteen

"I'm telling you, it won't fit," Matt said. "It's way too big."

Snowflakes fell on his head and shoulders as he dragged the seven-foot piñon out of the back of the SUV and stood it upright in the two-inch snowfall accumulation in the driveway, dozens of luminarias on the path and house lighting their way to the portico.

Dani had a grin a mile wide on her face, and her eyes were lit up with the spirit of the season. "No, it's perfect. I know just where to put it. In front of the living room windows, so we can see it all lit up when we get home at night."

"If you think so. You're the Christmas expert in residence."

"Yes, I am. So you have to do as I say for a change." She skipped ahead of him and opened the gate wide.

He half-dragged, half-carried the tree through the gate. "For a change?" He grunted. "Hah! The change…would be…that I…get to be the boss…at all."

She laughed. "You get to be boss at work. I'm giving you a break at home. I'll get the door. Oh!"

He didn't heard another word. "Dani? The tree's getting heavy. Is the door open? Dani?"

"Nice tree, Matthew."

Recognizing the honeyed southern drawl, Matt

dropped the tree, and it took out a dozen luminarias in its fall.

Dani's full mouth was drawn into a tight line across her face, her body a wall of anger as she glared at his former lover, Arienne Dubois Cartwright. Dressed in furs and silks, with four matching pieces of expensive luggage artfully arranged around her, Arienne lifted one perfectly shaped brow at him, then stood, as still and cold as a finely chiseled marble statue.

He looked from woman to woman. A better example of fire and ice he had never seen. Neither looked happy, and both stared at him with a look that demanded he do something about it.

"Arienne?" The tree forgotten, he moved to stand by Dani's side and slid his arm around her waist, which didn't escape Arienne's slitted blue eyes. "What are you doing here?"

"Why else would I come here? To see you, of course." Her five-foot nine-inch, model-stature frame, taller because of the designer heels, sauntered over to him.

He felt the tension zipping through Dani's body. Knew she was a breath away from kicking Arienne's ass all the way to the airport and depositing her on a plane bound for hell.

"A few short months in this vulgar place, and you've completely lost your manners?" Arienne said, the tension in her voice saying how hard she was trying to control her anger. "Aren't you going to ask me in?"

****

Arienne's discarded fur draped across the back of the couch, her matching hat and leather gloves atop it, her tower of luggage by the door.

His former and present lovers sat at opposite ends of the couch, as different as night and day in coloring and character, but alike in spirit and temperament. Strong, feisty women who went after what they wanted. And what they both wanted—despite the polite smiles and low voices—was to strangle the other…and maybe him, too. Two sets of eyes—one fiery brown, one icy blue—pinned him when he joined them.

"Darlin', I'm famished. I'd adore a cognac and some caviar or something light to nibble on until dinner is served."

"Yes, Matt," Dani added. "Why don't you grab a couple of crackers for our guest to nibble on while she and I have a little chat."

Matt stood frozen on the rug, unsure what to do. On one hand, it wasn't safe to leave them alone. On the other, it wasn't safe for him to stay.

They continued to stare at him, and his body heated, sending sharp daggers into his balls. Feeling as welcome as a sixth toe on one foot, he shuffled into the kitchen to prepare snacks.

****

Dani wore the faded jeans and T-shirt she'd worn Christmas tree shopping, no makeup, and her hair in a ponytail. She felt like a common sunflower bloom next to the pampered hot-house orchid that was Arienne. The woman's blonde hair curled delicately around her bare shoulders, and her makeup expertly enhanced her crystal clear blue eyes and lush, pouty lips, hiding her remarkably few imperfections.

Dani thought about rushing into the bedroom to fix herself up but nixed it. She didn't want to leave the baracuda alone with Matt for a second, she didn't want to give Arienne the satisfaction of knowing she felt inadequate, and she had something important to say while Matt was still out of the room.

"Let's not insult each other by beating around the bush," Dani said. "The role you played in Matt's life is over. He's with me now. We're in love, and I'm moving to Dallas with him when his business here is finished."

Arienne laughed and leveled hate-filled eyes at Dani. "Let me explain to you about Matthew. He can have any woman he wants. They're all eager to tangle his sheets and slake his desires. He lets them." She shrugged. "He never stays with them, though. He returns to me. Always. I'm in his blood."

Though her heart was about to burst, Dani smiled at her nemesis. "You may have been in his blood, but I'm in his heart. He's in love with me. I'm in love with him. I'm the woman who can give him what he wants and needs, so the days of settling for an arrangement with a woman he doesn't love are over."

Arienne shook her head at Dani, as if she were the silliest little girl in the world. "Here's a little unsolicited advice. Have your little affair. Enjoy him. But know this. When it's over and he leaves, memories are all you'll have of him, because that's the only thing he can give to any woman."

Matt walked in, interrupting Dani's response. He set a tray carrying cheese, fruit, crackers, and two glasses of wine on the table. He handed one glass to Arienne, the other to Dani, and joined her on the couch opposite Arienne. He wrapped his arm around Dani, and she tucked against his side.

"When I heard your news, Matthew, I couldn't stay away," Arienne said.

"My news?" He took Dani's wine glass from her hand and sipped from it.

"Yes. I had to be the first to congratulate you. So, tell me, Danielle, when's the happy day?"

"The happy day?"

"Well, the wedding, of course, silly."

Dani immediately saw through the fake delight Arienne sent her way straight to the deviousness motivating the comment. It was clear that Arienne, who knew of Matt's aversion to marriage, brought up the topic to remind her of the impermanence of the relationship.

Dani took the glass from Matt and drank deeply.

"Arienne." Matt warned, obviously also seeing through his former lover's scheme.

"Don't Arienne me, Matthew. You and your lover both told me you're desperately in love, so naturally, I assumed a wedding is imminent."

Dani lifted her chin an inch, held her head high, even managed a small smile. "When we're ready to share that information, you'll be the first one we tell."

"Well, don't I feel special," she said, her teeth gritting behind her smile. "What precious babies you two will make," she gushed with faux glee. "Your lovely dark hair and Matthew's amazing green eyes." She rolled her eyes heavenward for emphasis.

At the silence in the room, Arienne spoke again. "Oh, my. If I've said anything inappropriate, I sincerely apologize." She opened her baby blues wide and placed her hand on her heart to bolster her words.

Matt squeezed Dani's shoulder. "That's enough,

Arienne."

Arienne smiled, as if she were enjoying being the cause of the discomfort pulsing in the room. "If that's your oh-so-diplomatic way of asking me to change the subject…heard and understood." She released a chuckle, then patted her hair in place as if worried the chuckle had messed it. "Very well. What are we doing tomorrow, Matthew? I'm sure there's at least one interesting thing to see in this town."

Matt cleared his throat and leaned forward, toward Arienne. "About that… You're welcome to stay the night, but thereafter, I'd prefer you stay in a hotel. Dani and I are in a committed relationship, and it's uncomfortable, for both of us, to have you here, considering…"

"Considering you and I are long-time lovers."

"Were," Matt said firmly.

Arienne looked as though she were chewing on glass, but her voice was cotton-candy sweet. "When Natalia invited me to stay here in *her* home while I'm in town to visit you, my dear friend, I had no idea it would put such a burden on y'all." She dropped her gaze to her lap and gave a little chuckle. "I'm so embarrassed." Her face even blushed demurely on cue. "I'll leave in the morning."

Dani drained her glass. She wanted Arienne gone now, but she'd let it go because Matt had sent Arienne packing without her having to deploy the "she goes or I go" threat. That he chose her and their relationship comforted her, made her feel loved, like he'd be on her side no matter what.

"Thanks for understanding," Matt said and stood. "Well, it's late, and Dani and I have work tomorrow."

He took Dani's hand and helped her to her feet, then curled his arm around her shoulders.

"Help yourself to whatever's in the kitchen," he said to Arienne. "Watch TV. Read. Whatever. Goodnight."

"I hate to impose further," Arienne said before they could turn, "but would you mind writing out a list of decent hotels and limo services for me?" The woman had perfected the pout and the sad eyes. "This being my first time here, I have no way of knowing who is reputable and who isn't. Heaven forbid I find myself in gang territory."

"I'll leave some numbers for you before I leave in the morning."

"Would you mind doing it now? I might have other questions. Like your cell number in case I get lost. And if you could show me where things are in the kitchen in case I need to get up in the middle of the night. I wouldn't want to take a wrong turn and accidentally wander into your bedroom."

His mouth tightened into an annoyed line before he released a low sigh that said he was as wise to her game as Dani was. "Sure," he said, then looked at Dani in time to see her roll her eyes. "I'll write out the list, then lock up."

Arienne's smug smile made Dani's blood boil. But for her to protest now, insisting that she would assist Arienne while Matt locked up, would be to admit that she was worried that Arienne meant something to him.

"I'll be right in." He leaned in and kissed her, and she pulled him closer and pressed a branding kiss on his lips.

"Make it quick," she whispered when they broke

for air. "Goodnight, Arienne," she added, then turned and walked to the bedroom, forcing herself not to glance back at the two of them.

In the bedroom, she undressed and pulled on a robe, brushed her teeth, washed her face, and paced the floor, on pins and needles waiting to hear Matt's footsteps in the hall outside their room. Two minutes passed. Five. Then ten.

Arienne's words rang shrill in her ears, *I'm in his blood, he always returns to me.* Dani left the room.

The house was dark, except for a faint light coming from the opposite side of the house. From the other bedroom. She padded through the living room, the dining room, and around the corner to the guest bedroom. Her soul drained from her, and cold washed over her. Matt stood at the doorway to the bedroom. Arienne's arms slid around his waist, and she kissed him.

Chapter Nineteen

Dani's heart froze, and she felt as if the wind had been knocked out of her. Matt must have heard her because he pushed away from Arienne and stepped back.

Finally finding her voice, she spoke, her words calmer than she imagined they would be considering the anger that pulsed through her veins. "Looks like she found where everything is."

Matt spun around, a *caught* look on his face. That, and Arienne's smile, told her she had interrupted more than him helping Arienne settle in.

"Dani—"

She stormed back to the bedroom, slamming the door so loud the neighbors probably heard it.

He pushed the door open seconds after she'd yanked off her robe.

"I know what it looked like but—"

"It looked like you were kissing your lover." She pulled her jeans and T-shirt back on. "How close am I?" As she spat out each word, her voice grew louder. She grabbed clothes and toiletries and threw them into an overnight bag.

He grabbed her arm. "Would you be still for one second and let me explain."

"I don't need any explanations about why you were kissing her." She struggled against his grip, but he was too strong. "It was clear. You're not finished with her."

"You're going to hear me out. I won't let you give in to your fears and give up on us."

She threw herself at him, pounding his chest with balled fists. "There is no us, you son of a bitch. Not after seeing you making out with that fucking woman right under my nose."

He took the first few hits, then grabbed her arms and yanked her to him, trapping them against his chest. "I was answering her question about one of the hotels I recommended when she lunged at me and kissed me. She kissed me. Not the other way around."

"This is why we can't be together. You're just like…" Shit. She couldn't believe she'd almost blurted out *You're just like my father*. She pushed away from him, grabbed her bag, and headed for the door.

He blocked her way. "Like who? I'm just like who? Elliott?"

She couldn't answer. Better to let him think *Elliott* than to have *that* conversation. Not now.

"I'm not him, baby. I love you. I'm committed to you. Only you."

She pushed past him and headed for the door.

"Where are you going?" He stopped her again.

"I can't stay here, Matt. The whole thing makes me sick to my stomach." She tried to go around him, but he blocked her at every turn.

"I'm not letting you walk out on us. Every time you don't want to talk about something, you shut down or storm off. This time we're going to stay and talk it out, yell it out if we must, until it's solved. I don't fucking care who's here to hear it. We're worth fighting for, and I won't let you take the best part of my life from me."

She threw her bag down. "The only problem we have at the moment is Arienne and you."

He gripped her shoulders. "Baby. There *is* no Arienne and me. There's only you and me."

He looked and sounded so sincere. She was tempted to believe him. She saw how Arienne was with him. She wanted him. It made sense that she'd make a pass at him. Thinking back to the image of that kiss, she realized that his hands hadn't been on her, that he'd stepped back from Arienne when she kissed him and before Dani announced herself. Maybe he was telling the truth. She could give him the benefit of the doubt. She owed him that. But she didn't have it in her right now to do it gracefully.

"I can't talk about this anymore tonight." She left his arms and undressed, and for the first time since they'd been together, she slipped a gown on before climbing into bed.

He pulled his clothes off and joined her. He reached out and slid his arm around her waist.

She rolled away from him. "Don't touch me. Not while you have her smell, her fingerprints, and her spit on your body."

He let go and sat up. "Fine. I'll go take a shower."

"Fine, but I'm not having sex with you while she's in this house." She kept her back to him.

"Maybe I should sleep on the fucking couch tonight?" His voice was rough and tight, like he was chewing on his tongue to keep from taking his anger and frustration out on her.

"Sleep wherever the fuck you want."

With a curse, he got out of bed, making her heart

lurch, making her head turn toward him. Instead of storming out the door like she thought he'd do, he headed to the bathroom. She lay in bed, listening to the shower and picturing him in there, naked, washing Arienne off his body. For her. Minutes later, he came out and lay in bed next to her but not touching.

"I love you, Dani. Only you," he whispered in the dark. "Have some faith in me. I think I've earned it."

Everything inside her told her to turn to him, respond to him, love him, but she let her anger and suspicion and jealousy and insecurity win. When she finally fell asleep, it was with her back to him. And he didn't touch her all night.

****

Dani rose early the next morning after an unsatisfying night of sleep. She showered and dressed and was out the door for work before Matt finished his shower. At this point, she didn't give much of a thought to leaving the two of them together alone in the house. They would do what they wanted to do whether she was there or not.

"You agreed to the bamboo flooring precisely because of its green benefits," she said to Clint Masters from Saguaro Spas, Meganlin's wealthiest client out of Phoenix. She had handled the account before she was promoted to assistant director, and he'd threatened to take his business elsewhere if she handed him over to someone else, so this was the only case she had kept. She hadn't been in the office an hour before Clint called. "The quoted cost is for bamboo. If you now want teak, that's going to increase the cost and strip you of the green incentive."

She paced while listening to Clint's response.

"What can I say?" he said. "Estevan has concerns about the durability of bamboo when he saw how easily the sample scratched."

"I mentioned early on that bamboo might not stand up in high-traffic areas."

"Yes, well, he wants you here tomorrow morning to discuss different options and costs."

Frustrated by this latest change amidst at least two dozen others since they'd signed off on the estimates and materials, she pressed the phone to her chest and grumbled a curse under her breath, counting to ten but giving up before she'd reached five. "You know the benefits and costs of the various options as well as I do from the last presentation I made. Why can't you explain—"

"You're the only one who can explain to his satisfaction," Clint said as a quick rap sounded on her door and Matt walked in. She looked up in recognition of him, but then couldn't pry her gaze from him. They'd made love every night since they'd gotten together. Even one night apart, like last night, made her feel empty, deprived, anxious, and out of balance, and had put her in an all-around shitty mood.

"Hellooo? Are you still there?" Clint said, reminding her that she'd stared at Matt longer than she thought.

"I'll consult with my experts and call you in an hour with the plan." She hung up. "Shit," she mumbled.

"Everything okay?" Matt said.

"Estevan Saguaro changed his mind about the materials. Again. He said he doesn't care about the additional cost."

"He wants what he wants." Matt said.

"Yeah, and what he wants is me in Phoenix tomorrow morning to discuss the pros and cons of the materials he's interested in."

"Clint's his assistant. Let him handle that."

"He wants to hear it from me, or at least that's what Clint says. My guess is that Clint is tired of dealing with his boss' wishy-washy decision making. I need to consult with my materials guy and book a flight to Phoenix."

He walked to her desk and picked up her desk phone and began punching numbers.

"What are you doing?"

"Calling Saguaro to get this bullshit straightened out. There's no need for you to fly all the way there to discuss options you've already discussed numerous times. It's not a good use of your time. You're an assistant director. Send a customer rep."

She took the phone from him and hung up. "This is still my account, and I'll deal with it. I'll be back tomorrow afternoon in time for the board meeting."

He cupped his hand at her neck. "I don't think I can go another night without making love to you." He was about to pull her into his arms when a knock sounded at her door.

Karen walked in, eyes going from Dani to Matt. "Excuse the interruption. Dani, I need to go over some points with you about your meeting with Estevan Saguaro."

Just like Clint to do the run-around and go right to Karen. Bastard. "I'll be right there."

Karen gave them both another quick look and left, leaving the door open.

"Call me tonight when you get settled in." This

time he did pull her into his chest. And she let him.

She hadn't felt his arms around her, his body inside hers, last night. Feeling him against her now reminded her how much she had missed him, but her heart and ego were still sore and bruised from the Arienne drama, and she wasn't feeling particularly forgiving. "I will."

He moved to kiss her lips, and she accepted it but quickly eased out of his arms, grabbed the necessary file, and headed for the door.

"Dani?"

She stopped and turned toward him.

"I love you."

"I know." Fighting the annoying urge to cry, she hurried to Karen' office, the feeling of resounding despair sitting heavy in her chest. Now was so not the best time to go away. All she wanted to do was go home, wrap herself around Matt, let his warmth and love ease her fears.

****

Matt shifted in his chair again. In anxiety, in anticipation, in annoyance, in frustration. The board members had arrived early for the meeting, and only slightly more than half of them had bothered to show up, but at least they had a quorum. The projector unit in the large conference room wasn't working, forcing them to meet in this small conference room near his office, the one with the hard-ass chairs.

And he was crawling-out-of-his-skin eager to see Dani. She was expected any time now, and he couldn't wait. As soon as the meeting ended, he would kick the board out and spread Dani out on this table, bury his face in her pussy and eat her until she came in his mouth, then fuck her with his two-day hard-on until she screamed the roof down. He heard his name. But it wasn't Dani's voice.

Pulling himself out of his vision, he focused on the board. The chairman apparently had asked him a question, which he couldn't answer because he hadn't heard it. He opened his mouth to ask him to repeat it when the door opened and Arienne strolled in.

"Forgive the interruption, gentlemen, but I have important business with Mr. Collins that can't wait."

Matt stood, jaw working to hold back his anger. "Excuse me," he said to the group and joined her, firmly taking her arm at the elbow and leading her out of the room.

"You simply must hire new staff, Matthew. They're all idiots," she babbled as he marched her to the empty larger conference room down the hall.

He closed the door behind them. "What the hell are you doing here?"

She smoothed her hands up his lapels, then slid them over his shoulders. "I had to see you before I left. I only came here for you, and we haven't had a moment alone."

He grabbed her wrists and pulled them away from him. "Goddammit, Arienne! I've tried to be nice about this, but nothing's getting through to you. Listen to me this time. I love Dani. I'm with Dani. Only Dani. You and I are through. For good." He spoke right into her face to make sure she heard him. "I never want to see you again." He said the biting words slowly and sharply, keeping his eyes tight on hers to make sure they hit their mark, then released her wrists with more force than he'd intended. "You got that?"

She leaned in and smashed her mouth against his,

one hand looping around his neck, the other gripping his cock through his pants.

****

Dani had the taxi drop her off at the office instead of taking time to go home first. She'd be a few minutes late to the board meeting, but fortunately, she'd been able to complete her progress report on the flight home and could present it whenever called on.

She headed directly to the boardroom so she wouldn't miss any more of the meeting than she already had. Her heart did a cartwheel in her chest at the thought of seeing Matt. Even a night away from him was too long.

A smile lit her face when she remembered him telling her last night on the phone he'd dropped Arienne at a hotel before work that morning and that she planned to fly back to Dallas today. It had started to extinguish the sliver of jealousy and mistrust living in the dark corner of her heart that questioned the permanence of their relationship.

Leaving her luggage in the small office off the boardroom, she made a final check of her hair and makeup in the decorative mirror on the wall, grabbed her briefcase, then quietly opened the boardroom door so as not to disturb the meeting in progress.

The open door admitted a swath of light into the dark room, spotlighting the tall blonde standing with Matt, mere inches separating them. They weren't touching, weren't kissing, but they had the look of it, like they had just done it or were about to, and there was enough heat between them to rival the sun.

She stared at her lover and his lover and felt something break inside her, leaving her insides mangled and her outside numb from the pain of betrayal. Her briefcase dropped from her hand to the carpet along with her dead heart, leaving her feeling like a dry, empty gourd.

Matt spun toward the light, his face a mask of surprise and dread.

"Christ! Dani?"

He reached out his hand to her as he said her name, but she slammed the door before he could touch her. Head on fire with pain, eyes burning, she ran toward the stairs, not wanting to waste time grabbing her luggage or waiting for an elevator. She heard him calling her name, but she didn't slow her retreat.

He caught up with her one floor down but had to grab her arm and step in front of her to get her to stop.

She jerked away from him, and the slap of her hand on his face echoed in the stairwell, stunning them both into stillness. Seeing the crimson patch blooming on his cheek in the shape of her hand made her stomach roll. Never in her life had she struck anyone so violently. It shocked the blind rage from her, and she turned her face away, palms flat on the cold roughness of the wall, her throbbing head pressed into the backs of her hands.

"Dani, she showed up uninvited. I took her into the board room to ream her out about it, and was about to escort her off the premises."

Bile rose in her throat at the sound of him again explaining his indiscretions with that woman. At the smell of his lover on his clothes. Her mind tried to sift through his words to find truth in them, but it was too filled with pain to see it.

"Wipe the lipstick from your mouth before you go back into your meeting," she said, her voice low and rough.

"Fuck." He swiped his hand over his mouth, wiping at something that wasn't there, telling her all she needed to know. She shook her head and closed her eyes.

"You have to believe me. Baby, I don't want Arienne. I want you. Only you."

Only you.

Her father had said the same thing to her mother, all the time. *You're the only one I love, dulce. Those other women don't mean anything to me. You're the one I always come home to.*

Dani's legs suddenly felt boneless, her body devoid of energy. She didn't want to fight. She didn't want to think. She didn't want to talk.

"Say something. Please," he said.

She opened her eyes and found his. Anguish sparked in their green depths. Worry stiffened his mouth.

Swallowing against the bitter taste of betrayal in her throat, she stiffened her spine. "I can't do this now."

"I'll take you home."

She held out a hand. "No."

He grabbed it. "Dani—"

She jerked it back. "Dammit, Matt, just go back to your…meeting!" Hearing her voice crackling with pain and fury, she reined it in and cushioned the statement that followed. "We'll talk later. But not now, when I'd rather hurt you than listen to you."

The courage it took to move one foot in front of the other down the stairs, away from him, while holding in her tears, depleted the minute she left the building. Running on pure pain, she stumbled down the sidewalk, unsure where she was headed. The first drops of rain on her head didn't register, but when the downpour hit, she ducked into the first building she came to.

Via the glow of neon beer signs, Dani found her way to a small corner booth in the back of the bar. She removed her cross-body purse and tossed it onto the seat beside her. Her phone rang. It was Matt. She rejected it. Too many bees buzzing in her head to speak sensibly to him. To anyone but the bartender to order a flight of tequila. To anyone but Liz to ask for help.

Dani was on the second shot when Liz rushed into the bar, rain dripping from her hair and sloshing in her new designer shoes, Dani's suitcase and briefcase in her hands. A better friend there never was.

"Of all the bars you could have stumbled into, it had to be this one?" Liz's eyes darted around the cave-like biker bar dive as she carefully slid into the booth, trying not to touch anything.

Dani's weak chuckle broke to pieces as the tears fell from her eyes.

"Oh, honey." Liz jumped up from her seat and slid in next to her, pulling her into her embrace. Dani dropped her head on her shoulder and allowed herself a moment to cry and feel sorry for herself. Then she shifted back, wiped away her tears, and downed the throat-burning drink.

Liz grabbed one of the shots and smelled it. "Tossing back the rough stuff, huh?"

Dani nodded as Liz held her nose and downed the liquid fire. She pounded the table as it went down. "Whoa! This stuff'll numb every nerve in your body."

"I'm counting on it." Dani grabbed the last shot and held it aloft to her friend. "Here's to the best friend

I've ever had, who comes to my rescue even in the middle of a downpour, risking the ruin of her new shoes."

"You owe me." Liz clinked her empty glass to hers and watched her down the shot in one gulp. Even through glassy wet eyes, Dani recognized the concern on her friend's face.

"What happened?" Liz asked.

Dani drew a shaky breath and released it slowly. "I caught Matt and Arienne kissing in the boardroom."

"What? Are you sure?"

"I didn't actually see them kissing, but I know they did."

"What did he say?"

"The same tired story I heard the last time I found them making out. It was her, not me."

"I totally believe him."

"Whose side are you on?"

"Yours, of course. I'm just saying you know what a trouble-making bitch she is and how much Matt loves you."

"I know what I saw."

"What are you going to do?"

"I swore I'd never be with a man who won't commit, who won't be faithful, and I've already given him one chance too many."

"So, you're leaving him?"

"What else can I do?"

"Nothing. Dump the bastard."

Dump him? Dani's insides clenched at the idea that seemed ridiculous and impossible now that she'd heard it said out loud. Yet, what other choice did she have? Live with a man who wouldn't commit to her? Suffer the pain of his betrayal again and again, for the rest of her life until she died of heartache when she couldn't take it anymore? Like her mom.

She nodded.

Liz squeezed her hand.

"I need a minute to freshen up. But then would you take me home?"

"I'll call Karen and let her know we'll be out for the rest of the day." Liz got up to allow Dani to slide out of the booth. When she left the table and headed to the bathroom to freshen up, Liz was making the call.

She stared at her reflection in the dirty mirror, looking for answers. What she saw was a woman whose heart was in pieces in her chest because she had to throw away the love of her life because *she* wasn't the love of *his*.

"Oh, Matt. How could you do this? I believed you when you said I was all you wanted," she whispered as the image of his face appeared in the mirror. Images of them laughing, loving, living a life together. Then the image of him kissing Arienne appeared, erasing the pretty pictures.

Her decision was obvious.

She grabbed a wad of rough toilet paper and wiped the tear-smeared makeup from her red eyes. She applied lip balm. A squirt of mouth spray cut some of the bitterness of the tequila. A dollop of hand sanitizer vanished some of the sludge clinging to her. As she headed toward the door on shaky legs, she felt as drained as the shot glasses she'd flipped upside down on the table.

Back at the table, she grabbed her purse and slipped it over her shoulder, ready to go, but the bartender set a martini down in front of Liz.

"Let me finish this, and we'll head out." She brought the glass to her lips for a sip, then glanced toward the door when it opened to admit a fury of rain...and Matt.

Dani's eyes met his, and the air inside the tiny bar crackled with heat and electricity she felt to her core, like he was the center of the storm. He moved toward her, water dripping from his hair, his face, his clothes onto the scuffed wood floor. He exchanged a look and a nod with Liz before again focusing his gaze solely on her. In a heartbeat he stood before her.

"Come home with me, baby. Give me a chance to explain." There was a pleading tone to his low voice she'd never heard before. The tone of a man who was about to lose something he desperately wanted to hold on to? His face carried the same emotion, dark brows knitted in pain over liquid eyes, rain-wet mouth tense.

At her silence, he tacked on, "If you're not satisfied with my explanation, I'll...I'll do whatever you want." His voice caught, as if he couldn't bear the thought of what she might do. He glanced away for a second, his jaw tensing, as if he were grinding his teeth, trying to rein in emotions stirring too close to the surface.

Dani fought with her own set of emotions. Was what she'd seen a simple misunderstanding? Or was Matt just like her father, able to love many women without feeling any remorse for the pain his actions brought to them, able to sweet talk his way back into their hearts? Her mother's sad face floated before her.

I understood now, Momma, why you didn't leave daddy. He had your heart, and you couldn't live without it...or without him.

"Okay," she whispered, the word so quiet he didn't immediately react.

"Okay?" he repeated, just to be sure.

She nodded.

He exhaled, as if he had been holding his breath on her response. He hugged her rigid body to his. She looked over his shoulder at Liz, who nodded as if telling her she'd made the right choice. Dani didn't know whether to thank her or tell her off for calling him. She did neither, just watched her best friend hand her luggage to Matt before going to pay the bar tab.

On the way home, the SUV's heater on high, Matt explained to a shivering and soaked Dani how Arienne had showed up unwelcome and unannounced to the board meeting. How he'd pulled her into the boardroom so no one could hear him ream her out about persisting with her attempts to get back with him, despite his repeatedly telling her it wasn't going to happen. How she had thrown herself at him and he had pushed her back right before Dani had opened the door. How sorry he was he'd hurt her. How something like this would never happen again because he would never see Arienne again and she would never be welcome in their home. How he loved her and would do anything to regain her trust.

Through it all, Dani was silent. She wanted to believe him. With all her heart and soul she wanted to. But she wasn't sure she did. He loved her. She was sure of that. What she wasn't sure of was his ability to be faithful. Would there always be women coming out of his past, coming on to him, catching him unaware and planting a kiss on his mouth, finding a way into his arms, into his bed?

Most men, when they found "the one," wanted to put a ring on her finger, marry her, fill her stomach with babies to show she was his and off the market. But not Matt. He didn't seem to want any outward appearances of commitment. Maybe it was because, deep down, he didn't really want to settle down with just one woman. He was used to the life of a bachelor, where he could enjoy as many women as he wanted, whenever he wanted. Maybe she was expecting too much from him. Maybe they just weren't right for each other. Maybe.

So what was she to do? Be with him until he broke up with her and broke her heart? Or be with him, enjoy him, now, while he was here, knowing that when he left he'd go alone? Or leave him before she got hurt even worse?

When they got home, he carried her to their bedroom and peeled the sodden clothes from her body before shedding his own. He started the shower and pulled her in with him, briskly rubbing his hands up and down her chilled flesh. Instead of warming her, the hot water released a new wave of shivers. Pulling her close, his heat wrapped around her front, her back to the spray, he enveloped her in heat.

There was nothing sexual in his touch, in his movements, in his intentions, but hunger ignited inside Dani all the same, in an explosion of consuming need and hurt. She pressed him up against the back wall of the shower and pulled his face to hers, capturing his mouth with a fierceness meant to destroy all trace of Arienne. Her teeth ground against his mouth. She bit his lips and sucked the bruised flesh into her mouth. Her tongue plunged his mouth, fought with his tongue. She stole the breath from his lungs and pulled it into her own. She was rough, punishing, driven to scour the essence of Arienne from his cells, from his memory, from between them.

He absorbed her assaults and gave back gently. She didn't want gentle. She wanted rough. She wanted it now. She pressed in, scraping her mouth over his, harder, deeper, demanding more. When they gasped for air, she swallowed his breath and gave it back so they could keep going, keep this passion burning.

Finally, he gripped her hard, yanked her even closer, and returned her kisses, her touches, greedily, eagerly, fanning the flames, taking both of them over. His tongue thrust into her mouth like she wanted his cock to in her pussy, and she couldn't wait anymore.

"Get on the floor," she said, her voice harsh and quick. "On your ass."

He seemed confused about what she wanted, but he did as she asked, sitting with his back against the wall, his hard cock sticking straight up from between his legs, ready for her. She straddled him and, gripping his shoulders, impaled herself on the long, thick rod. He gave it all to her, touching the very top of her.

As his hands gripped her ass, she rocked and rolled and bounced on him, scratching for her release, wanting to feel his hot cum shooting into her as he growled. She wanted to see the fucking hot look that took his face when he came inside her, like he was seeing the face of God.

Stars burst inside her and her orgasm rumbled hard through her, on and on, until she was shattering into a million pieces. She heard him cry out with a gasping shout and knew he was in pieces on the floor of the wet shower with her.

Too wrung out and breathless to kiss him, she tucked her head against his forehead, and they breathed each other. She felt his hand gently at her face, and she looked at him. Love for him burst open inside her, showing her the truth. She loved him, but now she knew. This mind-blowing, soul-sharing sex was the ceiling for them. It was all they could have. She would leave him before he destroyed her completely.

She cried, soft tears at first, then great, wracking sobs that shook her body. Through it all, he held her, loved her, whispered sweet sounds of love into her ear.

Later, when her well of tears had dried up, he dried them off and led her to their bed, where their bodies clung around each other like peel around fruit.

Trailing his hand up and down her arm, he kissed her head. "Forgive me, Dani."

They hadn't spoken since the shower, and that had been at least fifteen minutes ago, so his voice breaking the silence jolted her.

"For what?"

"For allowing someone to come between us, for hurting you by not handling the problem better. I won't make that mistake again. Ever. You have my word on it."

Cuddling deeper into his arms, she kissed him. "I forgive you."

She did forgive him. But forgiveness wouldn't change the fact that she was leaving him.

****

"Have you told him you're not moving?" Liz's breathing was stretched due to the seven-minute-mile pace they were keeping, but she and Dani both were able to carry on a halted conversation and keep to their pace.

"Not yet."

"Why not?"

"I'm waiting for the right time."

"No, you're waiting to give yourself time to change your mind." When Dani didn't respond, Liz took her friend's arm. "This isn't you. Giving up what you want in life just so he can have what he wants. What's next? Him making all your decisions and you sitting there nodding your head like a good little mistress?"

Dani jerked her arm away and grabbed the water bottle attached to her hip. She took a long pull on it, then dumped some of it on her head and wiped the water from her eyes. "I love him, Liz. It's not that easy to just walk away."

"Maybe not, but do you want to live your entire life unmarried and childless? That's what you'll be doing if you go with him. I mean, that's okay if that's what you want, but if it's not…"

"He loves me, and I love him. Maybe after a while he could change his mind about—"

"Don't you dare do that! He's made it perfectly clear where he stands on marriage and kids. If you're hoping if you just love him enough, he'll change his mind, you can stop that fantasy right now."

"You're the one who told me to go for it when I first contemplated a relationship with him."

"So it's my fault you're in this fucked up relationship?"

"I didn't say that."

"Look. It's not right that he's putting restrictions and conditions on your love."

"Then what the hell am I supposed to do?" Dani

angrily brushed sweaty tendrils of hair from her face.

"If you can live without marriage and kids, then Matt's your man and you should go with him to Dallas. If you can't live without marriage and kids, then you let him go alone. It's as simple as that."

"It's *not* that simple." She sighed. "But you're right."

"Have you ever told him about why it's so important to you to have a husband and kids?"

"No. It didn't seem important after he dropped the no wife, no kids condition."

She huffed. "You guys need to stop fucking long enough to talk for five minutes." She grinned. "Or talk while you're fucking, like I do."

Dani shook her head, giving her a little grin, and Liz hugged her. "It'll work out how it's supposed to. I promise. Now, let's go home. I have a date with Jon to get ready for."

She dropped Liz off and, on the way home, thought about what she'd told her friend, that her needs—husband and kids—weren't important after she'd heard Matt's conditions. Of course they were important. To her. But not to him. She had been willing to put aside what she wanted so he could have what he wanted. What had he given up for her? What would he be willing to give up for her? She knew the answer to that. Her decision was clear.

Chapter Twenty

Dani's suitcases, overnight bag, briefcase, and purse sitting in the hallway were the last things Matt expected to see when he got home. He twisted his brain, trying to recall whether she had mentioned an upcoming trip. Had she been called back to Phoenix for another meeting?

He dropped his keys next to her set in the oval basket on the hall table and moved into the living room. She sat on the couch, facing the wall of windows that displayed the sparkling city lights at night and the mountains during the day.

Instead of her yoga pants and T-shirt he'd imagined she'd be wearing, she wore jeans, T-shirt, jean jacket, and boots. She never wore shoes in the house. Matt felt a sharp slice of anxiety jab into him. He removed his suit jacket and laid it across the back of the couch, then topped it with the tie he had unfastened on his way out of the office building.

"Hey, baby. You going somewhere?"

She turned her head toward him but didn't look him in the eyes. Her face wore a veil of grief, and she had been crying, evidenced by the tears spiking her lashes. He wanted to rush to her side to comfort her, hold her, kiss away her sadness, but after her growing aloofness over the past week he wasn't sure whether his attention would help or hurt. The eyes that gently touched his were filled with sadness and pain.

"It's time," she said. "You've achieved what you came here for. You solved the mystery of the financial irregularities and you've sold the company. It's time for you—and me—to move on." She stood and headed for the hallway and her waiting bags. "My house keys are in the basket. I don't think I've forgotten anything, but if I have...I can replace it."

He hooked her arm as she walked past him. "If you're throwing away our relationship, I have a right to know why. You owe me that much." He wondered if she could hear the panic in his voice that anger was trying to disguise.

She released a shaky sigh, but her voice was strong. "I finally got it. I finally faced the reality that we want vastly different things. Things that neither of us is willing to give up. I want marriage and children...a family. I know that now. One hundred percent. You don't want either. That's a fundamental difference that can't be resolved."

"There's so much about us that works, yet you're willing to walk away from it over one small issue? That's a little selfish, don't you think?"

"Having a marriage and children with the man I love is no small issue to me. Nor is it being selfish. If anyone is selfish here, it's—" She must have seen the pain dart across his eyes because she stopped. "You have so much to offer a child."

"Having kids just to have them is what would be selfish. What kind of life would that be, for them or me? Believe me, kids know when they're wanted and when they're not."

"I see your point...truly, I do. And you're right. If

you don't want children, you shouldn't have them. If you don't want a wife, you shouldn't have one. I respect your reasoning. And your choices. I'm asking you to respect mine. I want kids. I want a husband. I want a family. I want them with you, but since that's not possible, I need to move on. If I stay with you, I'll never get what I want."

Fear, sandpaper rough, gritted across his heart. His stomach heaved. She was leaving him. "You love me. I love you. Why can't that be enough?"

"I do love you, Matt, more than I've ever loved anyone…but it's not enough."

"There's got to be a compromise in here somewhere that can help us save what we have."

"Matt—"

"Marriage and kids are the issues…okay, for taking kids off the table, I'll agree to consider marriage. It's a fair compromise. We both get something we want." The stupidity and insensitivity of his panicked words brought his hand up to his forehead in frustration. Grasping at the last threads of his cherished relationship wasn't a sane place to be, and it was turning him inside out and shutting off his brain to rational thought.

Her body stiffened, and her voice came out angry and rough. "This isn't a business negotiation. It's my life, my happiness, my future. I don't want to negotiate that, and neither should you. If we do, we'll come to resent each other. And I don't want that."

They stared at each other in silence, the look in her eyes telling him this was the end. Dani wiping away more tears was his undoing. Swallowing hard, he gritted his teeth and squeezed his jaw to hold his own tears at bay.

"Dani." He whispered her name and moved to her, his hand outstretched toward her.

Her arm shot out to stay him. "No, don't touch me. If you touch me I won't be able to do this, and I have to do this." Her words begged him to stay away, but her face showed her heart's desire to be in his arms.

He slipped an arm around her waist. "And I have to do this." He pulled her gently to him and kissed her eyes to dislodge the tears that had pooled there. She held her arms between their bodies, keeping herself apart, stiff. He slid his other arm around her, willing her to feel his warmth and love. It was like hugging a wall, but he didn't let go.

Surrendering with a deep wracking sob, she fell into his embrace, wrapping her arms around him, clinging.

They held to each other, rocking, for a long moment. He dropped warm kisses on her face. At the corner of her eye. On her cheek. Along her jaw. Down her neck. He found her lips with his and gently pressed them. She didn't return the kiss, but she didn't push him away either. She simply, calmly, accepted the last rites of his love for her. He kissed her again and again, her top lip, then her bottom lip, then both. In the circle of his arms, he could feel her body respond. It was an opening up, a warming, a releasing that signaled her acceptance of his attention. She returned his kiss.

Love for this woman—his woman—rushed throughout his body like an earthquake. She was the heartbeat that kept him alive. How was he going to live without her in his arms, in his life? He had one last chance to get her to change her mind.

"Stay with me tonight. Lie beside me in our bed

and let me make love to you. Let me show you how much I love you. Let me remind you what you're giving up. If you still want to leave in the morning, I…I won't stop you."

Dani slowly backed out of Matt's arms and walked to her suitcases in the hall. She picked them up and stood with them, feeling the impossible weight of them in her hands, and wrestled with the voices in her head.

Get out while you can. A clean break now will be easier than leaving him the morning after spending hours in the pleasure of his arms.

One more night with the man you love. Tomorrow is soon enough to begin the sorrow that will last a lifetime.

There was only one choice.

She dropped her bags to the floor, bent over, pulled off her boots and stood them against the wall, then took off her jacket, laying it atop the bags.

Tonight she would enjoy the man who had given her more love than she thought she'd ever get, a man she loved more than she ever thought she could love someone, a man who had breathed life into her very soul. The man who taught her what real love felt like.

In the morning she would tell him goodbye.

"Tonight," she said. "Just tonight."

****

Matt scooped her up into his arms, and carried her to their bedroom. She had given him tonight. A few hours. To try to convince her to stay. Tonight would be about making sure she enjoyed every touch, every taste, every smell, every kiss, every pleasurable sensation. About savoring these precious sensations and committing them to memory in case the worst-case scenario happened and he failed in his attempt to keep her with him.

He set her next to the bed and grabbed the hem of her T-shirt, lifting it over her head, letting it fall to the floor. His fingers moved to the front hook of her bra. In one move, he had it undone and off.

His hands slid down her sides to the band of her jeans. The button unsnapped, and the zipper whispered down in less than a heartbeat. He pushed down the jeans, and she stepped out of them, sweeping them away with her foot.

Sliding his fingers inside the band of her panties, he took a moment to cup her, feel her heat, her wetness, tease her with his fingertips before tugging the panties down her legs and off.

She stood before him wearing nothing but soft moonlight filtering in through the window. He kissed her lips, thoroughly, tenderly, before beginning his slow exploration of her body. The ever-present heat between them began to fuse them into one being, one body, one breath. He captured her face between his hands and smoothed his thumb at the edge of her lips, then kissed her again, breathed her in, their tongues twirling and dancing while his hands crawled over her shoulders and down her arms.

She broke the kiss but not their gaze and put her fingers to the buttons of his shirt. Her hands slid into the part in the shirt and smoothed over his stomach, his bare chest, then up to his shoulders. His nipples hardened at her touch and his stomach contracted. His cock stiffened in his pants, and electricity sizzled inside him. She pushed the shirt down his arms, and he flung it across the room.

Her hands moved to his belt and unbuckled it, giving her easy access to his fly. Unbuttoned and unzipped, the pants easily slid to the floor with a little push from her. He kicked them away as she had done her jeans.

The last barrier keeping their bodies apart was his boxer briefs, and they would fall soon, too. But first she touched him through the fabric, making him feel as if he were spinning. He was hard and ready as she cupped his balls and dragged her palm up his cock to tease the wet cockhead.

Not able to wait any longer, he peeled off his underwear, then took her hand and climbed onto the bed, drawing her along with him. He lay on her and again found her mouth. His lips slid across hers, nipping, sucking, softly, relentlessly. His hands moved down the body he knew as well as his own.

Her breasts were like ripe fruit in his hands, heavy, sweet, her nipples ready and begging for the touch of his lips and tongue. He sucked and laved their puckered points, wanting to remember the taste of her breasts in his mouth. Inch by slow inch, his hands continued their trek downward, across her taut stomach and lower to tease and stroke her wetness. She eagerly parted her legs to him.

Going in for a deeper exploration, he stopped first at her clit, greeting it gently with his fingers. She closed her eyes and drew in a sharp breath, telling him that the tiny touch had raised her hunger to a higher level. Before this night was through, he would take her higher, higher, to the crest and above it, many times.

Dani's hands were as busy as his, matching his gentle and slow pace. Reaching for him, she wrapped her fingers around his cock. He was hard and desperate for her to surround him. Drops of pre-cum appeared at the tip, and she smoothed the moisture over the slit with her thumb, making his dick jerk and his balls climb up tight inside him. She tugged him toward her pussy, letting him brush against her opening, enticing him to come inside.

But it was too soon. He had more building to do. More pleasure to give. So much more. He inched down her body, leaving kisses on her stomach, licks to her belly button, nips on her smooth parted thighs, before settling his head between her legs. He breathed deeply to imprint the soft scent of her in his mind.

The feel of him between her legs, his breath against her sex always propelled her several notches on the pleasure scale. In their months together, he'd learned just what to do to make her come. Every time. His lips tugged at her pussy lips, and his tongue darted over and circled the tiny coil of pleasure sensors, alternately lapping her wet slit.

He knew she was at the peak by the small sounds emanating from her, by the way her hips rose to his mouth, by the tightening of her pelvic region. At her release, he drank her in greedily, wanting to relish her taste, her scent and implant them in his mind. When she had ridden out the wave, he moved back up to face her. "Open your eyes, Dani. I want you to see how much I love you."

She opened her eyes and tears rolled out. "I love you, Matt."

Slowly, he entered her, then just as slowly, pulled back and pushed forward, letting them feel every bit of each other. Together they drove higher and higher, absorbed each other so fully that they became a single entity with a single purpose.

Being inside Dani was the only heaven he'd ever get to. And that was fine with him. At this moment, he was perfect, the best man he could be, the happiest man who ever lived. Because of her. Sheathed inside her, he knew peace and joy and everything good most people took for granted.

Feeling the urgency of her need, he increased the pace of the rhythm, sliding in and out, hard and fast, until he thought he'd lose his mind. She arched, her pussy clutching him, and growled her released. He followed her to the top, feeling her nails cut into his back through the powerful, shuddering explosion rocking them.

They caressed and kissed and enjoyed the extreme satisfaction of the afterglow, their bodies humming with intense pleasure that they had only experienced with each other.

They turned to each other again and again in the night, some rough, some gentle, but each sweeter and more satisfying than the time before. Both felt the undertones of urgency in their touches, instinctively knowing these were their last chances to be together this way.

As much as he wished the night to never end, the sun rose on schedule, shining a harsh, unwelcome light of reality on them. Her head resting on his chest, he felt her warm breath, and he swore he heard her heart beating, slow and steady, through the fingertips she trailed across his skin.

While they had dozed here and there throughout the night, neither had wanted to waste the final precious moments with each other on sleep. And now their final moments were clicking down. The lovemaking had been better than ever, but somehow he knew it wasn't going to be enough. With the exception of marrying her and giving her children, he had tried everything he could to get her to stay, and it was up to her whether she tore them apart or kept them safe and united. If what he *could* give wasn't enough, then maybe she should leave.

****

Dani moved her hands lightly up and down Matt's stomach and side and chest, wishing she could stop time and keep him here, in this spot, forever. She raised her face to his and looked into his eyes. He brought his mouth to hers and kissed her lips with a clinging tenderness she was afraid she would never again feel.

Their night had been more passionate, loving, and fulfilling than it had ever been, but it hadn't erased or minimized the issue at heart. As much as she loved him, as much as she knew he loved her, she couldn't continue a relationship that went no further than living together. She had postponed the inevitable for a few blissful hours, but it was time to face the truth. He had been clear. She would never be his wife or the mother of his children. She had been clear, too. Being his lover wasn't enough. She wanted more. She deserved more.

Even knowing she might never find a love like this again, she said the words that started the countdown to the end. "Matt." She whispered the word against his mouth and knew she would miss the sweet sound of his name rolling from her lips.

"Dani."

She rolled on top of him and looked into his face, committing to memory every plane, every angle, every pore, every hair, every little line. The flecks of teal in his green eyes. The tiny white scar at his chin. The straight slope of his nose. The dimple in one cheek. The fullness of his lips. Ah, those delicious, giving lips that had pleasured every inch of her body. She pressed her mouth to them and committed to memory their feel and taste.

"I love you so much," she whispered, and it felt as if their breathing had stopped. For an instant, neither of them moved. This was the moment. Stay. Or go.

It took everything inside her to pull herself away. His arms instinctively tightened around her, but she rolled out of his embrace and left their bed. He sat up and started to get out of bed.

"No, don't get up," she said. "Please just let me—"

"Don't go."

She nearly collapsed in pain at the love and anguish she heard in his voice. He sounded like a man whose last chance to live was to pray, softly and reverently, using only the most important, most powerful words. Her response caught in her throat, and she silenced a sob. Turning her back to him, she quickly dressed and left the bedroom before the misery in his eyes, the warmth of his touch, the taste of his kiss on her lips changed her mind. True to his word from last night, he didn't follow her.

At the front door, she pulled on her boots and jacket, not daring to stop to wipe away tears. Hesitation now would only lead her back to his arms, his bed, his life. As much as she loved him, as deeply as her heart felt the wound of leaving him, she had to go.

Through a misty veil, she grabbed her bags. Taking a deep, sobbing breath, she walked through the door. As it clicked solidly closed behind her, forever barring her, she leaned against the rough outside adobe wall and released the wracking sobs that filled her.

As she drove away, she felt the empty finality of her choice and wondered what it would end up costing her. She already felt as if she had lost everything.

****

Matt stayed in bed long after Dani had left, trying to make sense of the situation, of the pain exploding in his chest. He'd had relationships end before. Women he'd cared for had left him. He had even missed a few of them. But never before had he felt as if his heart had been speared, ripped from his chest, and crushed into tiny smears of red matter on the floor until the moment Dani left their bed, left him, left behind their life together as easily as she would toss away a crumpled, used paper cup.

Dani. He loved her. More than he'd ever loved anyone. Even Jessica. He pulled her pillow to him, inhaling the scent of her clinging there. The image of her beautiful face floated before him. That smile that lit up his heart every time she graced him with it. Her voice that hummed through him like an electrical current, energizing him and making him feel whole and worthwhile.

The quiet of the house without her was oppressive, squeezing in on him, choking him, punishing him for making such a stupid mistake in letting her go.

I tried to get her to stay, dammit. She's the one who chose to go.

You didn't even go after her.

She didn't want me to.

Of course she did.

She didn't want me just because I don't want kids or marriage? That's not right. What we have is fucking fantastic. She's the one who blew it. Not me. I gave her everything I had to give…and it wasn't enough.

She's the best thing that ever happened to you, and you let her walk out the door. You're an idiot.

I'm an idiot.

The weight of the realization that Dani was gone from his life forever hit him squarely in the stomach, and he couldn't catch his breath. It was suddenly too hot and too claustrophobic in the big house, and he felt as if his chest were being crushed.

Unable to stand it any longer, he jumped out of bed, threw on his running clothes, and headed out for a hard, pounding run to clear his head of the woman he'd never be able to forget.

****

The moment Liz opened the door, Dani spoke quickly in order to get her sentence out while she could still speak. "I couldn't face the empty condo."

"You left him?"

Dani nodded.

Liz pulled her into a comforting hug, and she leaned into the embrace, releasing a fresh batch of tears.

Liz led her to the couch and curled up beside her. She reached for the box of tissues on the side table and handed it to her friend.

A dozen or so tissues later, and Dani had wiped most of the tears from her face, blown her nose, and told Liz everything.

"When I left our bed and he told me he loved me, my heart shattered into a million pieces. And I know his did, too. Oh, Liz, what have I done?"

"You decided not to settle for less than you want and deserve."

"But I love him. I love him like I've never loved anyone. What if I never find another love like him? What if…what if I can't even have children? I will have given up the best thing in my life for nothing."

"You can't grab what you really want if you're fearfully holding on to what you already have. You said you couldn't imagine your life without a husband and children. You let go of Matt so you could find someone who wants those things, too."

"How am I going to get over him long enough to even look for someone else?"

"You just will. Right now it seems impossible, but in time you'll realize it was the best decision for both of you. That's when you'll get out there. But don't move too fast to find Mr. Right. Your wounds need time to heal."

"I had Mr. Right."

"If he was Mr. Right, you'd still be in bed with him instead of crying on my couch, using up all my tissues."

Dani laughed and sobbed at the same time and snatched another tissue from the box to wipe her nose.

"Remember when you and Elliott broke up that night?" Liz held out the trash bag so Dani could toss in the used tissue. "You were upset then, but you went to Vegas and you found someone else, someone so much better. Do you know what that tells me?"

"What?"

"We need to go to Vegas!" Liz threw her arms up in the air and wiggled jubilantly.

"You're insane!" Dani smiled through her tears at her friend's outrageous attempt to cheer her up.

"No, I'm crazy, not insane. There's a difference, you know."

The two talked until late into the day, ate a little, drank a lot. And when she went home the following morning, she assured Liz she was all right, but lying in her bed that day, alone, with nothing but her arms by her side, thoughts of Matt filling her mind and the crushing pain in her heart, she knew she was not all right and that she wouldn't be for a long, long time.

Leaving Elliott had been like getting a brazillian—sharp but short-term pain. Leaving Matt was like losing the ability to breathe—intense pain that rolls on and on, neverending.

What are you doing right this second, Matt?

Are you lying awake missing me as much as I miss you?

Are you hearing my voice between the gaps in the silence?

Are you feeling my touch on your skin?

Do you feel like you're dying of heartbreak and wish that God would just end the torture and take you?

Or are you glad to be rid of me, already hunting for a new woman to fill your bed?

Or calling Arienne to tell her to ready her bed for your return?

Thinking of Matt with Arienne, with another woman, stabbed another spear into her heart. With a soft groan, she rolled onto her side, curled up into a protective fetal position, and cried herself to sleep.

Chapter Twenty-One

"Liz, I need to see you a moment."

Matt's request came out sounding like an order. The group of co-workers Liz was chatting with in the break room scattered back to their offices, leaving her to fend for herself.

She turned to the coffee machine and poured herself a cup of coffee. "Can I pour you a cup of decaf, boss? You seem a little edgy."

He stepped closer to her and lowered his voice. "You're Dani's best friend. She listens to you. Can't you talk to her, convince her we're meant to be together?"

"How can I do that when I'm not convinced?"

His mouth clamped into a tight seam, and he gritted his teeth. "I love her."

"She loves you, too. But sometimes that's not enough."

"What can I do to change her mind?"

"Uh, how about sacrificing something you want for the good of the relationship instead of expecting her to do it all?"

"I'm sure she told you about my past. I'd do almost anything to make Dani happy, but I can't give on those two issues."

"All I know is that you don't want marriage and kids. Have you ever asked her why she does?"

He stared at her, at a loss for words. Why didn't he know that?

She tossed an ugly laugh his way. "Of course you haven't. Like most men, you automatically assume women think of nothing but marriage and kids all the time, that their lives are incomplete without it. Well, as far as Dani's concerned, there's a reason for the panic she feels about being with a man who won't commit to her in marriage."

"Tell me."

"Talk to Dani."

Dani had taken a week off after their breakup and all his attempts to reach her had gone unanswered. "She won't answer my calls or emails or texts, and she won't see me. Liz, help us fix this."

She poured the bitter coffee into the sink and tossed the paper cup into the trash. "Buy me a cup of good coffee, and I'll tell you what I know...though she'll probably kill me for it."

****

The good stuff steaming in white, wide-mouth mugs in their hands, Liz told him about the Dani he didn't know existed.

"Dani grew up in some hippie commune near Taos. Her dad was a spirited guy, charming, full of life. He loved her mom, but the free-love doctrine they lived by in the commune really appealed to him. He moved out of the house several times a year for a week at a time, sharing his love with various women."

"His wife didn't mind?'

"They weren't married, and yes, Dani's mom was devastated, cried all the time he was gone, wouldn't leave the house. Dani was furious at her dad for leaving her mom to go sleep with other women, and at her mom for not demanding that he be true to only her."

Liz took a sip of her latte and sighed.

"She said she constantly yelled at both of them, saying that if they'd only get married, things wouldn't be so messed up all the time. She said she hated how they lived their lives and was going to leave as soon as she could."

"When did she leave?" Matt watched Liz's face intently, fascinated by what he was learning about Dani and wondering why she'd never told him. Why he'd never asked.

"Two days after her mother killed herself."

"What?"

"Her dad had gone off again with another woman, and I guess it was the final straw for her mom. The *curandera*—the healer—said it looked like she had brewed a tea from a poisonous plant and drank it. Dani blamed her dad, saying that her mom had died of a broken heart."

He stared into his cup, picturing the young girl she had been, heartsick over her loss. "How old was she when she left?"

"Thirteen. A change of clothes, a jacket, and an old letter from her mother's sister is all she took, stuffed in a backpack. She hitched a ride to Taos and called her aunt, telling her that her mom was dead and that she couldn't live there anymore. Her aunt paid her bus ticket to Boston, where she started a new life."

Christ. A thirteen-year-old on her own. No wonder she had such a take-charge attitude. She'd had to. "Did she ever go back?"

"Once. Her dad was sick, on his deathbed, and he

begged her to come home so he could see her one last time. He told her it was after her mother was gone that he realized how much he loved her. He said if he could have had her back, he'd have done anything—even marry her—to make sure she was happy."

Liz took a sip of her coffee. "Dani ended up staying a month to help her sister with her dad until he died. She was going to college in Boston at the time, but she dropped out of her classes so she could make peace with him. With her mother, too, for that matter. Dani carried around a lot of guilt about how she yelled at her mom the day she died, said some horrible things to her. In a way, she blames herself for her mom's death. The day her mother was buried, Dani promised her that she'd never be with a man who wouldn't marry her and commit just to her. And she's kept that promise. Until you."

Matt dug his fingers into his forehead and tried to rub out his thoughts. "In my mind, I always referred to Elliott as the asshole who hurt her. Now I see I was wrong. The honor's all mine."

Liz put her hand on his, and his gaze lifted to hers. "She was crazy about Elliott, even saw a future with him. She *loves* you, more than she ever loved anyone, but she's terrified of ending up like her mother. And when she caught you with Arienne...twice... Well, to her, it was proof she was headed down that same path, and it scared the shit out of her. She had to let you go to save herself."

He felt Liz's judgment in her tone and in her eyes when she gave him the once over, but he said nothing to defend himself. He'd fucked up. Plain and simple.

"So, Matt? Does that explain Dani's intense,

almost overwhelming desire for security, stability, and commitment of marriage from the man she loves? Do you understand why she left you? Do you understand how incredible it is that she stayed with you as long as she did? Do you realize how hard she tried to give up what she needed just to be with you?"

He nodded. "Yes."

"Good. Now what are you going to do about it?"

He could fix things with Dani. Right now. All he had to do was go to her, the woman he loved, and tell her what she needed to hear. *Marry me. Have my children.* A sudden ice storm invaded his veins at the very thought of doing it. Petrified him. The loss and emptiness left by Justin's death had been consuming. He loved Dani, trusted her, but then he'd loved and trusted Jessica, too, though not nearly to the same extent. And she'd left him a broken man. He couldn't go through the past few years again. It would kill him.

"I don't know," he said finally.

Liz shook her head. "*I don't know?*" she scoffed. "That's the same as *nothing.* You don't deserve her." She stood and walked out the door.

****

The small conference room was filled to standing room only. Introductions of the new owners had already been made, and Matt was wrapping up his goodbye speech. As he spoke, he scanned the crowd for a glimpse of Dani. He finally pinpointed her in the back, her eyes glued to his, a proud, half-smile on her face.

The crowd applauded when he finished, giving him a standing ovation for the job he'd done on the investigation and in managing the successful sale of the business to a company who would not be making

Sophia Ryan

dramatic, sweeping changes to the fifty-year-old institution.

He shook dozens of hands, accepted numerous congratulations and farewells, smiled way too many smiles before the one person he wanted to see stood before him.

"Congratulations, Matt. You did a great thing for Meganlin." She chuckled. "I mean, Rivera Builders."

He took her hand in his, almost unable to breathe from the sheer joy of touching her, hearing her laugh, smelling her skin again. It made him smile. "It'll take some getting used to, but I'm sure as their new director, you'll lead everyone into the future quite easily."

She held tightly to his gaze. "And I'm sure you'll be equally successful in your next venture. Best of luck to you."

As she went to pull her hand away, he held on to it and leaned in an inch or two. "Stay behind for a minute." At the hesitation in her eyes, he whispered, "Please."

She dropped her gaze, nodded, and stepped away so the next person in line could have a shot at wishing the exiting boss well.

Ten minutes later, the new owners announced the open-bar and hors d'oeuvres reception in the large conference room. Everyone filed out, and the door shut, leaving him alone with Dani for the first time since she'd left their bed—was it really only two weeks ago?

They stood on opposite sides of the oval conference table, their eyes connected, and he felt the heat flaming between them. Her nipples pouted hard against her silk blouse, and his cock stirred in his pants as if saying, hey, I know her and I'm ready to go. He wanted to go to her, wrap her tight in his arms, kiss her, palm her breast, press his ready cock against her mound. But he had no right. He had given up that right. But he would say goodbye, and he would say it the right way—in her arms.

He moved toward her, slowly so as to not freak her out. She stepped forward, too. They met in the middle, went into each other's arms in a familiar motion, and held each other.

It was the last time he'd see her. He breathed in the scent of her and stopped himself from kissing her. He didn't have the words to say what he really wanted to say to her, here in their last moment together. And it seemed like she didn't either, because she remained quiet.

She pulled back way too soon and just stared at him, her gaze roaming over his face, his eyes, his mouth, his nose. Was she trying to memorize his shapes, colors, textures, smells? That's what he was doing with her.

Silence surrounded them and pulled in the edges, and he fought the force that was pushing him to take her into his arms because it wasn't fair to her. She held her hands tightly to each other, gripping. To keep them from reaching out to touch him? That's why his hands were in his pockets.

"Come with me, Dani," is what he wanted to say.

"Take me with you, Matt," is what he saw in her eyes.

But in the end, what each of them said was hollow because it could have come from anyone.

"I wish you all the best, Matt."

"You, too, Dani."

She moved forward and laid her hands on his chest. His heart raced at her touch, and it seemed as if his breath was being held captive in his lungs. She leaned in and kissed the corner of his mouth, and his heart trembled.

"Thank you," she said.

"For?"

"For sharing your life with me for a while. It meant everything to me." Slowly, she lowered her hands to her sides, stepped back from him, and turned to go, cutting the final thread in their life as a couple.

He caught her hand. "I'm sorry."

"For?"

"That we didn't find a way to make it work."

She squeezed his hand as her response, then let it go and turned again. At the door, she stopped and glanced back at him. Then she moved on through the door and out of the conference room.

Though it killed him, he let her go.

Chapter Twenty-Two

"You've walked around with that long face since you got home. What has you so upset?"

Matt looked up from the paper and met his mother's eyes before quickly looking away. "Other than the Cowboys losing the Super Bowl?" he said, trying to read the paper but failing because his mind was on other things.

Megan Linton shook her head at him. "Your sadness has nothing to do with football. You look like you lost something very precious to you. Don't deny it. A mother knows these things." She sipped her tea.

Matt gave a nonchalant little shrug, but his heart was racing. He did not want to have the conversation she was hinting at. "Business matters."

"Look at me, Matthew," she said, and he did, using the stone face mask he used in business. She narrowed her eyes at him, and he knew she was looking for the truth behind the curtain he'd put up. "You're lying. Tell me what happened in Albuquerque. Tell me about Danielle."

Unable to hide his shock, Matt dropped the paper to the floor beside him and sat back in his chair. How in the hell did she know?

She smiled. "Don't look so surprised. Your old momma hasn't lost her mind yet."

She also likely hadn't lost her connection to the

social gossip line either. Even he had heard the buzz about his break-up with Arienne and her slurs against Dani. He returned his mother's smile. "No. In fact, she's too smart for her own good."

"Tell me about her." Her tone softened into a concerned mother's voice.

"Dani is…" He stared into nothing, seeing Dani's face materialize in front of his eyes. "…the love of my life."

"Then why aren't you together?"

He dropped his head back, closed his eyes. "She wants things I can't give her."

"Things? What things? Boats and jets? Diamonds and cattle?"

"Marriage and children."

"Oh, for Pete's sake. You threw your ridiculous 'no marriage, no children' rule at her and like any decent woman would do, she ripped it up and threw it back in your face, then she left you, your rule intact but your heart broken into a million pieces."

Matt nodded, looking sheepish that his mother could so easily see through him.

She furrowed her dark eyebrows. "Matthew Collins Linton, you need to go to your woman and beg her, on your knees, to forgive your stupidity and to marry you and have your babies."

"It's not that simple. I love her. I just don't know if I have it in me to give her what she wants."

"I know why you think you don't want marriage or children. You're afraid because of what happened with Jessica and Justin." She put her hand on his and squeezed it at the mention of her only grandchild's name. "But it doesn't mean it'll be that way this time. Son, Jessica was

302

always a little, shall we say, unstable. The poor girl had demons that clawed inside her all the time, and I don't mean demons like that poor Dean Winchester has to deal with. She trapped you into marriage because she thought your love and money could make her whole again. But all the love and money and pretty things in the world couldn't change how she felt about herself deep down inside."

He opened his mouth to speak up for his late wife, but his mom held up her hand to stop him. "Oh, I know it wasn't totally her fault. Growing up with an alcoholic father and a drug-addict slut for a mother made her clingy, needy, never truly able to love and trust anyone fully. Not even you. She loved the idea of you, of who she thought she could be with you. I know you cared about her, but you didn't really love her. You do love this woman, this Dani, with all your heart and soul. I can see it in your eyes. Hear it in your voice as you talk about her."

"I love her more than I've loved anyone."

"And she loves you?"

"Yes. Well, she did. Now…who knows."

"If you can love her that much without marriage, then you can love her that much or more in marriage. If you can love her that much without a child, you can love her even more with one, or six. If the love is there, it's there, no matter what else it shares space with. You see? Simple."

Speech over, she reached for her cup and went back to sipping her tea, but he saw her smile as he came to his senses.

****

"Have you completely lost your mind?" Hands on

her hips, Dani glared at Liz for her insane suggestion that she go to Matt. "I broke up with him for good reasons...reasons you supported."

"You're miserable. Everyone can see it. Get your ass on a plane and go to him. Guys like him don't come along every day."

Karen walked in on their conversation. "I agree," she said. "And if you don't go to him and try to work things out, I'll have to fire you."

Dani frowned. "You can't fire me for what I do or don't do in my personal life."

"I can when your personal life is affecting your work life." She walked over to Dani's phone, jabbed in a few numbers. "Yes, this is President Rutledge. Please have the jet ready in an hour. Danielle Parker is flying to Dallas on important business."

She hung up and turned to Dani. "Be at the airport in forty-five minutes." She walked out, a smile on her face. "I expect an invitation to the wedding."

****

Thanks to Karen's call, Brenda, Matt's assistant, was waiting for Dani when she arrived at his office building, and she showed her to his office to wait.

"He's running late this morning," she said. "Which is unusual for him. Coffee?"

She was already wired. Coffee would make her explode. "No thanks."

When Brenda left, Dani sat in Matt's big leather desk chair. She could smell him, almost feel him around her. Her gaze traveled around his office. Abstract artwork in various slashes of deep, bold color. A couple of Remington bronzes. Books, mostly on law, construction, and Texas history. Certificates of achievement, college diplomas, professional honors. One photo. A small one. Of him and his son.

Justin.

She picked up the photo, looked into the little face that resembled the man she loved. The green eyes. The way he held his mouth. The little dimple in one cheek. The eyebrows. Even the shape of the ears were the same.

He had lost this child, and the pain of it had made him vow to never have another. Panic ripped through her at the thought that she'd never have a child that looked like him or like her or like them. She came here convinced she was ready to give up her dream of having a child, of being his wife, but now that she was here, a few remaining doubts tumbled like dice against each other in her stomach. Her hands were ice as they set the photo back in its place.

"You're late, boss," Brenda said in the hall, kindly warning her of Matt's approach.

"I stopped by the store this morning. And my damn phone's dead again."

At hearing his voice, the love in her heart for him melted the panic, dissolved the dice. She stayed in the chair, remained faced away from the door so he couldn't see her.

"Brenda, would you get me a charger?" He was in the office now, digging around in one of the drawers of the credenza across the room. "And I'm going to need a flight to Albuquerque as soon as possible."

"Here you go," Brenda must have handed him the charger because Dani heard beeps as the phone slurped juice.

"C'mon. C'mon. This is taking too fucking long."

He soon began pushing buttons.

Dani smiled as the phone in her jacket pocket began to vibrate.

She brought the phone to her mouth as she slowly turned in the chair.

"Hello?"

Matt spun toward her.

The intense love in his face took her breath away, and she knew she'd made the right decision. As long as she had him, she had love, and as long as she had love, she had everything she ever wanted. She hoped he still wanted her.

"What are you doing here?" he said into the phone, then, realizing what he was doing, hung up and rushed toward her.

She put her phone down, stood, and met him half way. They didn't hug or touch. They stared at each other, looking as giddy and shy as two teenagers who just realized they were in love.

"Why are you calling me?" she asked.

"I…" He laughed. She'd never seen him so red-faced and tongue-tied. It was endearing. "I called to ask you…something."

"Ask me what?"

His pulse was throbbing in his neck. Whatever it was, was big. Then he slowly dropped to one knee and pulled a ring box from his pocket, and her own pulse throbbed. She felt her eyes going round in surprise, her mouth hanging open until she remembered to close it.

"Baby, it took losing you for me to realize that our love for each other is all that matters to me," he said, his eyes on hers, his voice strong and surprisingly calm for the topic he was expounding. "If I have you, your love, I have everything I ever wanted." He opened the ring box, revealing a diamond the size of Texas set in a thin platinum band. "Marry me, Dani. Be my wife. Have my children. As many as you want. Just say you'll love me forever."

Tears threatened, but she choked them back. "You're not the marrying kind."

"That was before I knew the right woman was out there. Now that I've found her, found you, I'm ready. And I don't want to wait a minute longer to begin the rest of our life together."

She looked into his face, his eyes, his heart and knew she had found someone who could commit to her and commit to keeping their love alive and vibrant. Someone she could trust with her whole being. Someone she could love forever. With or without marriage. Or children. Or money. Or anything. It was odd how they'd both come to the same conclusion at the same time, like the universe had a hand in making them see the light. The joy of it made her smile. Then giggle. Then throw her head back and laugh so hard she was wiping away tears.

Matt shifted uncomfortably on his knee. "That's not the response I expected," he said, looking perplexed and a bit annoyed at her unexpected reaction to his heartfelt proposal.

She knelt, face-to-face with him, and wrapped her arms around him. "About two seconds after you'd left town, I realized how stupid I'd been. I had perfect love and I let it go. I want you in my life, Matt. Today. Tomorrow. Forever. I came here to take you up on your offer to move here with you. Be with you. Whatever your conditions. Because if I have you, if I have your love, I have everything. That's why I was laughing. The words I was going to say to you were the very words you just said to me."

He smiled. Chuckled. Then laughed, too.

"Thank God you've both come to your senses," Brenda said. "Now kiss each other and get on with your happily ever after. We have work to do." Smiling, she closed the office door.

They kissed each other with a passion forged during that first kiss at the birth of their Sin City affair, grown in the love they'd shared in Albuquerque.

"You know our engagement isn't official until I put the ring on your finger," he whispered against her mouth.

"We'll worry about that later," she said, taking him to the floor. "Much later."

And then he was where he should be, his body next to hers, the taste of his kisses on her lips.

Later…much later…he slid the ring where it belonged.

Epilogue

Soft post-sex laughter drifted through the semidark living room where Dani lay entwined with Matt on a blanket in front of the wall of windows looking out over the Dallas skyline. Half a dozen fat candles burned in the fireplace, bathing their naked bodies in a flickering golden glow. Two empty champagne flutes and a half-finished bottle of bubbly sat on the coffee table.

"Ah, my love. You're insatiable." Matt pulled Dani's lips into a wet kiss before rolling off her and collapsing back onto the blanket with a contented sigh. "I'm not going to have enough energy for the game tomorrow."

She lazily rose on her elbow and smiled down at him. "Fortunately, little league coaches don't need a lot of energy on the field, so they can expend most of their supply trying to satisfy their insatiable wives."

At his little groan of agreement, she sat up, straddled him, and fit his softening dick between her slick pussy lips.

His hands caressed her hips. "You're going to kill me, woman." His shining eyes and soft grin told her his complaints about her constant hunger for him weren't genuine. "But I can't think of a better way to go."

"Good answer, Collins." Fitting her mouth to his, she rolled her tongue with his, tasting the champagne and her essence. She flexed her hips against his, and she swore his dick twitched even though they'd both come minutes before. Truth was, he was as insatiable as she was, making them a perfect match.

Matt rolled them over so he was on top, breaking the kiss. He brushed her hair from her face with his fingertips and caressed her cheek with his thumb. His gaze captured hers, a soft grin in place. "If I didn't know better, I'd say you're glad I talked you into marrying me."

She laughed. "You talked me into it? Not sure you're remembering it right, husband."

"No? How do you remember it, wife?"

"I remember falling in love with you the night you pretended to be my husband. I remember pestering you day and night after that until you gave in and married me. I remember—"

He shook his head. "You've sure gotten good at spinning wild Texas tales, sugar," he said in an exaggerated drawl.

She pinched his nipple. "I learned from the best."

He chuckled. "The God's honest truth is, no matter how hard I tried to get you to believe happily-every-after with me was possible, you fought it. It took a lot of convincing before you agreed to be my woman."

She'd felt like his woman from the first night they met, but he was right that she hadn't believed they could have a future. Until she lost him. "Oh, it didn't take that much convincing."

"That's my story, and I'm sticking to it. So answer my question."

"What was the question?"

"Are you glad I talked you into marrying me?"

"Of course."

"Why?"

She trailed her fingers through his thick hair, licked her grinning lips. "Because you're fucking hot."

His eyes lit up as if her statement pleased him. "So you love me just for my hot body and pretty face?"

"Not just that."

"What else?"

She slid her hand between them and grabbed his dick, which was still wet with her cum, his. "You're very good with this," she said, fondling him, feeling him swell in response.

"And?"

The low and sexy *and* rumbled through her, and her chest swelled with love and desire at what the *and* entailed.

"Because of you I'm whole, and happier than anyone has a right to be." All teasing was gone from her voice, and she hoped he heard the sincerity in it. Matt was everything she'd ever wanted—in a man, a lover, a husband, a partner—and everyday, in his every word and deed, he made her believe it more.

He kissed her, softly, lovingly, acknowledging her words and the deep sentiment they revealed.

Wanting to see his face, see his eyes, see his emotions, she broke the kiss. "What about you? Are you glad you talked me into marrying you?"

"It's the best return on investment I ever had."

She rolled her eyes. "Oh, be still my beating heart."

He chuckled at her flat reaction to his teasing and captured her face with his hands. "Everything I thought our life would be pales in comparison to the life we've lived these past five years."

"Is that good or bad?"

"The best. I thought I knew happiness before you, Dani, but I was wrong. You, our life, means everything to me. And baby, I'll do anything and everything to keep it."

The sincerity, the love in his words, his eyes, his face, his body flooded her with joy and brought tears to her eyes. Love, happiness, respect, belonging only to each other, working together as a solid, unbreakable force. That was their story today, no matter how it had begun. And like him, she'd do anything to keep it alive.

She wrapped her legs around his waist. "I love you, husband."

"I love you, my beautiful wife."

The clock chimed twelve times as they kissed.

"Happy anniversary," they whispered in tandem, their lips just touching, not yet ready to pull out of the kiss.

"Do you want your present now or in the morning?" he asked, his voice filled with desire.

She had the best gift anyone could ever have, right here in her arms. "All I want right now is for you to make love to me all night in our bed, like you did the first night we met."

"Eh, I got you that last year," he teased. "And the year before that."

"And the year before that," she said. "It's what I want every year."

"Most wives want jewelry. You want me."

She didn't miss the pride in his voice. "Got a problem with that?"

"Not a one." He stared deep into her eyes, and she reveled in the love there. "I'm a lucky, lucky man."

"Yes, you are. Now take me to bed."

A grin on his face, he stood and held out his hands to her. She grabbed them, and he helped her to her feet. He put the champagne bottle and flutes in the kitchen and she blew out the candles, then he lifted her in his arms and headed to their bedroom.

On the way, they stopped by the room next to theirs and quietly peeked in. Four-year-old Jack and three-year-old Will lay dreaming in the twin beds decorated with bedspreads sporting the city's namesake football team...courtesy of their father. Matt was already turning their sons into raving sports fanatics.

As she watched her sons sleep, she reflected over how much her life had changed in a short five years. The thought she'd almost missed this because she'd almost given up Matt over her fears sent a chill down her back, and she shivered. She felt Matt's arms tighten around her, felt his warmth at her back, his erection at her ass, his love surrounding her, and peace returned. She'd never expected to have a perfect life, but somehow she'd managed it. It was a gift, a miracle, one she'd fight hard to keep.

Matt kissed her neck and nipped her earlobe, sending her emotions spiraling down a different, more fiery path.

"Are you ready for number three, Mrs. Collins?" he whispered so as to not wake the boys.

She turned her head and shot him a surprised smile. "Three?"

He smiled. "A girl this time I can spoil."

"First, I can't get you to have kids. Now, I can't get you to stop."

"I realized how good I am at it."

"Making them or being their daddy?"

"Both." His hand moved lower and cupped her mound, one long finger expertly finding her throbbing clit.

She dropped her head back. "I can't argue with that," she said before his kiss swallowed her moans of desire.

Slowly, she broke the kiss, turned in his arms, and held him tight to her. "Let's go make a baby, Mr. Collins."

About the Author

I write the kind of books I like to read: stories where sexual heat sizzles off the page and the characters fall hard into lust and soft into love.

When I'm not writing about passion, I'm indulging in it—yoga, hiking, laughing with friends over hot chili and cold beer, being crazy and lazy with the family, and, of course, writing.

Learn more about me at
http://sophiaryan.webs.com

To chat with Sophia Ryan and other Wild Rose Press authors of erotic romance, join us at www.groups.yahoo.com/group/thewilderroses.

Also Available

Dirty Little Secrets

by

Sophia Ryan

http://amzn.com/B00R6ZWOGA

Angela Abbott lives the best life her parents' money can buy, but a life of privilege has rules. The first rule is don't fall for a bad boy from the wrong side of the tracks. Sexy, hot, and dangerous, Nick Spencer is everything she should stay away from, but the more she sneaks off to be with him, the harder and faster she falls. The sex is mind-blowing, and so is the way he strips Angela of her stifling, rich-girl shell until the real her is bare before him, beneath him, atop him. She'll do anything to keep Nick in her life as long as he remains her dirty little secret.

But Nick has a secret of his own, and when both are revealed, Angela will have to come clean about what she wants most—the trappings of her privileged lifestyle or the love of the bad boy who's oh-so-good for her.

This title was previously published as In the Bad Boy's Bed but has been completely revised and expanded for The Wild Rose Press, Inc.

Also Read

To-Do Him List

by

Denise Marie

Lipstick Diaries
Book One

http://amzn.com/B0100NNM6K

With her life expectancy most likely measured in weeks, Isabelle Chambers jettisons her risk-free, missionary-position life for a to-do list that is short on dull and long on passion.

Cole Davies may be living his dream as lead singer for Scandals complete with fame, fortune, and unlimited female attention, but life still feels incomplete. So when Isabelle takes her list viral on Twitter he can't resist her appeal.

From flying to bondage and touring with the band to getting it on in public, Isabelle's To-Do Him List turns them both inside out. Then things get hotter than either planned and they both need to decide what they'll risk for love.